ABOUT THE AUTHOR

Cathryn Hein is a best-selling author of rural romance and romantic adventure novels, a Romance Writers of Australia Romantic Book of the Year finalist with *Santa and the Saddler*, and a regular Australian Romance Reader Awards finalist.

A South Australian country girl by birth, Cathryn loves nothing more than a rugged rural hero who's as good with his heart as he is with his hands, which is probably why she writes them! Her romances are warm and emotional, and feature themes that don't flinch from the tougher side of life but are often happily tempered by the antics of naughty animals. Her aim is to make you smile, sigh, and perhaps sniffle a little, but most of all feel wonderful.

Cathryn lives in Newcastle, Australia, with her partner of many years, Jim. When she's not writing, she plays golf (ineptly), cooks (well), and in football season barracks (rowdily) for her beloved Sydney Swans AFL team.

To discover more about Cathryn and her books, visit cathrynhein.com

Facebook: facebook.com/cathrynhein
Twitter: @CathrynHein

Rural Romance

Eddie and the Show Queen

Elsa's Stand

The Country Girl

Chrissy and the Burroughs Boy

Wayward Heart

Santa and the Saddler

April's Rainbow

Summer and the Groomsman

The Falls

Rocking Horse Hill

Heartland

Heart of the Valley

The Horseman's Promise

Romantic Adventure

The French Prize

Eddie and
THE SHOW QUEEN

CATHRYN HEIN

First published 2019

ISBN 9780648000587

Eddie and the Show Queen is a work of fiction. All names, people, places, businesses, events or incidences, are fictitious and a product of the author's imagination. Any similarities to actual people, living or dead, or actual places or events are entirely coincidental.

Cover Art by Kellie Dennis at Book Cover by Design
www.bookcoverbydesign.co.uk

For Jim

ONE

MELANIE ARGYLE SNAPPED her fingers at her sulking son. 'Come along, Eddie. I haven't got all day.'

Eddie groaned. He really did not want to go to Lindner's. Even the thought of it made his goolies shrink up protectively.

'Don't you groan at me, Edmond Argyle. Put your boots on.'

'But I haven't finished my morning tea.'

She snatched the remaining bite of lemon slice off his plate and popped it into her mouth. 'Have now.'

Eddie's brother, Harry, who was standing behind her, grinned. Eddie threw him a sneer, then gave a longing look at his empty plate. He'd been enjoying that slice.

'Why can't Harry do it? He's always bragging how much bigger and stronger he is.' Which he wasn't. Not much, anyway.

'Your brother has work to do.'

'And I don't?'

'You do. Coming with me.'

There was never any defying Melanie Argyle when she

wanted something. Eddie straightened from the kitchen table and dragged his socked feet to the door. His mum didn't allow dirty farm boots in the house. The only dirty things allowed were looks, and then only from her, although Eddie and his brother exchanged their fair share with each other behind their mum's back.

Harry was still grinning. Not that that was anything unusual these days. Since meeting his girlfriend, Summer, jug-eared Harry had turned into an even bigger bumbling twit than he'd been before.

'You'll keep,' Eddie muttered, earning himself a cuff under the ear from his mum.

'What did I say about fighting in the house?'

Harry's grin turned even broader. There would be pain when Eddie got him alone, serious pain.

Hat pulled down and hands shoved deep into the pockets of his jeans, Eddie followed his mum out to his ute. Why she needed him was anyone's guess. Lindner's was a well-run garden centre. There was always someone on hand to hoist potting mix or whatever, and while his mother might be half the size of her gigantic sons, she was strong. You didn't help run a farm or raise two strapping boys without developing a muscle or two.

She was up to something. He hoped like hell it had nothing to do with Alice Lindner.

Eddie sulked the entire drive into Levenham. His mum ignored him, humming along to the radio and checking Facebook on her phone, all with her mouth half lifted in one of her smug you-can-sook-all-you-like, doesn't-bother-me smiles.

Mondays were the nursery's quietest day and the carpark held only a few cars near the entrance. Eddie chose a space a bit further away, in a patch of sun. Autumn was fast drifting into winter, and the air was chilly despite the clear sky. At least the wind wasn't up. Levenham was a small town only twenty or so kilometres from South Australia's isolated southernmost coast, and that separating strip of land did nothing to warm a wind that could sweep straight at them from the frozen plains of Antarctica, when the mood took it.

Though an Antarctic wind would probably feel cosy compared to any welcome he'd get at Lindner's.

Eddie dug his fists deeper into his pockets as he followed his mum to the entrance. Lindner's had been operating for over twenty-five years and the entrance was a showcase of Ross Lindner's expertise. A shaded stone path with bright moss growing between the joints led to a lush, leafy bower and pond spanned by a sturdy timber bridge. The effect was like entering a room where the only sound was the plinkety-plink of water as it tumbled over a raised rock formation. It was pretty, ridiculously so, but the sound of all that running water made Eddie wish he'd gone to the loo before he left home.

Like he wasn't uncomfortable enough.

At the end of the bridge a pair of automatic doors slid open, gusting out a warm peaty smell. Eddie trailed his mum inside, his gaze darting immediately to the counter and the information desk. He breathed out. Maybe he was in luck and Alice was out the back or not working today.

There were plenty of places she could hide, though. The indoor area was well lit thanks to skylights in the roof and industrial pendulum lamps, but Alice was tiny, an energetic blonde pixie who could be anywhere among the lush plants, stacks of pots and shelves of garden paraphernalia.

'Oh, look,' said his mum, 'there's Ross. Just the man. Grab me some snail pellets, would you, Eddie? I won't be long.' Without waiting for an answer, she hurried through another set of glass sliding doors to the outdoor section.

Eddie took a long look around. Still no Alice. He sauntered towards a likely looking shelf and peered at the multiple options for snail destruction. A hand-written sign dangled from below the boxes of pellets. He recognised Alice's loopy script and experienced a painful tug on his heart. Once upon a time, she'd written him notes and cards in that same script. Words telling him how much she loved him. How they'd be together forever. Teenage stuff – stupid but nice.

Did you know, read the sign, *that there are non-chemical ways to get rid of snails? Simple solutions using things you already have at home. Just ask!*

He fingered the sign for a few seconds and with a quiet sigh picked up a box and scanned the back. The active ingredient sounded hellish.

'You could try crushed eggshells instead of chemical warfare, you know.'

Eddie muttered a mental *shit* and closed his eyes. Taking a breath, he shoved the box back on to the shelf and turned.

Alice regarded him with folded arms. Eddie was a big bloke. Really big. Six feet five and one-quarter – that quarter mattered – and built, as his equally enormous gramps liked to joke, like a concrete blockhouse. Yet this tiny person had the capacity to hurt him like no other.

'Alice.'

'Eddie,' she replied, without a scrap of warmth.

'I'm just waiting for Mum.'

Why did he say that? It made him sound like a tool, as if he didn't have anything better to do than hang around a garden centre, waiting for his mother. He had plenty of better things to do. They were drenching cattle this week, and as soon as the paddocks had dried out enough after their recent soaking, Eddie planned to be out on the tractor seeding.

'You might be waiting a while. She just disappeared into the roses with Dad.'

Bugger. If there was one thing his mum was mad for, it was roses. The front garden at Talanga was a maze of the thorny things, though they did look good in bloom.

Alice stepped closer and Eddie's lungs locked, then she reached around him and straightened the snail pellet box he'd hastily dumped. Casting him a look he couldn't interpret, she swung towards the counter, the end of her long blonde ponytail clipping him across the chest as she went.

Eddie's focus dropped immediately to her body. Even in her uniform of heavy-duty khaki work trousers, matching shirt and steel-capped boots, she was glorious. Fine-boned, slim and pert, but strong, too. A fascinating combination of female softness and athleticism. He'd once spent ages tracing his hands over her curves, marvelling at her beauty, at how, despite their size difference, she perfectly fitted him.

His Alice of the wonderland.

She slid behind the counter and started tapping at the computer.

Eddie scratched his head. Maybe he should go find his mum before she really got lost in roses stuff. Or maybe he could stop behaving like his bumbling brother and talk to Alice. They used to talk for hours when they were an item, surely they could make civilised conversation for ten minutes?

He wandered over to the counter. Alice glanced up, pursed her pretty lips and went back to whatever she was doing.

Another tug hurt his heart. With everyone else, Alice was a cute-as-a-button girl whose sweet bubbliness was so infectious people couldn't help but smile in her presence. With him she was stiff and cold, and nothing like the Alice he once had loved.

Still loved.

In front of the till was a raffle book with its cover folded back and a pen jammed in the join to keep it open at the next ticket. Eddie bent to read the details and let out an amused *humph* when he realised it was promoting the Show Queen contest.

'Something funny?' asked Alice.

'Just this Show Queen thing. Bit stupid, isn't it?'

'What's so stupid about raising money for local charities?'

'Well nothing, but it's all a bit …'

Old-fashioned, is what Eddie thought. A Show Queen competition? Where the winner was crowned at a big ceremony and expected to parade about like royalty afterwards, shaking hands and kissing babies? That kind of stuff went the day of the dodo years ago. It didn't matter that the Levenham Wine Show committee, who were running the event, had made it open slather, with every man and his dog – literally – eligible to enter, and the winner determined solely by who raised the most money, it was still pretty dumb.

But from the way Alice was standing, arms folded and weight cocked on one hip, saying so might not be smart.

'Just because you don't care about anything, doesn't mean you can make fun of others who do. Oh, sorry,' she touched a finger to her chin, 'silly me. You do care about one thing. Pity it's just where your next easy lay is coming from.'

'Hey, hang on.'

That wasn't fair, on either count. Eddie cared about a lot of things. The farm, his family. His mates. His football team, the Gerrinton Giants. His cricket team. His red kelpie, Blue.

Her.

As for easy lays, there hadn't been one of those for a long time.

She waved a dismissal. 'Don't bother defending yourself, Eddie. I've seen you in action, remember.'

Eddie gritted his teeth. 'That was ...'

Hard to explain. And now wasn't the time for it.

'Yes?'

He shook his head. What was the point? Alice wouldn't believe him anyway.

Eddie picked up the raffle book and read the fine print. Bugger. He'd forgotten that the new cancer centre at the hospital was one of the charities. Alice's mum, Kate, had been diagnosed with a grade-three brain tumour the year Eddie and Alice started going out and it had claimed her life barely three years later.

Kate and her family had been fortunate, if you could call it that that. Most sufferers of her kind of tumour were lucky to survive a year or two. Local oncology services had been minimal to non-existent then, and Kate's endurance was more a testament to willpower than any medical intervention. No wonder Alice was defending the Show Queen competition. She wouldn't want anyone to suffer like her mum.

'I care about more than you realise,' he said, flicking through the raffle book and counting. He pulled out his wallet and checked his cash supply. He had enough. 'I'll take the rest of the book.'

For a heartbeat, Alice's expression seemed to soften. Then she looked away. 'Nice gesture.'

'It's not a gesture. I want to help.'

'A few raffle tickets won't make much difference.'

He glanced at her. Something in her tone suggested that she wasn't referring to the charity. 'What would, then?'

'Nothing you could do.'

'You'd be surprised.'

For a long moment, Alice remained quiet. Eddie held his breath as her gaze raked over his face. A chance was all he wanted, to prove that he wasn't whom she thought, and to make amends for the hurt he'd somehow caused her and still didn't understand.

That he was still the bloke she'd once loved.

'Go on, then,' she said finally. 'Surprise me.'

He tapped the raffle book. 'This Show Queen thing is open to anyone. I could have a go.'

Alice laughed. Eddie didn't. He'd considered it quite a clever idea.

'What's so funny about me entering? No reason I couldn't win this thing.'

'You? As Show Queen?'

'King, not queen.' There was nothing queenly about Eddie. 'And why not? It's not like it takes any special skill. It's just running a few raffles.'

'Just a few raffles, huh?'

He shrugged. 'Maybe a sausage sizzle.'

Alice's blue eyes took on a dangerous glitter. 'Do it, then. Enter. I dare you.'

He didn't like that glitter. It made him nervous. 'I bloody might.'

'Might? Thought so. All talk.' She returned her gaze to the computer and began clicking the mouse.

'All right, I will.'

'Sure. Whatever.' She kept clicking. A printer whirred. 'Will.'

Alice bobbed down then rose holding a piece of paper. She slapped the printout on the counter and banged a pen on top of it. Eddie eyed both warily.

'Show Queen entry,' she said.

Bugger. Now he'd have to fill it in, and everything in Alice's expression told Eddie that he had no idea what he was committing himself to.

She pushed the pen and paper closer and arched a fine blonde eyebrow.

Eddie rubbed his mouth to hide a grimace. This is what you got for being a big-mouthed idiot still crazy about your ex-girlfriend four years after you'd split up. With a shallow sigh, he picked up the pen.

When he'd finished, Alice snatched up the form and checked it through. Satisfied, she passed it back. 'You need to drop it in to the Tourist Office. They'll pass it on to the Wine Show committee.'

Eddie folded the sheet and pocketed it, only for Alice to curl her fingers in a 'gimme' gesture. Assuming she meant the form, he reached for it.

'Not that. Money for the raffle tickets. You were going to buy the rest of the book, remember?'

Oh yeah. So he was. Eddie dug out his wallet and handed over the cash, wishing he'd never looked at the rotten raffle book. Too late now, and at least filling out his name and address and tearing off tickets gave him some-thing to do besides freak out over the Show Queen thing.

Harry would piss himself laughing when he found out. As for the footy boys, that didn't bear thinking about. His mum? She was too aware of Eddie's feelings for Alice and would know straightaway that he was up to something. Perhaps that wasn't a bad thing. If he asked nicely, she might even lend him a hand.

He'd bloody need it if he was to pull off this stunt.

Alice didn't say a word, but he could feel her gaze lasering the top of his head and had to stop himself from scratching at the itchy feeling it left.

'Who's running this raffle anyway?' he asked as he tore off the final ticket.

'Who do you think?' Alice leaned forward, eyes wide in her biggest 'derr' look. 'Me, Eddie. You've just helped fund your greatest Show Queen rival.'

TWO

'LET'S GO TO THE PUB,' said Alice, linking arms with her best friends Chrissy James and Paige de Bruin, and practically skipping them across the carpark of Wallace Park, Levenham's netball and tennis complex.

Their Rebels Netball Club team meeting had taken less time than anticipated and now Friday night stretched emptily ahead. They had a game tomorrow and Alice had a dozen Show Queen chores to attend to at home, but home meant quiet and too much opportunity for Eddie to slither into her mind, and she'd had enough of that great lump tangling her brain for one week. A drink or two in the cosy back bar of the Australian Arms with friends, surrounded by people and laughter, was much more appealing.

'I shouldn't,' said Chrissy.

'A couple of drinks won't hurt,' said Paige, bumping her hip against Chrissy's and causing her to stumble a step.

Where Alice was small, slight and fast, Paige was tall, strong and statuesque thanks to her Dutch ancestry. She was also as smart as a whip. Alice considered her magnificent and desperately wished some gorgeous local bloke would hurry up and discover the same. Her friend hadn't had the easiest of upbringings, and if anyone deserved everlasting love it was Paige.

'Didn't do any harm last week,' Paige reminded her.

'Or the week before,' said Alice, squeezing Chrissy's arm. 'And I'll buy.'

Chrissy narrowed her eyes. 'This had better not be one of your tricks.'

'Nope, purely spur of the moment.' Which was true, but if Chrissy happened to bump into Nick Burroughs then that would be an excellent bonus.

Alice was getting a marvellous kick out of Nick's pursuit of Chrissy. His efforts, which had so far included a hilarious, attention-grabbing parade and a glittery, hand-decorated card, were ridiculously romantic. Even better, Nick was using Alice as a conduit, which meant she got to watch it all unfold up close. The view was so wonderful it was almost enough to make a girl want it for herself.

Chrissy's expression stayed suspicious. 'It'd better be.'

'Why are you being so funny about Nick anyway?' asked Paige. 'I thought you said the card was cute.'

'It was.'

'And?' said Alice. Cute wouldn't cut it. Yes, Chrissy had a right to be a little miffed that Nick barely had acknowledged her existence at school, especially after all the embarrassing things she'd done to get his attention, but he was doing his best to make up for it. And school was school. They were in their twenties now, grown up. This had the potential to be the real deal.

'And nothing. It was one card.' She sniffed. 'I sent him at least four.'

'Must do better, huh?' said Paige.

'Exactly.'

'Well,' said Alice, 'I think it was gorgeous of him to send one, and a handmade one at that. There aren't too many men in this world who'd do that.'

A softening of Chrissy's expression showed her point had hit home.

'Pub, then?'

'Why not?' said Chrissy, laughing and forging onwards.

As usual, the pub was crowded with Friday-night revellers – people hanging out at the bar, waiting for the night's Australian Rules Football game to start on the big screen, meeting friends or enjoying a comforting meal at the pub's excellent bistro.

Spotting a small gap at the bar, Alice shot into it, popping up in front of Nick's equally dreamy and sadly now off-the-dating-market brother, Danny, like a jack-in-the-box.

'Three glasses of shiraz, please,' she said, leaning her elbows on the countertop, cupping her cheeks and blinking coyly at him. Like Nick, Danny was a sweetheart, and Alice's play-flirts usually earned her a smile, and occasionally an extra slosh of wine.

'You sure you're old enough to drink, little girl?'

Alice screwed up her nose at him. 'Everyone's a smartypants.'

Danny laughed and reached above the bar for the wineglasses.

Alice took a moment to scan the crowd. No Nick. No Eddie either, thank God. One encounter was enough for the week.

She turned back to Danny. 'Hey, tell Beth to keep Friday the nineteenth free.'

'What are you stealing my girlfriend for this time?'

'Girl's Night In at the netball clubrooms.'

'For the Show Queen comp?'

Alice nodded.

Danny gave her a look as he poured. 'An all-girls night? Sounds dangerous.'

'Silly man. That's the whole idea.' She hoisted herself up on tiptoe and leaned closer. 'By the way, Chrissy's here.'

'And?'

'And your brother.' She rolled her eyes. '*Honestly*. How am I supposed to vicariously live their romance if you won't help them see each other?'

Danny lifted the wineglasses closer to Alice. 'Yeah, all right. I'll let him know.'

'Thank you. And Beth about the nineteenth. Don't forget her.'

'Never.' His smile at the mention of his girlfriend made Alice feel slightly gooey. There was nothing so gorgeous as a man in love.

She found the girls in the lounge bar near the open fire. Settling on to the stool they'd snagged for her, Alice raised her glass in a toast. 'To the Rebels and another win tomorrow.'

'And to your Show Queen quest,' added Paige as they touched glasses.

'Speaking of which,' said Alice, 'I had an idea for another fundraiser. A second-hand book sale. We could hold it at the library, in one of the event rooms, maybe combine it with a talk or something.' She checked Paige, who was one of the librarians at Levenham's popular council-run library. 'What do you think? Doable?'

'I can't see why not.' Paige considered for a moment. 'What about a book swap rather than a sale, where people pay a fee scaled on how many books they bring? We could lay on wine and cheese to make it more fun, and keep people browsing and talking.'

'Or add some live music,' threw in Chrissy, warming to the theme, which was no surprise. As marketing manager for Ryan's Winery, promo was her thing. Alice was enormously grateful to have Chrissy on board for her assault on the Show Queen crown.

'Or a poetry slam,' said Alice.

'Yes!' said Paige. 'You would not believe how many closet poets there are out there, and because the opportunity arises so rarely, most of them would jump at the chance to read their work in public. It's the sort of event that would attract all ages and sexes, too. You could advertise it as catering for any kind of poetry, from limericks to bush ballads, with the only requirement being that they're entertaining.'

'Brilliant!' said Chrissy. She clutched Alice's arm, her eyes wide. 'Alice, this could be huge. Just think, you could host a whole range of open-mike-type nights. Comedy, music. Speed painting.'

'Theatre sports!' Alice clapped her hands and jiggled. Her friends were amazing.

More ideas were tossed around, Alice tapping notes into her phone as the girls talked faster and faster about the events she could host, and the money they'd raise. Before long, their wineglasses were empty.

Chrissy gathered up the empties. 'I'll get this round.'

'I said I was buying!'

'Leave her,' said Paige. 'She just wants to check if Nick's here.'

'Do not.'

'Do so!' said Alice.

'We'll keep an eye out this side, then, shall we?' Paige

called out as Chrissy stomped off haughtily, causing Alice and her to lean against one another as they cracked up.

'There's a good chance Nick'll be there, too,' said Alice when she'd finished giggling. 'I told Danny she was here. He said he'd let Nick know.'

Paige turned suddenly wistful. 'He's nuts about her, isn't he?'

Alice sighed. 'Completely. If she wasn't our friend, I'd hate her.'

'Me too.'

They shared a smile.

'Don't worry, you'll still have me in old spinsterhood,' joked Alice, bumping her shoulder fondly against Paige's.

'You're too kind.' Paige scanned the crowd. 'You know, the boyfriend thing I can give or take, but right now I would bloody kill for a decent one-night stand. Maybe a two-nighter. Some proper sweaty, fun sex. The kind that leaves you tingly for days and feeling great about yourself.'

'Yes,' said Alice, feeling wistful herself. It had been ages since she'd had sex. Her last experience had been with an irrigation supplies sales rep who'd since moved territories and still occasionally texted to say hello. Sadly, there'd been no toe-curling passion for either of them and both were content to stay friends. 'The trouble with awesome sex like that is it makes you want more, which kind of defeats the purpose of a no-strings one-nighter.'

'True. Anyway, it's all beside the point, isn't it? There's no one on offer. Danny's taken, Nick's gaga over Chrissy.'

There was Eddie, thought Alice, then blinked. Where the hell had that come from? That wine must have gone straight to her head.

She stood. 'I'm going to get some water. Do you want some?'

'I wouldn't mind. Thanks.'

Deciding to look in on Chrissy, Alice headed for the front-bar water dispenser. As she turned the corner, she halted so suddenly someone crashed into her back.

'Shit, sorry,' whoever it was said, but Alice didn't acknowledge the apology. Her gaze was locked on the end of the bar where a dark-haired giant with coffee-coloured eyes was enthusiastically hugging a pretty brunette.

Eddie.

'Crap,' said Alice.

'Fuck,' said the man behind her.

Fists clenched, she stalked towards the bar, eyes not leaving her prey for a second. If that slimy rat thought for one moment he could come on to Chrissy, he was about to learn otherwise.

Danny reached Chrissy's section of the bar just as Alice approached.

'Jesus, Chrissy,' he said. 'Don't talk to him. He's a sleaze.'

Eddie puffed out his chest like the peacock he was. 'Am not.'

'Are so,' said Alice, a response echoed by the man behind her, whose voice she now recognised as belonging to Nick Burroughs. Good. With Nick around, Eddie wouldn't stand a chance.

Eddie grinned at Nick, only for his smile to falter and disappear completely when he spied Alice. He nodded at her. 'Alice.'

'Eddie.'

For a pause, no one said anything. Alice stared at Eddie, while Chrissy's gaze shunted between Nick and Alice, becoming more worried with each cycle.

Danny broke the standoff with a knuckle rap on the bar

top. 'Are you guys going to stand there like a bunch of bunnies or is anyone going to order?'

'Sorry,' said Chrissy. 'Three glasses of—'

Nick grabbed her hand. 'Can I have a quick word first?'

Alice pushed her towards him. 'You go with Nick. I'll get the drinks.'

'Are you sure?'

'Yes. I said tonight was my shout.' She gave her another shove. 'Now go.'

Chrissy glanced at Eddie and back at Alice. 'Only if you're sure.'

'Yes! Go!'

Nick led Chrissy off, shooting Alice a wink of thanks over his shoulder as he left. Alice smiled and turned to the bar. 'Three glasses of shiraz, and can you do us some iced water, too, please?'

Ignoring Eddie wasn't easy when he was so big and so close. His beer was on the bar, and from the corner of her eye she could see his long fingers circling the glass. Worse, she could feel his gaze on her. Alice wished he'd go away. His presence was spoiling her excitement over Nick and Chrissy.

'I entered,' he said.

Her head whipped around so hard it shot a pain through her neck. 'You what?'

'The Show Queen thing. I entered.'

Alice could only stare. Eddie had entered? Oh, no, no, no. That was *not* meant to happen. The thing with the form was just to rile him. He wasn't actually meant to go through with it.

A line formed between his brows. 'What's wrong?'

'Nothing.' She focused on the mirrored back of the bar and the fragments of stupid, silly blonde girl reflected there.

Eddie was popular, good-looking and practical, and even though he'd be joining the competition a few weeks late, he was more than capable of making up lost ground. Threats didn't come much bigger than this. 'Nothing at all.'

'Alice.' He lowered onto his elbows, his deep voice hushed. Danny glanced at Alice as he continued to pour, letting her know he'd pull rank if needed. Alice was fine. Eddie would never hurt her. Not that way. 'I thought it was what you wanted.'

He was so close she could smell him. The familiar scents of the soap and washing powder he used. Her heart sped up in recognition. Alice tightened her jaw against it. This was the man who'd taken advantage when she'd been desperate for love and understanding, then compounded the hurt by sleeping with every bit of skirt he could find after they broke up, as if Alice had been nothing special at all. She would not want him again. She would not.

'It was. Is. The more money we raise the better.'

'That was my take too.' He continued to study her, and his voice lowered even further. 'I can pull out.'

'Why would you do that?'

His gaze flicked one last time over hers, then he straightened and shrugged.

'Here you go,' said Danny, setting a tray on the bar and loading it with wine and water glasses.

'Thanks.' Alice went to dig into her handbag and found air. She looked to her side, where it normally hung, and smacked her forehead. 'I'm so sorry. I left my purse with Paige. Can you hang on? I'll be back in a jiffy.'

Not waiting for an answer, she scurried off, cheeks flaming. Of all the silly things, and in front of Eddie, too. His fault. If he hadn't distracted her with his announcement and flustered her with his concern, she would have realised earlier.

'Chrissy went off with Nick,' she said in response to Paige's raised eyebrow at her empty-handed return. 'I said I'd grab the drinks, only I didn't have my bag.' She scrabbled inside her purse and pulled out a fifty-dollar note.

'Alice,' said Paige, tipping her head to indicate behind Alice's back.

'What?'

Paige's sympathetic smile revealed the answer. Alice closed her eyes. Of course he'd paid for the drinks. Eddie might be a man-whore, but he was a chivalrous one. Melanie Argyle had made sure of that.

He set the tray down. 'I figured it'd be easier if I fixed it up.'

'Thanks,' said Alice. She thrust the fifty towards him. 'I don't have anything smaller.'

Eddie shoved his hands into his pockets and shook his head. 'Don't worry about it.'

'Don't be ridiculous.'

'I think I have change,' said Paige, rummaging in her own purse, but Eddie was already stepping backwards.

'Think of it as a donation. For your Show Queen fund.'

Paige stopped her rummaging. 'The donate-to-the-favourite-cause trick, huh? Come on, Eddie, surely a man of your vast experience can sleaze better than that.'

Eddie shot her a glare then looked at Alice. 'Good luck at netball tomorrow. I'll see you around.'

He stomped off, hands deep in his pockets, shoulders hunched in a very un-Eddie-like way. Alice watched until he disappeared around the corner and then slumped onto her stool. Eddie was only being nice and she'd been mean. Twice now, if she added her current lack of graciousness to

Monday's silly prank. No wonder it had backfired. Karma hated a meanie.

Paige regarded Alice with eyes turned to slits. 'You. Eddie. Spill.'

'It's nothing.'

'Didn't look like nothing.' She leaned forward. 'Alice, you've barely said two words to one another since you broke up and he just bought us drinks and wished you luck at netball.'

Alice toyed with telling Paige the mess she'd made and decided against it. It'd require too much explanation. Namely, why she'd goaded Eddie into joining the Show Queen competition in the first place. That would only encourage lengthy analysis and Alice would rather scrub Lindner's customer toilets for a year than suffer a session of that.

Besides, she didn't understand it herself.

'It's nothing. Really. He was just being Eddie. You know what he's like.'

Paige humphed. 'Maybe, but my gut tells me he's up to something.'

Oh, he absolutely was. And Alice only had herself to blame for it.

THREE

LEVENHAM'S HISTORIC MECHANICS' INSTITUTE was a sober grey limestone building tucked behind the main street, half a block from the town's biggest supermarket. Once the town's first library and educational centre, it was now used for community groups and the occasional lecture. Alice's older brothers, both now in the navy, had attended Scout meetings there when they were boys, after a fire destroyed the Scout's old timber clubhouse, and her mum had done yoga classes in one of the upstairs rooms before she'd become sick. Now it was Show Queen HQ.

With all the closest kerbside spaces taken, Alice parked at the supermarket and walked back, her bright-pink down jacket zipped up to the neck and her hands curled in its pockets. It was freezing thanks to a nasty southerly, but Alice took her time, scanning the street for Eddie's car. As a Show Queen entrant, he was obliged to attend the committee's fortnightly Monday meetings. Trouble was, she had no idea what he drove these days, and he could be using any number of the farm's vehicles. With a bit of luck, he would be already inside and she'd be able to slide into a seat at the back, as far away from him as possible.

Though light glowed through the ground-floor windows, the looming two-storey institute looked as gloomy as she felt. The Rebels had another win on Saturday, and the garden centre's Sunday takings had been above average for this time of year. She'd sold another book full of raffle tickets and Nick had texted to say that he'd drop by at lunchtime tomorrow with another gift for Chrissy. Normally, all these things would have Alice on a high, but since Eddie's announcement on Friday night she'd been flat.

Flat and worried.

What could Eddie possibly want to achieve by entering the Show Queen contest? Alice might have goaded him into it, but Eddie wasn't a total sheep. Nor did he have to save face. He could have played along at the garden centre, not bothered to lodge the entry and left it at that. No one other than Alice would have known.

As for local causes, since when did he care about those? His beloved football team, the Gerrinton Giants, didn't count. All the boys did what they could for the club; however, a football team was hardly a charity. To be fair, she'd had next to no contact with Eddie for four years, but Levenham was home to only seventeen thousand people and their social circles tended to overlap, which was how Alice knew all about Eddie's rampant skirt-chasing. Yet she'd heard nothing about this side of him.

It was flummoxing.

Alice pushed open the door and stood in the foyer listening as she unzipped her jacket. She could hear Sarah Nolan, Levenham Wine Show's committee chairperson, calling for everyone to take a seat. Alice waited until chairs had stopped scraping and the general hubbub had died down before entering.

'Hi, everyone,' she called out. 'Sorry I'm late. How horrible is this wind? It's freezing out there!'

The room filled with return cheerios and grumbling agreement about the weather. Not one voice belonged to Eddie.

So much for her cunning plan.

Two rows of chairs faced a large whiteboard already marked up with entrants' names. Three seats remained unoccupied, all next to each other at the end of the front row. Alice took the one adjacent to Steph Albrecht, who worked at a local car dealership and whom Alice knew from Steph's regular visits to Lindner's. She smiled at Steph as she settled down.

Sarah usually ran the meetings with council's tourism officer, Tiffany Duncan, except tonight, sitting like an empress on a chair beside the table, was town matriarch and Wine Show patron Audrey Wallace. She nodded regally at Alice, who grinned and waved back.

More than a few people found Mrs Wallace and her old-money wealth and attitude intimidating. Not Alice. The elderly lady might be almost comically posh, but she was also intelligent, glamorous, and harboured zero tolerance for fools and vegetarians. Glaucoma had destroyed most of the vision in her left eye. To compensate, Mrs Wallace peered at people with an intensity that left many unnerved. Alice thought her formidable yet marvellous. A person who made things happen. The Wine Show wouldn't exist without Mrs Wallace's relentless efforts to get it up and running. Nor would many other local events.

'I had hoped to introduce our new entrant,' said Sarah, 'but it appears he's been waylaid.'

'Nah, I'm here,' said Eddie, tipping his wide-brimmed hat as he strode in. His colossal size made the high-ceilinged institute feel small. 'G'day,' he drawled, sounding like an Aussie tourism advert.

Margot Shulte, who seemed to be more in the Show Queen for the attention than any urge to help the community, tittered. Alice felt an overwhelming desire to shoot daggers at her. She hadn't liked Margot much at school and her laziness so far in the competition had done nothing to change that opinion.

Even Alice had to admit that, with his broad smile and undeniable rugged handsomeness, Eddie was a total country-boy hottie. That he'd clearly come straight from farm work only added to his appeal. He wore jeans tucked into a pair of calf-high heavy-duty leather boots, a checked flannelette shirt with the cuffs folded up one turn, and a sheepskin-lined oilskin vest with a thread of blue baler twine dangling from one of its pockets. Eddie looked capable, trustworthy, fit and more than a bit sexy.

'Eddie Argyle. Sorry I'm late. We're still calving at home and the little sods have no respect for meetings. Or dinnertime.' His gaze connected with Alice's. He waved his hat her way. 'You can blame Alice here for me joining in the fun.'

Several whispers sounded. Steph regarded Alice with a furrowed brow. Alice glared at him, her cheeks on fire, but unlike every other recent encounter Eddie's grin didn't falter.

'Granny B!' he said, spotting Audrey Wallace.

Alice wondered how he was familiar enough to use her nickname, then remembered that Eddie and his brother, Harry, played football with Mrs Wallace's grandson-in-law,

Josh Sinclair. Harry had even been groomsman at Josh's and Emily Wallace-Jones's wedding.

Mrs Wallace lifted her cheek and Eddie dutifully planted a kiss on it. 'Looking flash as always. Hey, Tiff, how's things? Great dress. Another of your own creations?'

To Alice's annoyance, he kissed her, too, then Sarah. Mrs Wallace was the only one who didn't blush like a schoolgirl.

He took the seat next to Alice, scraping the chair over a fraction when his bulk overflowed into her space.

'Sorry,' he said, not sounding even remotely apologetic.

He leaned forward, his focus on Sarah and twirling his hat in his hands, oozing eager energy, like a giant sheepdog puppy.

Alice wanted to hiss at him, but she couldn't. Especially after his announcement that his involvement was her fault. What was the story with that?

What was the story with Eddie altogether?

She fixed her attention on Sarah. The point of these meetings was to ensure events didn't clash, that no one scheduled something the committee deemed inappropriate, to discuss media opportunities, and to promote a sense of competition by ranking everyone on a leaderboard.

As far as Alice was concerned, it was a good way for others to steal fundraising ideas and had said as much to Mrs Wallace when she had bumped into her in McArthur Street, Levenham's main thoroughfare, a few days after the first Show Queen meeting. Her complaint had been shooed away.

'It will keep you on your toes,' Mrs Wallace had claimed in her clipped, aristocratic voice.

'But won't the leaderboard put the less successful fundraisers off?'

Mrs Wallace had smiled. 'Perhaps.'

Alice had stared at her. 'You *want* them to pull out?'

'Clever chap, Darwin,' Mrs Wallace had replied, before extracting a cigar and lighter from the pocket of her long fur coat and striding off.

It had taken Alice some time to puzzle out her reasoning. In the end she thought she understood. As the also-rans dropped away, rivalry between the frontrunners would increase, cranking up the pressure to hold events that were not only unique and media worthy, but wallet-opening. With fewer entrants and events and a tighter, more exciting competition, the risk of fundraising fatigue in the local population also was reduced.

The Show Queen competition wasn't a cute country festivity. It was a blood sport.

'Okay,' said Sarah when she'd finished the preliminaries. 'What's everyone got scheduled for this fortnight? Eddie, perhaps you can start us off.'

Eddie looked momentarily startled. Then he stood and faced the group. 'I have a sausage sizzle planned for after footy training this Thursday night. That ought to be good for a bit of cash. The boys love a sausage.'

'Don't we all,' murmured Steph, forcing Alice to muffle a laugh.

'Anything else?' prompted Sarah.

Eddie scratched at his jaw. 'S'pose I could raffle a slab of beer?'

A couple of entrants snickered. Someone coughed. People shifted in their seats and exchanged smiles. Sarah had her lips rolled together so tightly they'd almost disappeared.

'What?' he said, frowning at Sarah and then at Alice.

His expression was so little-boy-lost, Alice felt a pang of sympathy. Eddie really didn't have a clue.

'That's fine, Eddie,' said Sarah. 'There's no shame in a modest start. I'm sure you'll wow us all with some amazing activities in the future. Now, Chelsea and Willow? Perhaps you can go next.'

Alice edged onto her hip to look behind, where the Phillips twins stood in the back row, dressed in the same clothes and indistinguishable from one another. The pair had signed up as a team, which should have been against the rules but had been permitted given their twin-ness. With their long, wavy, golden-brown hair, beautiful white teeth, gold-flecked hazel eyes and fresh young faces, they would make photogenic Show Queens. Until Eddie, Alice had considered them her main rivals.

'Wednesday we're holding a clothes swap,' said one twin.

'And Sunday,' chimed in the other, 'is our scavenger hunt. Then our dance marathon starts the following Friday.'

'With our craft stall on the Sunday.'

'If we can still stand after all that dancing.'

The pair exchanged a look and giggled.

Alice glanced at Eddie. The man was swallowing like he'd just inhaled a fly. His discomfort should have made her feel smug, but it didn't. All she felt was mean again. Despite their past, Alice was well aware that Eddie's big body contained a big heart. She'd once been the benefi-ciary of it and it had been special and beautiful, until it warped.

'Good work,' said Sarah. She regarded Tiffany. 'We have media sorted for that?'

Tiffany scrolled through her tablet and then nodded. 'Community radio is covering the whole of the danceathon, and the *Leader* is sending a photographer to cover both it and the scavenger hunt.'

'Excellent.' Sarah zoned in on Michael Perryman, who, upon reading the conditions of entry and realising they were so inclusive they'd failed to exempt non-humans, had entered his black-and-tan kelpie, Missy, for a lark. 'What's Missy up to this week, Mick?'

Mick was in his late seventies, with walnut skin, a balding, age-spot-speckled head, and knees that had seen better days. He rose slowly, bones clicking audibly. Missy watched his every move until a gesture saw her trotting to the front, where she regarded the gathering with intelligent brown eyes before barking three times.

'Missy says she has the dog-and-spoon race Sunday week.' Missy made a whingeing noise, lowered her head and wrapped a paw over her snout. 'She also apologises for not organising more.' The dog straightened and woofed. 'But a girl has a farm to work.'

Everyone clapped. They all adored Missy and Mick's performances.

So far Mick had organised few events, saving up for the big one in the Show Queen's final week when he planned to hold a dog puissance – a dog high-jump competition – in Civic Park. Sponsorship had already hit nine thousand dollars and was still growing. Even with costs taken out, that would still leave a lot for prize money, and as Missy had won the Kelpie High Jump at Casterton's famous Kelpie Muster two years before, she was prime dog to bag it.

'Should have entered Blue in this thing instead of me,' muttered Eddie. 'He'd stand a better chance.'

'You still could,' said Steph.

Eddie shook his head. 'I'm in enough trouble without adding my dog to the mix.'

The others detailed their events, each announcement seeing Eddie's shoulders sag lower. Alice felt a strange urge to pat his knee in sympathy. Why she'd want to do that was unfathomable. The last thing she wanted was Eddie comforted. Instead of quitting the game, he might take it as encouragement.

Finally, it was Alice's turn.

She spread her hands in apology. 'Other than my ongoing raffle, I don't have anything scheduled until our Girls' Night In on the nineteenth. Tickets for that sold out on Saturday, which I'm thrilled about. Don't worry, I have *lots* of things planned for the coming months. They are going to be huge!' She raised her arms and performed an excited shimmy then sobered as she scanned the faces of her fellow entrants. 'I know we're in competition, but I hope you'll join in the fun. Not just my events. All our activities. The charities we're supporting are important to our town and to its people. We're not raising money for far-off strangers. We're raising money for organisations that assist people we know, people we love.' She flattened her palm on her chest. '*Our* people. That means the more we collectively raise the better. We're in competition yes, but don't let this blind us to what the Show Queen is really about.'

Missy woofed.

Alice laughed. 'Thanks, Missy. And don't worry, I'll make sure you can come along to every event, too, even if I have to smuggle you in.'

'Thank you, Alice, for that timely reminder of why we're here,' said Sarah. 'And I'm certainly looking forward to hearing what you have planned. I'm sure it'll be even more exciting than you say. Remember, everyone, we can't approve any of your fundraising activities or events unless you submit via the online form, so make sure you get those in well in advance. Now,' she clapped her hands, 'the tallies as they stand so far. Tiffany?'

Tiffany stood with her tablet in one hand and a white-board marker in the other. 'In last place we have Eddie on zero.' She smiled kindly at him. *Too kindly*, Alice thought. Tiffany was a pretty divorcee in her early thirties with a penchant for bright clothes that, according to Paige, who knew her from Tiffany's work with the library, she designed and made herself. Just the sort Eddie was likely to chase. Not that she cared what Eddie did, but surely there was some rule about fraternising with entrants? 'I'm sure this figure will be very different next meeting.'

She went through the remaining dozen contestants. As Alice expected, the twins were in the lead with almost two thousand dollars to their names, which was as worrying as it was impressive, seeing as they'd barely got started. Alice was a close second thanks to the previous month's car-wash, balloon-pop and wetlands-hike events. A few others hovered around the thousand-dollar mark, with the remainder scoring in the mid-hundreds.

With the tally done, Sarah closed the meeting. Chairs scraped as people stood and started moving off or grouped for a chat. Despite Tiffany's smile, Eddie remained seated, his big body hunched.

He caught Alice staring and shook his head. 'I'll never catch up.'

'You might, if you put the work in.'

'I had no idea it'd be so ...' He looked up at the institute's ornate pressed-tin ceiling.

'Cutthroat?'

'Yeah.' He rubbed his mouth. 'This isn't a joke, is it? It matters. To Levenham.' He paused. 'To you.'

'Yes.'

Eddie contemplated his hat, circling the brim in his big hands. 'Right, then.' He shoved the hat on his head and stood. 'Better get my A game on if I'm going to win this thing. Catch you later.'

He sauntered off, leaving Alice fuming at her stupidity. Why had she encouraged him? Why, why, why? Eddie had his competitive juices up now.

'I do hope Edmond gets his act together,' said Mrs Wallace, joining Alice, her focus unembarrassedly on Eddie's rear. 'A man of his attractiveness would make a splendid king, don't you think?'

'No, I do not. Anyway, I thought you were on my side?'

Mrs Wallace's mouth curled in a sly smile. 'Only when it suits me, dear Alice. Only when it suits me.'

FOUR

'YOU,' said Paige, jabbing a finger towards Alice, 'are in serious trouble.'

Alice's heart slumped. She'd known this was coming but had hoped to delay Paige's interrogation for another day or so at least. There were no secrets in Levenham, however, and Paige encountered hundreds of people a day at the library.

Alice gave Chrissy another farewell wave and faced her friend. 'You heard.'

'Of course I bloody heard. This morning. From Nancy Treadwell, of all people. You though,' she gave her finger another schoolmarm waggle, 'have known for at least an entire evening and *did not say a thing*. Not cool, Alice. Not cool.'

'I know and I'm sorry.' She looped her arm through Paige's and steered her towards her car. The night was cold, and they were sweaty from netball practice. If Paige insisted on discussing Eddie, Alice wanted to do it somewhere warm.

'Are we talking sorry-sorry or sorry-not-sorry here?'

'We're talking a grovelling truly-rooly sorry for not telling my best friend in the whole wide world what my sleazebucket ex has done.' And herself. If Alice hadn't been such a smartypants this wouldn't be happening.

Paige sniffed. 'I should hope so.' They walked a few steps. 'I know you don't like talking about Eddie, but this is the Show Queen.'

'I know. I would have said something tonight I promise. I just didn't want to spoil Chrissy's surprise.' Nick had dropped off another card for Alice to deliver, which she'd done on arrival with much teasing, until Chrissy had wrestled the envelope out of Alice's grip and run off with it to her car. 'I don't want her worrying about me when she has so much on.'

'Friends are supposed to worry about each other. It's part of the deal.'

Alice squeezed Paige's arm then let go to dig out her keys.

'Okay. Spill,' ordered Paige when they were cosy inside Alice's car, with the engine running and the heater blasting.

The radio was playing Lorde's new single. Alice turned it down and rested her hands in her lap. She stared at them, not knowing where to start. With Eddie at the garden centre, or back further, to the aching mess that their breakup became.

She looked up as Paige stroked her hair.

'This is me, Alice. You can trust me with anything, you know that.'

'I know.' She breathed in deeply. 'Eddie came into the garden centre with his mum the Monday before last. He saw my Show Queen raffle. Made some comment about the competition being stupid. I bit back that just because he didn't care about anything other than his next lay, that didn't give him the right to laugh at others who did.'

'Ouch.'

'I know. You know I'm not normally an awful person, but Eddie ...' Alice lifted her hands and let them fall heavily into her lap. 'I can't think properly when I'm near him. He's so tangled up with Mum's death that if I think of him, I think of her, and it's like all the hurt comes rushing back.'

She still felt bad about the 'next lay' comment. It was petty and mean, and Eddie had looked genuinely wounded by it.

'What happened after that?'

'He muttered something about caring more than I realise, then bought the rest of the raffle tickets.'

'Did he now?' Paige's lips pursed. 'Interesting. Then he what? Announced he was going to enter the Show Queen, too?'

'Not exactly.' Although the car wasn't yet fully warm, guilt had made her hot. Alice turned down the heater, then the radio some more. Running out of anything else to fiddle with, she released her hair from its ponytail and played with the tie instead, revealing the details in a cringing rush as she pulled and twanged the band. 'I made some jibe about a few raffle tickets hardly making a difference and then he asked what would, and I replied nothing he could do, and he replied that I'd be surprised.'

Alice covered her face, braced for Paige's reproof.

'And you challenged him to surprise you.'

She nodded. 'It gets worse.'

'Okaay.'

She peeked through her fingers at Paige. 'When he mentioned having a go at the Show Queen, I laughed.'

Paige winced, but it was a sympathetic kind of wince.

'There's more.' Her voice became even smaller. 'I printed out an entry form and slapped it on the counter, daring him to enter.'

'Oh dear.' Paige covered her mouth, a giggle bursting through her fingers. 'I'm sorry. I know I shouldn't laugh.' She reached across to hug Alice around the shoulders. 'You really don't do things by halves, do you?'

'No, unfortunately. I honestly didn't expect him to go through with it. I mean, why would he? It's not like Eddie cares about the Show Queen, and the only person who would have known about the entry form was me. I thought he'd chuck it in the bin first chance he had. I couldn't believe it on Friday night when he told me he'd entered. Now he's determined to win and it's all my fault.'

'He won't. We'll make sure of it. That Show Queen crown belongs to you.'

Alice stared at the netball courts, where a few dedicated youngsters were practising passes and goal shooting under the lights. 'He offered to quit.'

Paige's eyes widened.

'At the Arms. I think he sensed how upset I was when he announced he'd entered. He got this confused look and said he'd thought it was what I wanted. I replied that it was.' She swallowed, remembering the concern on his face, the delicious smell of him, the memories it reignited. The want. How vulnerable it had made her feel. 'I mustn't have sounded very convincing because he offered to pull out.'

'And you told him not to.'

'How could I answer any other way? The whole idea of the Show Queen is to raise as much money as possible. Asking Eddie to quit just so I'd have a better chance of winning would be nothing but egoism.'

'But you want this, Alice. Really want it.'

'I do, and it would mean a huge amount if I did win. If Mum was alive she'd burst with pride, and I know Dad would love it, too. I want to make them proud. If I ask Eddie to pull out it'd be like cheating. I couldn't do that to them or myself, or the committee. They're working their bums off for this. I have to win on merit.'

'Which means you're stuck.'

'Yep.'

Lines began to form between Paige's brows. 'Do you think Eddie knows how much you want to win?'

'I assume so.'

'Hmm.' With each second, Paige's face scrunched further until it had morphed completely into one of her deep, contemplative looks.

The netballers left the courts. Alice supposed they should go too. She and Paige had work tomorrow and Alice wanted to look in on the twins' clothes swap tomorrow night, but Paige showed no sign of ending her mull. Her brow remained furrowed and the fingers of her left hand beat a rapid tattoo on her thigh.

'Alice,' she said carefully, 'you and Eddie ... What happened?'

Alice stared out the side window. She'd never told anyone the full truth about that time. It was too painful, and she wanted to remember only the beautiful moments of those short, final years with her mum. Not the ugly ones, when Eddie took Alice's clinginess and grief and used it to service his own needs.

To make her pain even worse, Kate Lindner had adored Eddie and wept over the milestones that death was stealing from her – Alice and Eddie's engagement and wedding, the children they'd have. The blessed, golden future her mum had been convinced lay ahead for them both. Alice had played along, torn between wanting her mum's dying dreams to come true, and wanting to lash out over her own heartbreak and festering anger at Eddie's selfishness.

Two days after the funeral, Alice had told the man she'd given her heart and body to, the man she'd loved to the point of worship, they were through, doubling her grief – for what had been with her mum, and what should have been with him.

'Alice?' Paige touched her shoulder. 'I know you said he let you down, but how? He loved you. Everyone could see that.'

'It was a lie.' She regarded her dearest friend, her eyes prickling with hot tears. 'He didn't love me. I was just a means to an end.'

'Oh, honey, maybe ...'

At Paige's tone, she shoved up her hand. 'Don't you dare defend him about this. I know what he was like. And I know what he did afterwards, shagging himself stupid as if he couldn't wait to prove how little I meant.'

The tears Alice had been trying to contain spilled over. Her lip wobbled as though she were five instead of twenty-five and she hated that Eddie could still do this to her. She swiped at them.

'My mother was dying, Paige. Right in front of me, in front of Dad and my brothers. Getting weaker and more pain-racked every day until I was too terrified to leave the room in case she passed alone, without me holding her hand or telling her I loved her. But she made me leave. She said I needed to keep living. For her. She'd push me off the bed and wave me towards Eddie, and I'd go because it made her happy.

'All I wanted in those moments was a bit of comfort, someone strong to hold me, to tell me I'd get through this, and what did Eddie want? Sex, that's what. From the moment we first did it, all he did was push for more. I thought ...' Her breath caught as the hurt returned, fresh and sharp. 'I thought I was ready, that giving my virginity to Eddie would have real meaning. A kind of symbolism, I guess. Like I was somehow doing what Mum wanted me to do. Learning. Living. Loving.' She shook her head in disgust, at her own naivety as much as Eddie's selfishness. 'There was no deeper meaning. He didn't love me. All he cared about was getting that big willie of his wet. It's all he still cares about.'

'I'm so sorry. I had no idea.' Paige looked anguished. 'I wish you'd said. I might have been able to help. The least I could have done was tell Eddie to pull his head in.' She gave a wan smile. 'Big and small.'

Alice smiled too. 'I could have done that myself.' She might have been an emotional ruin, but that didn't mean she'd been weak.

'Why didn't you?' Suddenly, Paige's eyes widened then sharpened scarily. 'Please don't tell me he forced himself on you, because I will take a staple gun to his gonads if he did.'

'No! Eddie would never do that. He was lovely.'

'Just as well. Even the thought makes my fingers trigger-happy. So how, then, if you didn't want to? Big willies are all very nice, but it takes more than a long staff to get me going.'

Alice blinked. 'Long staff?'

'Someone dumped a bagful of old-style sexy historical romances at the library. We didn't want them, so I took them home and have been devouring them like cupcakes. They're brilliant. Stiff staffs and rigid rods popping up all over the place.' She touched a finger to her chin. 'I still haven't recovered from jigglestick, though. That was one out of the box. Or in, as the case may be. Anyway, stop trying to change the subject. You, Eddie, the horizontal tango. Why yes instead of no?'

'Because I loved him. That and my body's a traitor.' She angled a look at Paige. 'Eddie's very good with his ...'

'Jigglestick?'

'Hands.'

'Oh.'

'And mouth.' She bit her bottom lip to hold back a smile at her friend's pained expression. 'Pretty expert at jiggling his long staff, too.'

'I'm not sure I needed to hear that.'

'I'm not sure I needed to remember.'

They both stared ahead. Then Alice sensed Paige twitching with suppressed laughter and her own rose in a bubble. Within seconds they were cackling like kookaburras.

'God,' said Paige when their giggles finally had worn off. 'I must be hormonal if I'm thinking those kinds of things about Eddie.'

'Me too.'

Although, over the years, Alice had thought many times about Eddie's magic hands, mouth and body. He'd been a wonderful lover and she was grateful he'd been her first. Another boy might not have been so careful. Even as a teenager, Eddie was big and strongly built, and with Alice so tiny in comparison, he'd been worried sick about hurting her. She'd loved him for that. She'd loved him for everything he was, until she had realised that the god she'd worshipped had feet made of clay.

Alice sniffed and reached into the console for the travel pack of tissues she kept there, wiped her eyes and blew her nose noisily. She tucked the tissue into the cup holder and slumped back, overwhelmed with fatigue. She'd been so stressed about Eddie she'd barely slept. Now, tears and belly laughter on top of netball training and a full day's work had drained the last of her energy.

'You'll be all right,' said Paige.

'Of course I will.'

With sudden certainty, Alice knew she would be. Sharing her secret with Paige had been tiring but cathartic. They'd be able to talk about it openly now, protected by the knowledge that Paige always would be on Alice's side, no matter what silliness entered Alice's head. And when Alice was hurting, Paige would soothe it with compassion and humour. Or a staple gun to Eddie's gonads should it prove necessary.

Paige patted her shoulder. 'Atta girl.' She opened the door, whooshing the car's cosy air into the night. Paige's legs were already out and planted on the asphalt when she suddenly twisted her upper body towards Alice. 'This winning-on-merit thing.'

'What about it?'

Her friend's grin was pure naughtiness.

'Paige,' warned Alice.

'What?'

'You know exactly what. You're thinking of playing dirty.'

'No one said I couldn't. Anyway, all's fair in love and show-queening, my friend.' She waggled a finger. 'Now you be a good little majesty, and I'll see you Thursday. Oh, and no thinking about Eddie. From here on in that's my prerogative.' She rubbed her palms together. 'And it won't be his jigglestick I'll be thinking of.'

FIVE

CHIN ON HIS HAND, Eddie stared at the pile of coins and notes stacked in front of him on the kitchen table. By the time he took out expenses, there'd be next to nothing left from his sausage sizzle and beer raffle to add to his Show Queen coffer.

He flicked a finger at the pile of dollar coins, then did the same with the two-dollar tower, collapsing both with a noisy jangle that did nothing to appease his mood.

The Phillips twins probably raised ten times that last night with their clothes swap, and they still had their scavenger hunt and danceathon to come, not to mention the dozens of other things they no doubt had in the pipeline. What did Eddie have? Sweet bugger-all.

His dad, Warren, walked into the kitchen and threw Eddie, then the coins, a look. 'Not much of a golden touch there, Midas.'

'Barely a silver one,' said Eddie, toppling his tower of fifty-cent pieces.

With a long sigh, he shook out a plastic ziplock bag and scooped the coins into it. He'd bank the takings tomorrow, as pathetic as they were. The expenses would come out of his own pocket. Call it a personal donation or something.

His mum ruffled his hair as she passed to switch on the kettle. 'You'll get there.'

'Not if I keep going like this I won't.' He folded the notes on top of the coins and pressed the ziplock closed. Despite his promise to Alice about getting his A game on, Eddie was stumped at what else he could do that the others weren't doing already.

'You know your trouble?' said his dad. 'You're thinking too small.'

'Your father's right. You need to think big. Host events that have wider appeal, that pull a crowd. Look at Alice's Girls' Night In. She sold out in days and those tickets weren't cheap, but she can afford to charge a lot because what's on offer is so unique.'

Unique? Surely a girls' night in wasn't much more than a bunch of women watching chick flicks and getting drunk on cheap wine?

'And if Paul Saunders is to be believed,' continued his mum, 'Stephanie Albrecht's golf tournament already has sixty players booked in. The Phillips girls are charging five dollars for song requests at their danceathon, and that's on top of what they'll get from the participants.'

'I know.' Eddie rubbed his face. 'I'll have a think.'

'Try googling. I bet you'll find plenty of ideas. You have lots of friends, the Giants and the cricket boys, your mates from school. Look for things that they'd get excited about. Fun things, like that motor-neurone-disease ice-bucket challenge, and the Movember movement.'

'That's the problem, though. All the good stuff has been done before. Or Alice and the twins have nicked it already.'

'Then you'll have to come up with something better.'

She bent to hug his shoulders, her mouth close to his ear. 'Buck up. How are you supposed to impress Alice if you don't put up a fight?'

Yep, no flies on his mum.

Eddie spent the rest of his evening on the computer, taking notes. Who'd have thought fundraising was such a competitive sport? There were millions of pages dedicated to the topic, and with each blog post and article, his mood lifted.

By the time he hauled himself into bed it was after midnight, but he had a list of twenty actionable ideas. Some more nuts than others, and one that could even be danger-ous. Dangerous could also prove very popular, however, and Eddie had a lot of fundraising to catch up on.

Besides, Eddie wasn't short on courage, and this was no longer about proving to Alice that he could care about more than getting laid. The stakes were much higher than that. He wanted her back. Watching her speak at Monday's Show Queen meeting had only hammered home what he'd lost — that passion, that kindness. That sexy gorgeousness. That *life*.

If putting himself in a bit of danger for the Show Queen cause was the cost of winning her heart, then so be it.

The Phillips twins' danceathon was rocking. Eddie stopped counting the number of dancers at thirty. There was too much movement and strobed lighting to keep going, but there had to be at least fifty people in the hall. With the cover charge set at a tenner, it was a handy money spinner.

His gaze settled back on Alice, who was doing some sort of weird funky-chicken thing with Paige on the illuminated floor. They were both wearing sparkly clothes and makeup, and sporting enormous, teased-up hairstyles. Alice had gone for big curls and every move sent them bouncing around her shoulders. He smiled as she crouched and flapped make-believe chicken wings, then tipped, laughing uproariously, onto her bum.

An arm that didn't belong to Paige reached out to pull her up.

Eddie's smile collapsed as he recognised Willow and Chelsea's older brother, Cameron. His eyes narrowed as Cam joined their dance, copying the girls' flapping and knee knocking. Alice's grin broadened as Cam's movements became more and more exaggerated. Why she was smiling was a mystery. The bloke looked like a dropkick.

Thankfully, the song was nearing its end. Eddie breathed out when they left the dancefloor and headed to the bar. He followed, not liking how close Cam was keeping to Alice. Normally it wouldn't bother him, but the sod was single now, having split up with his long-term girlfriend a couple of months ago. From what Eddie heard, it wasn't a nice breakup either.

Not that Eddie could chuck stones. His and Alice's split had hardly been painless.

Paige was first to spot him. 'Well, if it isn't Sleazy Eddie.'

Eddie tried not to bristle at the taunt. He frigging hated that name, but thanks to his past behaviour it had stuck. Even his mates liked to have cracks at him, and Eddie couldn't do a damn thing about it without looking like a can't-take-a-joke loser.

Alice greeted him with an expression that could have been puzzlement or annoyance, it was hard to tell in the low, constantly shifting light. 'Eddie. I didn't expect to see you here.'

He shrugged. 'You said Show Queen entrants should support one another, so I'm supporting.' He held out his hand to Cameron. Cam worked at the agricultural machinery dealership the Argyles used and played footy for Mount Pitt, the Gerrinton Giants' arch rivals, although Eddie wasn't so petty as to hold that against him. Alice, however, was another matter and it made his handshake firmer than usual. 'Cam, how's things?'

'Good. Yourself?'

'Not bad. Busy now we've started seeding.'

'I bet. Hey, that part finally came in this morning.'

'Good. Dad's been waiting on that. Mum'll be in town on Monday. She'll probably pick it up then.'

Eddie refocused on Alice. He hadn't seen her since last Sunday's scavenger hunt, and then it'd only been a glimpse. He'd made the mistake of partnering with his lumbering brother, who was a decent bloke when he wasn't calling Eddie shortarse, but not exactly the sharpest cue in the rack. To Eddie's annoyance, they'd finished near the tail of the field. Alice had teamed with brainiac Paige, giving them the combined advantage of speed and smarts, and they'd won. Eddie would have hung around after the presentation to congratulate them if Harry hadn't demanded they go home. Which was all right for him. Harry had Summer waiting in his bed. All Eddie had was his longing.

'How did your Girls' Night In go?' he asked.

'Brilliant! Ruby was amazing,' she said, referring to the guest speaker she'd engaged – a Paralympian and world champion para-triathlete whose strength of spirit had made her an inspiration to many, and whose presence had ensured the night sold out in record time. 'The others were great, too.' She glanced at Paige, smiling. 'I think everyone had a good time.'

'They did,' agreed Paige. 'Some more than others.'

'Especially if they happened to play for South Levenham.'

The pair giggled.

Eddie grinned. The South Levenham Saints were the Rebels' biggest rivals, and he knew from checking the draw that Alice's team had played them that afternoon. 'I thought nobbling the opposition was against the rules.'

Alice blinked innocent wide eyes. 'We didn't nobble them, did we, Paige?'

'Not at all. They had free will.'

'Exactly. All we did,' said Alice, maintaining a butter-wouldn't-melt look that made Eddie want to eat her up, 'was make available some excellent cocktails.'

'Truly excellent. Quite delicious. Very hard to stop at one.'

'Very hard,' agreed Alice.

'Some people have no control, though, do they, dear Alice?'

'No control at all.' She lifted her hands. 'But what can you do?'

'Very little.' Paige nodded, her expression a mask of seriousness. 'And who are we to deny other girls their fun?'

'Who indeed, friend Paige. Who indeed.'

Eddie laughed and shook his head. Then he heard Cam laughing too and Eddie's amusement withered. For a moment it had been just like the old days, when Alice and Paige would twist him in knots with their Tweedledum-and-Tweedledee routine. But this wasn't like then. He couldn't sling an arm around Alice and kiss her silly in thanks for making him laugh, then make her giggle and squirm with whispers of all the lovely things he wanted to do to her. All he could do was smile and pray that his plan to win her back would work.

He indicated the bar. 'What can I get everyone?' He looked at Alice. 'Diet Coke for you?' With the event being for all ages and unlicensed, the bar was soft drinks only.

'Thanks.'

After taking Paige's and Cam's orders, Eddie joined the queue then wished he hadn't been so chivalrous when Cam sidled too close to Alice again. Jaw set, he turned away. Cam was an okay bloke, if a bit short and weedy compared to Eddie, and Alice could talk to whoever she liked. Eddie just wished it was him.

By the time Eddie returned, Alice, Paige and Cam had been joined by the Phillips twins, looking very disco in matching white satin pantsuits. He handed over the drinks and kissed the twins hello. 'Looks like your danceathon's going great.'

'It is,' said Willow, who, like her sister, was helpfully wearing a name tag. They were as perky as each other, which was amazing given they were now over twenty-four hours into the danceathon, although Eddie suspected their thick makeup hid a lot of their tiredness.

'Sorry I wasn't here last night for the start. Needed my footy rest.'

'That's okay,' said Chelsea. 'You're here now.'

'And you came to our scavenger hunt,' said Willow.

'You'll dance with us later?'

'Sure. I'll show you some of my moves.' Eddie did a step and slide, ending it with a hip wiggle and wink, causing Paige to roll her eyes and mutter, 'Sleazebag' under her breath, and Eddie to retaliate with, 'Don't worry, Paige, I'll show them to you, too.'

Her reply was an even more exaggerated eye roll. 'Spare me.' She dumped her drink on a table and hooked her arm through Alice's. 'Come on, girls. The air's too thick with testosterone here. Time to slay this dancefloor again.'

'Good to know we're wanted,' said Cam.

'Yeah,' replied Eddie, and promptly changed the subject to the day's football results.

He watched Alice as they chatted. Where the hell she got her energy from was beyond him. She'd had a big night on Friday with her Girls' Night In, and like Eddie, Alice had played sport today, but while Eddie was feeling every hard tackle and sprint in his weary muscles, Alice appeared unaffected, twisting and whirling and wiggling like she could do it all night.

The music was universally lame. Stuff from before he was born that his mum still liked to play and dance to as she cooked. Once, when his mum had thought she was alone, Eddie had caught her belting out 'Total Eclipse of the Heart' like she was Bonnie Tyler in concert. Instead of stopping, embarrassed like a normal person would be, his mum had laughed at his appalled expression and continued to sing even louder while encouraging him to join in. Eddie adored his mum, yet there were times when she seemed to come from a different planet.

Finally, the music flipped to something half-decent.

'I'm going to bust some moves,' he said to Cam, hoping like hell Cam wouldn't follow, but was unsurprised when he did.

The twins had moved on, circling the dancefloor as they urged on anyone flagging. Spotting her brother's return, Chelsea skipped immediately over. 'Come help us out.'

'I was going to dance with Alice for a bit,' Cam said.

'Plenty of time for that later.' She pulled on his arm. 'Come on.'

Cam threw a last look at Alice then a wry one at Eddie, and with a shrug obeyed. Eddie had a hard time holding back his smugness as he grooved his way to Alice and Paige.

Despite his brag, Eddie wasn't much of a dancer. He had some idea of beat but possessed none of Alice's innate rhythm. She knew exactly when to sway or jig or raise her arms and shimmy. Eddie couldn't take his eyes off her.

'I forgot to ask how the Rebels went today,' he yelled over the Black Eyed Peas' 'I Gotta Feeling'.

'Won,' Alice yelled back. 'By four goals.'

'Well done.'

'You?'

'Flogged them. Thirty-seven points in the end. I got best-on-ground.'

'Really? That's twice this year, isn't it?'

Eddie stopped dancing. Alice had been keeping tabs on his performances? Like she used to? A fluttery feeling hit his chest and a grin began to form. Then he registered Alice's and Paige's slowing moves and curious looks and quickly got back into the groove.

'Yeah,' said Eddie, too shocked to come up with anything more articulate, and too scared to ask Alice how she knew in case she killed his high by saying the news had come from her dad.

Neither spoke for the rest of the song. Eddie could feel Paige's gaze burning into him and wondered what her problem was.

The music changed to a quieter song. Paige nudged Alice and mouthed something as she pointed to the toilets. Alice shook her head. Paige mouthed, 'Are you sure?' and when Alice nodded, she threw Eddie a quick look and headed off.

'How are your Show Queen plans going?' asked Alice, moving a little closer.

'Okay. Got a few ideas on the brew.'

'Oh yes? Like what?'

Eddie smiled. 'That'd be secret Show King business.'

'Show King?' She made a *phht* noise. 'Not going to happen.'

He chuckled. 'You think?'

Her expression turned as sweet as her voice. 'How was your sausage sizzle, Eddie?'

'Oof,' he said, clutching his lower belly. 'Low blow.' But again he was struck by how much she knew about him.

Alice chuckled and play-hit his arm. 'Idiot.'

He was. An idiot for her.

The song faded. Alice smiled and started to move off.

Eddie touched her arm. It had been years since they'd been this close and he didn't want it to end. 'One more?'

She waited for the next song to kick in and laughed when the opening bars of the Village People's 'Y.M.C.A.' came on. 'No thanks, this one's all yours.'

But before he could escape with Alice, the twins scooted across the dancefloor and took each of his arms.

'Dance with us, Eddie!' yelled Willow, raising his right arm and spinning under it.

'Come on, Eddie!' added Chelsea, swinging from his left.

Only an arsehole would refuse the twins when they were being cute, and an arsehole Eddie wasn't. He clapped and side-stepped and copied their moves, making Ys, Ms, Cs and As with his arms and body. Attempting a pirouette for the hell of it, he caught a glimpse of Alice and Paige laughing at him then lost them on the next spin. Not the most comforting of reactions, but at least she was watching, and he'd take a laugh over a sneer any day.

'Y.M.C.A.' gave way to more dumb songs that the twins seemed to know all the words and moves to and were hell-bent on teaching Eddie. He finally excused himself after deciding ABBA's 'Waterloo' was one step too far.

He stood near the bar gulping cold water and scanning the room for Alice. Eddie needed home and bed but didn't want to leave without saying goodbye. He found her on the dancefloor, dancing with Cam, while Paige danced nearby with an older bloke Eddie didn't recognise.

Eddie watched her for a while, pretending Cam wasn't there. Sod's Law had dictated that the moment 'Waterloo' ended, the music turned semi-decent, or at least more modern. Lady Gaga gave way to Katy Perry, Alice singing along as she danced, a smiling blonde pixie shimmering even brighter under the mirror ball.

Then some toolbag put on Taylor Swift's 'Wildest Dreams' and Eddie's mood plunged. Alice loved Taylor Swift, and Eddie would bet his ute that 'Wildest Dreams', with its steamy African-set music video, was one of her favourites.

Cam stepped smoothly closer, matching his body's movements to the pulsing music. Their faces neared as they sang the verse, then Alice moved teasingly away for the chorus, before moving back in again for the next verse, the delighted smile never leaving her pretty face.

By the time the song came to its finale, Alice and Cam were singing to each other with their mouths inches apart.

Eddie scraped his hand down his face. A wild dream, that's what getting Alice back was. Still, rival or not, Eddie wasn't without hope. Alice not only had danced with him, she'd talked to him and even teased him a bit. What's more, she knew he'd scored two best-on-grounds this year. That had to be a good sign.

His confidence bolstered, Eddie set off for the dance-floor to say goodbye.

What kind of bloke knew all the words to a Taylor Swift song anyway? Jeez.

SIX

'CAM'S A BIT KEEN,' said Paige. 'Not bad-looking either.'

Alice leaned against the wall next to her and sipped her drink. It was after eleven and the dancefloor had thinned, although the twins and danceathon diehards were still going strong, despite a playlist that could have been chosen by the twins' daggy dad, Trevor. What they'd be like by tomorrow morning, when the competition ended, was anyone's guess.

She replied around her straw with an ambiguous 'mmm'. Alice didn't have room in her head for Cam. It was too full of Eddie.

Paige eyed her. 'Not interested?'

'I don't have time to be interested in anyone right now.'

'What? Not even for a bit of jigglesticking?'

Alice smiled. 'Not even for that.'

Paige had jigglesticking on the brain, which wasn't helping Alice with her Eddie situation. Her mind would not leave him alone. She supposed it was because he kept surprising her. First by going ahead with his Show Queen entry and now by supporting the competition like it really meant something. He was being sweet, too. Big, lovable, unaffected, sweet Eddie, and she could feel herself being drawn to him in the same way she had been as a teenager. It had to stop. The only thing to be found at the end of that path was hurt.

Paige released a long sigh. 'Pity. I need to live vicariously through someone.'

'Chrissy and Nick will be having sex soon. You'll be able to pump her for details.'

'*Pump* being the operative word. I bet they won't do it for ages yet. Chrissy's too wary after that bastard Owen.'

Alice didn't agree and said so. Having colluded with Nick in his charm offensive, Alice had enjoyed a close-up view of both their infatuations. They were definitely in the sex-a-go-go-zone. Lucky darlings.

'Bet you a fiver it takes another fortnight, at least,' said Paige.

'You're on.'

They shook and resumed their dancefloor watch.

'I suppose it's a bit rude to bet on a friend's sex life,' said Paige after a while.

'Chrissy won't mind.' Alice slapped a hand over her mouth as an enormous yawn hit her, which then set Paige off and caused them both to smile. 'Home?'

'I thought you'd never ask, m'dear.'

'Eddie reckons he has a few things on the brew for his Show Queen assault,' said Alice as they crossed to the carpark. Despite the cold, it was a gorgeous night; there was only a slight breeze and the sky was glittery with stars and a fat, luminous moon.

'I noticed you two having quite the chat on the dancefloor.'

Alice shoved her fists deeper into her jacket. 'We were just talking stuff. Nothing important.'

'Eddie thought it was. His face when you said about him getting best-on-ground twice.' Paige shook her head. 'Stunned mullet.'

That had been a weird moment. Even under the disco lights, Alice could see his astonishment and then delight. She loved making people happy because happiness made the world beautiful, but Eddie's unbridled pleasure had shot a thrill down her spine and made her dance-quickened heart perform a slow tumble-turn. Not good.

'I was amazed you knew about it.'

She shrugged. 'Dad never stopped following Eddie's footy career. He always lets me know when he's gone well.' Alice looked aside into the velvety night, her voice quiet. 'Dad always liked him.'

'Everybody liked Eddie,' said Paige even more quietly.

'I know.' Alice swallowed the thickness in her throat. 'But that doesn't make him right for me.'

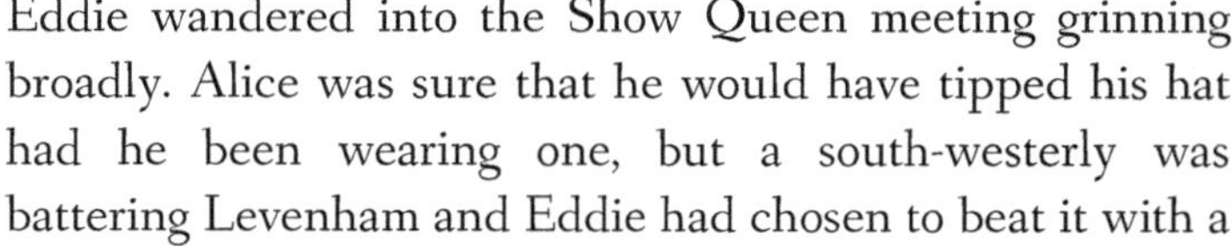

Eddie wandered into the Show Queen meeting grinning broadly. Alice was sure that he would have tipped his hat had he been wearing one, but a south-westerly was battering Levenham and Eddie had chosen to beat it with a fleecy Giants-team beanie. It should have been unflattering. Instead, he looked silly-cute.

After kissing Sarah and Tiffany and the unfairly energetic twins hello, he scanned the room, and spotting an empty chair next to Alice, quickly crossed to it. Before she knew it, Eddie had kissed her, too.

'Hey. Recovered from the weekend?'

Alice opened her mouth only for a croak to come out. Her cheeks hot, she cleared her throat and tried again. 'Yes. You?'

'Bit sore. But that's more from Harry than footy or dancing.'

'Harry?'

'Yeah. Tried to dunk me in a trough yesterday morning.'

'Why?'

Eddie shrugged. 'To prove he's stronger. Which he's not.'

'And did he?'

'What?'

'Dunk you in the trough.'

Eddie tugged off his beanie and concentrated on rolling it up. 'A bit,' he mumbled, shoving the hat deep into the pocket of his coat and not looking at her.

Alice grinned. The Argyle brothers had been play-fighting since birth. As far as she knew, Eddie had never won a bout.

Mrs Wallace swept in wrapped in a full-length fur coat that was probably worth the price of a new car. She took her usual position, regarded her watch with pursed lips and shot pointed looks at Sarah and Tiffany, who'd been happily chatting with Mick. Within a minute, everyone was in their chairs and the meeting open.

Sarah and Tiffany covered the usual stuff about positive media coverage and wine-show developments, and congrat-ulated those who'd held successful events over the previous fortnight. As he relaxed, Eddie began to spread into Alice's space.

Warmth seeped through the fabric of her jeans and into her leg. The hard muscles of his thigh flexed and unflexed as he twisted to smile or make faces at the others or leaned forward to concentrate on the committee.

It was nice. It was also driving her nuts.

'Sorry,' he whispered when she shifted away.

Moments later they were touching again. Having shed his jacket, Alice could smell the lovely combination of his Eddie-ness – farm-fresh air laced with a hint of lanolin, washing powder and man. She stared forward, breathing through her mouth, but the hyper-awareness remained.

'What have we planned for the next few weeks?' Sarah scanned their faces and settled on Alice. 'Alice, you must be keen for your next fundraiser after the huge success of your Girls' Night In.'

Alice shot to her feet, grateful for the excuse to break contact with Eddie. 'I am, but nothing quite so big for this fortnight. Just a pizza and ten-pin bowling night on the first of June, to celebrate the onset of winter. I had a meeting with Kai, the chef at Ryan's Winery, and Ryan's marketing manager, Chrissy James, on Sunday morning and we've booked high tea for Sunday, June eighteenth. Tickets for that will go on sale this week. I hope you'll all come. There'll be a fashion parade and a guest speaker that I know you'll love, and Kai's pastries are to die for.'

Missy woofed.

Alice laughed. 'Sorry, Missy. I did ask, but Kai was a definite no on dogs. Don't worry, I'll make you up a doggy bag of treats.'

'Excellent, excellent,' said Sarah, consulting her list as Alice sat down. She looked up and smiled indulgently at Eddie. Alice managed to hold back her eye roll. Eddie wasn't *that* good-looking. 'Eddie, thank you for your comprehensive list of proposals. The committee was very impressed by the work you've put in.'

Alice's gaze sharpened on Sarah. This didn't sound promising.

'Your "Dare Eddie" proposal gave us some pause, though. Perhaps you could explain a little more about it before we give final approval?'

He eased upright and faced the group. 'It's pretty straightforward. Someone proposes a dare, then everyone throws money at it depending on how much they'd like me to take it on. The higher the money on offer, the harder it'll be for me to refuse.'

'Yes, that's what we thought. Quite simple, as you say. However, we may have a few qualms. Tiffany?'

'The committee and council have one major concern,' said Tiffany. 'That neither the Show Queen competition nor the Levenham Wine Show, nor the council for that matter, be brought into any disrepute.'

'Wouldn't dream of it,' said Eddie.

'And, well, we know what boys are like. We wouldn't want to see you getting hurt doing a dare.'

'Neither would I. The Giants are at the top of the ladder. Can't have their star ruckman getting injured. Anyway, I'm not a boy anymore.' He winked cheekily, causing Tiffany to flush. 'I'm a man who knows what's what, but if you're worried, I could always run anything dodgy past Mum. She'd have my guts for garters if I killed myself doing something stupid.'

Giggles broke out. Even Mrs Wallace's mouth twitched.

'What?' asked Eddie. 'She can be bloody scary, my mum.'

'I believe you already have a dare lined up, Edmond,' said Mrs Wallace, putting an end to the laughter. 'Perhaps you could share?'

'Oh, yeah.' A lazy smile spread over his face. 'A few of

the lads have dared me to wear a pink fairy costume to the Arms on Saturday night. While it's a bit embarrassing, it's a shed-load better than the mankini they first proposed.'

A hush fell as everyone, including Alice, tried not to think of Eddie in a mankini.

'How much will that earn you?' asked Steph.

'I think the bidding was at four-fifty when I accepted.' He shrugged. 'It's not huge, but not bad for a couple of hours' work. I'm going to carry a donation tin. A gold coin for a touch of my wand.' At the horror on Tiffany's face he quickly added. 'My magic wand. Not ... you know. I could make it a stroke of my wings instead?'

'No,' squeaked Tiffany, cheeks almost as crimson as her stretch-velvet miniskirt. 'Wand is fine.'

'Okay, then? Sarah? Tiff?'

Sarah started and blinked, apparently still lost in Eddie's mankini.

Tiffany was surreptitiously fanning herself with her tablet. 'Er, yes. Yes, I think so.'

'A pink fairy sounds rather fun to me,' announced Mrs Wallace. 'In fact, the entire Dare Eddie project does.' She slapped a palm on the arm of her chair. 'Approved.'

Sarah opened her mouth then took in Mrs Wallace's expression and shut it again. She gave her eyebrow a rub, as though tending a nasty headache. 'That's fine, Eddie. Just keep in mind community expectations when you accept a dare, and your mother's counsel, and I'm sure there'll be no problems. Okay, Mick? What's happening with you?'

His moment over, Eddie sat. After a few minutes, he leaned close to Alice, his breath caressing the hair near her ear and shooting a thrill down her back. 'Want to dare me something?'

She shook her head, too afraid she'd squeak like Tiffany if she answered.

'Anything. Go on. Dare me.'

'No. Now pay attention.'

Which was easier said than done. Alice's mind was whirling with things she'd love to dare him. A few of them were painful, but most were things she shouldn't be thinking about at all.

Eddie had wings. Bright-pink wings with glittery centres and fluffy bits around the edges. The body of his costume was a pink leotard stretched to its limits over his big frame, with his modesty not very well protected by a stiff white net skirt speckled with glittery pink love hearts.

The front bar of the Arms was raucous with Giants players celebrating another win and their teammate making an idiot of himself. Alice had left Paige claiming a couple of seats near the fire in the lounge bar and gone to fetch drinks, and check if Eddie had made good on his dare. She'd never thought he wouldn't. Eddie wasn't one to back down from a challenge.

Unaware of her scrutiny, Eddie leaned over the bar to chat to Danny, who'd moved along to pour beers from the taps in front of him. The pose caused Eddie's stiff skirt to rear up, giving everyone behind an uninterrupted view of his long legs and the leotard that was wedged between the globes of his very taut backside. Tight pink ankle-length leggings left little to the imagination. It seemed like every woman's gaze, and some of the men's, was anchored on Eddie's rear. Alice was having trouble dragging hers away, too.

Eddie nonchalantly extracted the leotard wedgie from his bum and carried on talking, only for one of his Giants teammates to give his butt cheek a slap as he walked past.

'Oi,' yelled Eddie, shaking his pink collection tin. 'That'll cost you a gold coin.' One was duly flicked at his head. Eddie caught it with ease and slid it into the slot of his tin before turning back to grumble at Danny, 'My arse is worth more than a dollar.'

Alice had to agree. Eddie had his faults, but not with his butt cheeks. Or much else to do with his body. The man was a total hottie.

'Alice!' said Danny, finally spotting her. 'Didn't see you down there, sorry. Hey, great girls' night the other week. Beth's still going on about it, especially Ruby's talk. Said it was brilliant.'

'Oh, how lovely. Tell her thanks and I'll pass that on to Ruby. She'll be thrilled.'

'Shiraz?'

'Two, please.' She turned to Eddie while Danny organised her order and noticed the 'Show King Fairy' written in sequins across his chest. A fairy he unquestionably was, but Show King? Like hell. 'Nice outfit.'

'I thought so.' Then he leaned in and kissed her hello like it was the most natural thing in the world. Alice would have to remember to duck. This kissing business was getting out of hand. 'Like my sequins? Gran did them for me. Hey, bad news about Ryan's. How's Chrissy going?'

Mention of Chrissy and Ryan's had Alice sucking on her bottom lip. A fire on Tuesday night had gutted the winery and restaurant complex. Warehouse stock that had survived the initial fire was soon found to be undrinkable due to heat damage. Kai, the restaurant's acclaimed chef, was out of a job, as were all the wait staff. Wedding receptions and other events, including Alice's high tea, had been cancelled. Alice prayed that Chrissy's job wasn't next to go. She and Paige had only had their friend back a few months. It'd be awful to lose her again.

'She's okay. Doing her best to help the Ryans manage the situation.'

Eddie's big hand cupped her shoulder. 'She'll be all right.'

It was weird being comforted by an enormous man in a pink fairy suit, although Eddie's brown eyes were soft with sympathy and, bizarrely, it helped.

'She better be,' said Danny, lifting the wineglasses onto the bar. 'Nick'll go spare if he loses her.'

'Of course he would,' said Alice, handing over her payment. 'He loves her.' Not that Chrissy had revealed whether he'd said it or not, but everything Nick had done to win Chrissy spelled it out in neon lights.

She glanced up at Eddie to find him regarding her with an expression that once had been as familiar as breathing. Her lips parted in shock. For several seconds, Alice's heart thudded so hard and painfully her hand automatically went to her chest to calm it.

It wasn't what she imagined. It couldn't be. Not *that*. Even if it was, Alice couldn't go there again.

Mumbling her thanks to Danny, she snatched her change and the wine, and bolted.

'Are you all right?' asked Paige, taking the glasses from her and setting them on the low table, then peering suspiciously at Alice's face. 'You're all flushed.'

'You would be too if you'd just run into a man-sized pink fairy,' said Alice, collapsing on her stool.

'That bad?'

'His leotard's so tight he has a permanent wedgie.'

'Ouch.'

Alice tipped her glass against Paige's and sipped, then sipped some more as she debated whether to tell Paige about what she thought she'd seen. She decided against it. Eddie probably had indigestion or something, like when a baby gives you wind smiles. 'He has "Show King Fairy" sequinned on the front of his leotard.'

'Leotard wedgie, sequins ... This mental image keeps getting better and better.'

'I'm sure Eddie thinks he's impressive.'

Paige's eyes suddenly widened, then she broke into giggles. 'Oh, but he is. He absolutely is!'

Within seconds Eddie was at their table. He tapped his wand on Paige's head. 'A dollar for a touch of my special wand, little lady?'

'Eddie, Eddie, Eddie,' said Paige with an exaggerated sigh. 'There I was thinking how cute you were and then you go and spoil it by being a sleazebag.'

Eddie's grin disappeared. 'It was a—' He jerked around suddenly. 'Piss off, Sanders. You know the rules. No pinching.' He glared at his sniggering attacker and rubbed his bum. 'That hurt.'

'Poor fairy.'

'Poor bruised fairy.' He gave his tin a shake. 'Not interested? Your loss. My wand is magic.'

'Yes,' said Paige, 'I've heard that.'

Alice spluttered into her glass, heat rising from her neck to burn the tips of her ears.

Eddie frowned as if trying to work out whether Paige was taking the piss or not, but his mood clearly had been soured by that painful bum pinch.

'Like I said, your loss. I'll see you later.' With a final shake of his tin, he moved on.

'I knew I shouldn't have told you about him,' Alice hissed once Eddie was out of earshot.

'Sorry. Couldn't help myself.'

'That's no excuse.'

Paige lifted her chin. 'You used the same one when you blabbed to Nick about Chrissy being cheated on.'

'That was different!'

'Not.'

'Was.'

Alice poked her tongue out. Paige returned fire with one of her mean librarian scowls, which then had them both laughing. Soon they were sipping wine and chatting again like normal, their mini-feud buried.

Now and then, Alice's gaze shifted to where Eddie was working the room, and she'd feel strangely warmed. Getting your bum pinched or slapped every five minutes would test the toughest character, yet Eddie continued to smile and collect donations.

She wished he'd come back. She had change in her pocket from buying drinks and she was sorry for not throwing it in his tin. It wasn't much, and he'd bought fifty-five dollars' worth of her raffle tickets and hadn't blinked when it came to supporting any of the other competitors. Except when Eddie finished his tour he headed straight back to the front bar.

'Another?' asked Paige, pointing at Alice's empty glass.

Alice shook her head. It was almost eight and her dad had put a casserole for their evening meal in the slow cooker that morning, and she had work tomorrow. Sundays were busy at the nursery and she'd been leaving her dad in the lurch a lot lately. Lindner's had other staff to take up the slack, and Alice worked more than her fair share of over-time, but that didn't stop her feeling guilty. Evermore, the property behind the garden-centre complex that consisted of the house and gardens and an adjoining small acreage, was looking ragged and neglected, too. 'I only came down to see Eddie in his fairy suit.'

They slipped into their coats and gave the table a last sweep for phones or anything else left behind.

'Ready?' asked Paige.

'You go.' She plucked up the wineglasses. 'I'll take these to the bar. It'll save Danny some work.' And give Alice a chance to drop that change into Eddie's tin on the way out.

Paige gave her a dubious look. Thankfully, she chose to say nothing other than that they'd talk later.

The Giants still hogged the end of the bar where a football match was showing on the big screen, while the rest of the crowd had thinned, having headed off home, into the bistro or elsewhere.

Eddie was leaning against a window frame with his arms and legs crossed. His tin was on the sill, along with his wand. A slim brunette in skinny jeans and a silky white shirt stood in front of him. The girl was curling and uncurling her hair around a finger, her head tilted up to Eddie. From her vantage point near the door, it was hard for Alice to see the brunette's face, but a wobbly reflection in the window told her enough.

The girl was pretty, young, and Eddie was looking down at her like the cat who'd got the cream.

Alice left, the coins rattling in her pocket as once more her heart set like concrete against him.

SEVEN

EDDIE'S WINGS lay crumpled like a dead butterfly on his bedroom floor. He peeled off his leotard and leggings and chucked them on top, not caring if they crushed the wings further. The entire outfit would be going on the bonfire tomorrow, where it'd probably go up like a torch from all the alcohol spilled on it.

He inspected his bum in the mirror and winced at the purpling bruises on his cheeks. No wonder they hurt. His other bits weren't feeling great either. Fairy costumes weren't designed for blokes of his size. Eddie inspected his groin. It looked normal-ish, if you didn't count the red creases where the leotard had dug in, though he had the scary feeling he'd lowered his sperm count by billions.

The bed let out a loud creak as he collapsed on it and buried his face in his hands. What a frigging night. He'd thought he and Alice were getting along, until she'd given him this weird, half-panicked look at the bar and scuttled off with her drinks without a goodbye. When he'd later wandered over to her table hoping for a bit of a joke around,

Paige had called him sleazy, which was the last bloody thing he wanted Alice to remember about him.

Then, just to top off an already crappy night, Robbo's nineteen-year-old sister had cornered him in the front bar and Eddie could see no way of escaping without being rude, and that wasn't an option. He couldn't afford to have her complaining to her brother. Eddie was already in the shit with the Giants for threatening to belt that bum-pinching bastard Sanders if he even looked at Eddie's arse again.

All he'd really wanted to do was find Alice and talk to her without someone groping him or making a smart comment, but by the time he'd returned to the back bar she'd gone.

The only good result from the night was the amount of money he'd raised. A quick count of his donation tin totalled almost six hundred dollars in notes and coins. Not a bad dare all up, even if he did wake with an unfortunate rash tomorrow.

He gave his goolies another careful scratch, and with a wide yawn took his robe off the door hook and headed for a much-needed shower. Mick's dog-and-spoon race was tomorrow, and Eddie planned to take Blue along for a run.

With a bit of luck, his dog would run straight into Alice.

——— ♛ ———

Mick had booked Janet Mercia Park, a small greenspace towards the end of McArthur Street and one of the few local parks that was fully fenced.

Eddie arrived late, having been caught up in a wrestle with Harry over who'd rock a mankini better. From the success of his fairy costume, clearly it'd be Eddie, but Harry boasted that the size of his package would make him the winner. Biggest load of rot ever. Eddie's thankfully rash-free package would kick his brother's butt. Their wrestle ended when their mum marched out of the house to give them both a clip, followed by the order to shut their nonsense. When it came to filling out a mankini, their father would beat them both hands down, and as their mother, she'd know.

It had the desired effect. Completely grossed out, Harry had released Eddie from his headlock and wandered off, leaving Eddie to straighten his clothes and whistle for Blue, while his mum stood smiling smugly at the back door.

Mum psychology: the most dangerous weapon of all.

The fine, if chilly, day had brought locals out in force and the air was filled with barks, whines, shouts and the occasional bawl as parents tried to manage over-excited kids and dogs.

Eddie paused at the edge of the park and looked down at Blue, who regarded the mayhem with interest. 'Don't even think of acting like that,' warned Eddie, then laughed as Blue eyed him back with doggy disdain.

He paid his gate and competition fee and entered the fray. There was no sign of Alice, but the twins were out, looking cuter than ever in matching red ski suits, with their hair in plaited pigtails and the ends tied with red ribbons. Handily, their suits had their names embroidered over the chest. Chelsea was having her arm pulled by a boisterous springer spaniel who greeted Blue with an enthusiastic display of sniffing and tail wagging that Blue endured with polite stoicism.

Eddie kissed both hello. 'You look like a pair of snow bunnies. Nice dog.'

'His name's Cardiff,' said Willow.

'Cool name. This is Blue.'

The twins exchanged a smirk.

'Yeah, yeah. Not very original. Alice's fault. She named him.' He kept his tone nonchalant. 'Don't suppose you've seen her?'

The girls swapped another glance and shook their heads.

'Paige is here, though,' said Chelsea. She pointed towards the brightly coloured playground beside which a small tent had been set up and smoke rose from a barbecue. No wonder the dogs were ratty with those smells in the air. Even Eddie's stomach was perking at the aroma, and he'd had steak and eggs for breakfast.

'Are you racing?' asked Eddie.

'We're going to try,' said Willow, looking fondly at her dog. 'Although knowing Cardiff, he'll just eat the egg then try to hump all the other dogs. He's not very obedient.'

'We're hoping Mick will give us some tips on how to control him,' added Chelsea. 'Or maybe we should ask you instead? Blue's very disciplined.'

'Has to be. He's a working dog. But Mick's your man.' Eddie gestured towards the tent. 'Might grab myself a sausage. I'll see you bunnies later.'

'If it isn't the pink fairy,' said Paige when he greeted her. Eddie wasn't game to try a kiss in case she kneed him. His privates had suffered enough for one weekend. 'How's your bum?'

'Sexy as ever.'

Paige folded her arms and rolled her eyes. 'You are such a sleazebag.'

'You love it,' said Eddie, hiding his irritation with a joke and a wink. He wasn't in the mood for arguing, and other than saying he'd changed, Eddie had no defence anyway. 'Alice on her way, is she?'

'No, she's working.'

Eddie's heart dropped to dog height. 'I thought she might have come down to cheer Blue on in the race.'

'I think she's feeling bad about taking so much time off.'

'Yeah. This Show Queen business sucks a lot of time.' He frowned. 'What are you doing here, then?'

Paige rubbed her palms together and blew on them. 'I wish I knew. Freezing to death?' She smiled, reminding Eddie how attractive she could be when she wasn't being scary. 'Alice asked me to reconnoitre for her.'

A fox terrier with a sausage in its mouth and its leash trailing belted past, rapidly followed by a red-faced boy carrying a sausage-less sandwich. Eddie grinned as the foxy outwitted the boy, and everyone else giving chase.

'Wouldn't have thought there was anything to report.'

'There's always something to report,' said Paige, before pushing her forefinger into his chest. 'The real reason you entered the Show Queen would be a good start. And don't try to fob me off with an "Alice dared me" excuse. I know she dared you into it, but that didn't mean you had to go through with it.'

He shrugged. 'It's good for the town.'

'It is. However, the question I'm most interested in is why it's also good for you.' She emphasised the last word with a final firm poke.

Eddie opened his mouth then shut it as unease threaded his body. This was Paige. He had to be careful. 'Like I said, it's good for the town.' He waved vaguely towards the ring where Mick was instructing some children and their dogs. 'I should see if Mick needs a hand.'

Despite Paige's nosiness, the morning proved to be fun. Mick quickly put Eddie to work, chasing down loose dogs and the occasional child, and offering his own advice to owners when Mick was busy. Eddie mightn't have Mick's age and experience, but he'd been learning how to look after and train dogs since he was a baby on his gramps's knee.

The real entertainment began once the classes were over and the dog-and-spoon races began. There were four categories – junior, novice, intermediate and expert. Feeling cocky, Eddie had entered Blue in the expert category, not realising that, unlike in the other races, it was the dog who'd be holding the egg, not the owner, and in its mouth. Eddie could only pray that Blue wouldn't mistake his egg for a ball and crush it.

The junior race caused great hilarity, along with several spills as dogs tangled with egg-and-spoon-carrying kiddies, leaving raw egg splattered over both. The twins had entered Cardiff in the novice category, with Willow as handler. Unfortunately, the spaniel hadn't learned a thing from his earlier class and kept leaping for Willow's arm. The egg smashed onto the grass fifteen metres into the race, where Cardiff hoovered it up with his tail wagging until Willow dragged him away in disgust.

By the time Eddie and five others, including Mick and Missy, lined up for the expert race, Eddie was feeling sick with anxiety. Wearing a fairy outfit to the pub was one thing, but being humiliated by your supposedly well-trained dog was another. Most of the other competitors looked serious, too.

He crouched and held up the egg for Blue to inspect. The dog gave it a sniff and, thinking it was a snack, went to take it from his hand. 'No,' said Eddie. 'This is for carrying. You can eat it later. If you win.' He went through a few more commands until Blue held the egg in his mouth as though it was a fragile baby bird.

The intermediate and expert races included obstacles.

There were poles to weave through, a ramp to climb up and over, a fence to jump, and a short, plastic tunnel to crawl through. Because there wasn't enough equipment to go around, each competitor would be timed. Eddie had drawn third.

The first dog, a collie, galloped through the course without a worry, crossing the line and dropping the egg into its owner's hand to be passed to Mick for inspection. A galumphing multi-breed went next, its owner looking like Eddie felt – anxious as all hell. Sure enough, the dog crushed the egg at the end of the jump.

'Ready?' asked Mick when Eddie had led Blue to the start line.

Eddie nodded.

'Three, two, one, go!'

Eddie sprinted off, Blue galloping alongside. He directed Blue through the poles, then over the ramp, the dog bounding along as if he did this kind of thing every day. Eddie would have held his breath for the jump if he wasn't running so hard, but Blue landed with the egg still intact. They raced for the tunnel. Blue gave Eddie a look then crawled through, and with a whoop Eddie galloped to the finish.

He held out his hand for the egg, and Blue dutifully plopped it into his palm. Proud as punch, Eddie passed it to Mick.

'Sorry, lad,' said Mick, holding it up to reveal a crack. 'That's a five-second penalty.'

For a moment Eddie's shoulders slumped. Blue was already two seconds slower than the collie and Missy had yet to race. Then he perked up. 'Never mind, at least we weren't disqualified.' He crouched to give Blue a well-deserved scruff and cuddle. 'Who's a top boy, huh? Who's the best dog ever? You can have a hamburger for that. Two hamburgers even.'

As expected, Missy took out the race, beating the collie by four seconds, with Blue finishing a commendable fourth. Though he had a list of chores to do at home, after feeding Blue his promised hamburgers, Eddie hung around to help clean up.

When most of the heavy work was done, he shook hands with Mick, waved at the remaining helpers, and strode for his ute. He sat inside the warming cab and drummed his fingers on the wheel. The radio was playing some ex-boyband lead singer's new love song. Eddie tapped some more, then smiled wryly and put the car into gear.

His gran had put a lot of work into sequinning his leotard. It was only proper that he buy her a thankyou present. What better place to pick one up than Lindner's?

Alice was working the till, smiling and chatting in her usual life-lightening way. Eddie busied himself studying a vivid display of cyclamen, wondering whether his gran would prefer the plain variety or one with frilly petals. Alice would know. He'd ask when she was free.

Except she never seemed to be free. The moment she'd finished serving, Alice was off helping a customer. It went on for so long Eddie felt like calling out that he was a customer, too.

Finally, Alice stopped and took a breath, then she marched over, only for Eddie's bewilderment to deepen when she neatly ducked his kiss with a sideways step.

'What can I do for you, Eddie?'

Her arms were folded, her weight on one hip. Eddie wasn't always the quickest when it came to women, but even he could tell she was pissed off about something.

He scratched his jaw. 'I thought you might like to hear how Blue went today.'

'Perhaps later. I'm really busy. You know what Sundays are like.'

He made a show of looking around. Ross was chatting to the only browser Eddie could see, although there'd be plenty outside. 'It's quiet now. I reckon you could spare a couple of minutes.'

'There's more to running a nursery than ringing up the till, you know.'

'Yeah, I know,' he said, some of his frustration seeping through, even though he tried to bite it back. 'I used to help out here, but I guess you've forgotten that.'

She sucked hard on her lip and looked away, and he knew she was remembering her mum. Kate's illness had left the family exhausted. While Eddie knew bugger-all about nursery plants, he could lift stuff and quickly learned how to use the till and direct customers to the right area. His help wasn't much, but it had relieved some of the burden.

Eddie stroked a curled finger down her arm. 'Sorry.'

'It's okay. My fault.' She rubbed at her mouth. 'How did Blue go, then?'

'Finished fourth. He would have run third only he was hit with a five-second penalty for cracking his egg. I was bloody proud of him, though. He's sitting in the ute with a belly full of burgers, if you want to say hello.'

'No, I'm good. Thanks for letting me know. He's a lovely dog.'

'Yeah, he is.'

'I'd better go and ...' She gestured outside.

Eddie studied her. The skin beneath her eyes was puffy and bruised. She'd avoided his kiss and barely smiled, and she didn't even want to say hello to Blue, the puppy she'd named. What the hell had gone wrong?

'Yeah, sure. Before you disappear, can you sort this for me?' He picked up the nearest cyclamen. 'It's for Gran, for sewing my sequins.'

'For your gran? Not that one, then.' She plucked the pot from his arms and swapped it with one from the rear of the display. The petals were dark pink, with lacy white edges. 'Pink Splash. She'll like this one. It has character, like her.'

'Thanks.'

'Anything else?'

Eddie shook his head and followed her to the counter, unable to stop his gaze dropping to her slim waist and pert bum. Even in work gear and out of sorts, she remained Alice of the wonderland.

'Do you want it wrapped?'

'That'd be good, thanks.' Anything to extend their time together and give him half a chance to figure out what was wrong. 'Big week coming up?'

'Pretty quiet. You?'

'Same. Unless someone makes me a dare I can't refuse.'

She continued to arrange tissue paper and plastic, then cut a piece of ribbon to finish off.

'Alice ...'

At his tone, she glanced up and looked quickly back down.

Eddie lowered his voice further. 'What's wrong?'

She shook her head and knotted the ribbon.

'Was it the fairy costume?'

Alice didn't answer, apparently too busy using the scissors to stretch the ribbon into curls. The bow done, she set the plant in front of him. Eddie handed over a twenty and waited for his change.

She handed it back in silence.

Eddie jangled the coins. He'd let her get away with freezing him out after they broke up because his confidence was shot, and he was concerned with her own mental state after her mum's death. Not this time. 'Is this what I get now? The silent treatment, like we're twelve or something?'

Alice's eyes widened, then she pressed both hands over her face and held them there for a moment. 'I'm sorry,' she whispered through her fingers, then dropped them and smoothed a piece of tissue paper. 'I didn't get much sleep last night and this morning was really busy and I'm ...'

'What?' He crept his hand over the counter, closer to hers.

'Tired.' She smiled weakly. 'Nothing a good night's sleep won't fix.'

He didn't believe her. This was a girl who could work in the morning, play netball in the afternoon and dance all night. And those shadows around her eyes didn't come from just lack of sleep.

'You sure? I could hang around, help out. Blue won't mind. He'll enjoy the rest after his big morning.'

'I'm fine, Eddie.' Alice smiled again, this time with more heart. 'Really.'

He still didn't believe her, but sensed that pushing would only annoy her again. 'Okay. Take it easy, though. The last thing you need is to get run down and sick.'

'I know.' She passed him the cyclamen. 'Say hi to your gran for me.'

'Will do.' He hoisted the pot under his arm and went to head off, only to reverse and lean across the counter to kiss her cheek.

This time, she didn't duck.

EIGHT

ALICE WANDERED to a window and watched Eddie head across the carpark to his ute. He paused to ruffle Blue's ears then gave the dog a brief hug before opening the driver's door and sliding inside. Seconds later, he was gone.

She returned to the counter, slumped on a stool then leaned forward to press her burning face against the cool countertop.

Eddie was the last person she'd wanted to see today. Not after a night spent staring into the darkness with her jaw clenched while her brain conjured a thousand different images of him and that girl together. Alice had worked out who she was now – Griff Robertson's younger sister, Zoe. She played netball for the West Levenham Wanderers and was quite talented. She was also very, very pretty, which had twisted the jealousy inside Alice until it was as spiky and sharp as barbed wire.

It was ridiculous. Eddie could – and did – sleep with whomever he liked. Alice had no claim on him. They weren't going out. For God's sake, they'd just returned to speaking to one another. Yet, for some unfathomable reason, Alice had taken one look at Eddie and Zoe and felt betrayed all over again. If that wasn't stupid enough, she'd been so struck with anger at seeing him waltz cheerily through the nursery doors, she had deliberately avoided him. Then compounded her stupidity by acting like a sullen child when all Eddie wanted was to talk about Blue and buy a present for his gran.

Pathetic. Absolutely pathetic.

Alice let out a groan, sat upright and dusted her cheek. Sulking over her screw-ups wouldn't get any work done, and she'd need to be on the ball when she saw Paige tonight. Her friend could sniff upset at a hundred paces, and Alice wasn't ready to reveal her confused feelings over Eddie. No matter how much she teased him, Paige still liked Eddie and had stayed on friendly terms even when Alice and Eddie could barely acknowledge one another. What if Paige encouraged her to give it another go?

The idea shot hot flutters through her chest. Then the memory of last night froze them dead.

Alice's heart wasn't ready. It probably never would be.

⚜

'I had this idea,' said Alice.

Paige and Chrissy, the darlings, had arrived at Evermore early Sunday evening bearing Thai takeaway and were now seated around the Lindners' dining table, nursing glasses of the pinot gris Chrissy had brought. Which was, Alice had noted, not from Ryan's Winery. Her dad had offered to cook, but neither Chrissy nor Paige would hear of it. Thai was healthy and easy, and Alice and her dad had worked all day. Ross insisted on clearing up then retreated to the lounge to leave them to chat.

'I've been thinking about Eddie's fairy outfit.'

'Have you now,' said Paige, leaning back with folded arms and a tell-me-more smirk.

Alice threw her balled-up serviette at Paige's chest. 'Not like that. Remember the sequins?'

'How could I forget.' Paige turned to Chrissy. 'Cocky bugger had "Show King" sequinned across his chest.' She refocused on Alice. 'What about it?'

'I've been thinking we could do something similar.'

'Sequinned Show Queen leotards?' asked Chrissy. 'Maybe in the privacy of our own homes ...'

Alice wished she had another serviette to throw. 'No, smartypants. More like t-shirts. They're easy to source and might generate a nice profit if we make them fun enough. We could decorate them with Warhol-style images of Queen Elizabeth with "Queens Rule" on them, or "Dream Queen" in a swirly font or something. Inspirational messages for women, from little girls to teenagers to adults, encouraging them to aim high.'

'Queen power,' said Chrissy, serious now. 'I like it.'

Paige had her chin on her curled first, her brow furrowed.

'What?' asked Alice.

'I think we should steer away from the queen quotes. It's too easy to interpret them as something else.'

'Surely not?'

Paige regarded her. 'Queens Rule? Dream Queen?'

'Yeah, as in dream to be a queen. Oh.' Alice slumped. 'I see what you mean. It's a bit porny, isn't it?' She drummed her pen on her notepad. 'We could just stick to Show Queen.'

'We could,' said Chrissy. 'Or we could commission something original. A one-off design that people will actually wear and keep, not just buy out of kindness or for the novelty.'

'Expensive,' said Paige.

'I'm sure if we explained it was for charity we could persuade someone to help.'

Alice drummed her pen again then suddenly stopped as the obvious answer hit home. 'Leave it with me. I know just who to ask.' She pulled her list closer and ticked off the first item. 'Now, about rescheduling the high tea. I thought we could perhaps transform it into a teddy bears' picnic. What do you think?'

'In a Levenham winter?' asked Chrissy.

A good point. 'We'll keeping hunting for another venue.'

They hashed through the remaining items and closed the meeting. Alice offered tea and Tim-Tams, but the girls caught her smothered yawn and picked up their bags, chattering about busy weeks ahead and beauty sleep.

As Alice had feared, Paige had known all along she was out of sorts.

'Okay, spill,' her friend demanded as they huddled on the verandah waving Chrissy goodbye, their breaths puffing clouds into the chilly air.

'Spill what?'

'Whatever's wrong with you.'

'Garden-variety lack of sleep,' said Alice, covering her mouth as a giant yawn stretched it. It wasn't a lie; she really was tired. 'Anyway, I'm more concerned about Chrissy. Poor thing's worried sick about Ryan's.'

Paige grimaced. 'I'm hearing whispers they're not going to rebuild.'

'But they'd still need Chrissy, wouldn't they?'

'I don't know. I hope so.'

Alice stared at the now empty driveway and sucked on her lip. Poor Chrissy. She must be so scared, and for this to happen so soon after she and Nick had found each other. It wasn't fair. 'We'll look after her.' She nudged Paige. 'We're good at that.'

'We are.' Brow furrowed, she studied Alice's face. 'Are you sure you're okay?'

'Perfectly. Nothing a proper night's sleep won't fix.' She hugged her dearest friend. 'Thank you.'

'For what?'

'Caring, you silly moo!'

'It's my job.' Paige squeezed Alice hard, let her go and rubbed her hands together vigorously. 'Right, a girl's not a polar bear. Talk to you tomorrow.'

Twenty minutes later, Alice had tidied away the last of their rubbish, bid her dad goodnight and was snuggled in bed, wearing her favourite flannelette pyjamas and soaking up the warmth from her electric blanket. She hoped Chrissy was being warmed by Nick tonight. Chrissy needed the comfort and Alice imagined that Nick would be wonderfully comforting.

Which, annoyingly, only made her think of Eddie.

She humphed, rolled over and fluffed her pillow into shape. Eddie could take his lovely smiles and tight bum and sequined chest and dance off like a sugarplum fairy. Alice had a Show Queen title to win.

⚜

'A local artist?' mused Mrs Wallace when Alice phoned her

on Monday morning. 'We're hardly short of those in Leven-ham, but for a t-shirt design?'

Alice could practically hear the scrunch of Mrs Wallace's nose wrinkling, as if one of her artists would *dare* lower themselves to t-shirt design. Alice held in her sigh. 'It was just an idea. I thought you might be able to help.'

'Really, Alice, pull yourself together. I simply can't abide defeatist women. I never said I wouldn't help.'

Alice wasn't about to fill the pause in case she said something else that was dumb.

'As a matter of fact, I know the perfect person. I shall be in touch.' Mrs Wallace hung up.

Alice stared at her phone then laughed. Mrs Wallace was unique, that was for sure. Not expecting to hear from her for a few days at least, Alice pocketed her phone and returned to arranging some newly arrived pots of hellebores into a pretty display. Ten minutes later, Mrs Wallace called back.

'You may pick me up from Camrick at eleven.' Camrick being the Wallace family mansion in the heart of Levenham.

Alice made a choked sound. It was already after ten. 'I'm working today.'

Cold silence.

She winced. It was her own fault for not anticipating how fast Mrs Wallace would respond. Which was exactly what Alice needed to do right now before the old duck got it into her head to withdraw her help. 'All right.'

Any doubts that their excursion would be in vain disap-peared the moment Alice stepped into Scarlett Ash's studio. It was housed in a converted dairy, eight kilometres to the south-west of Levenham, and surrounded by lush countryside and Friesian cows with bony hips and pendulous udders.

Like the landscape around it, the inside was alight with vivid colours and textures. Layers of canvases were propped against every wall. Some bore only outlines, others were covered in intricate line work. The northern wall appeared to be home to finished works: complicated, intense paintings filled with jewel-like colours that must have taken hours to paint and left the artist with hand cramps. The images were eye-popping too, feminine and fantastical and very, very intimate.

She stared at a particularly startling self-portrait and swallowed. Surely Mrs Wallace wouldn't approve of *that* on a Show Queen t-shirt?

Scarlett was as eye-popping as her artwork. Her clothes were simple – khaki camouflage-patterned cargo pants, heavy lace-up work boots, and a black, paint-splattered fine-wool jumper. But it was her hair, eyes and skin that made her spectacular. Everything seemed overdone, from the cascading dark curls to the greenness of her eyes and the porcelain beauty of her face. Dramatic and finely drawn, like her art, and probably just as complicated.

Alice also suspected she was more than a little drunk. A cosy-covered teapot sat on a bench, along with a sugar bowl and a half-empty bottle of gin. Having greeted Mrs Wallace with undisguised mistrust and Alice with strange interest, Scarlett now paced the studio, sipping from a delicate teacup and sliding narrow glances at Mrs Wallace as the older lady flicked through canvases.

'I don't do free, as you well know, Audrey.'

Alice had no idea what the relationship between these two was, but the use of Mrs Wallace's first name suggested a long association. She hoped that was a good sign.

'This would be a favour.' Mrs Wallace smiled in a way that reminded Alice of a politician. 'To me.'

Scarlett's gaze sharpened even further. 'Calling one in, are you?'

Mrs Wallace's expression remained benign.

Scarlett's attention switched to Alice. She gave her the same up and down that she had on arrival. It didn't seem critical, more curious. 'Are you expecting to model for it?'

'Model?' Alice couldn't help her glance at one of the more revealing canvases. 'No. Not at all.' Not those bits anyway.

Which caused Scarlett to snort with laughter. 'Don't worry, I didn't have that in mind.'

'I should hope not,' said Mrs Wallace. 'You'd give Councillor Herriot conniptions, and she's having enough of those as it is. One expects that from a wowser vegetarian, though. Ridiculous woman. I take it we have an agreement?'

Scarlett downed the rest of her tea, set the cup on its saucer and waggled a blue-nailed finger at Mrs Wallace. 'Not yet we don't. We have a licensing, among other matters, to negotiate.'

Alice reassessed her drunk theory. Perhaps the gin bottle was only for show.

Mrs Wallace took Scarlett's defiance with good humour. 'Excellent. Shall we prepare a fresh pot? I'd quite like some date biscuits, if you have any. I find they go rather well with gin. Oh,' she said, acknowledging Alice as though she'd forgotten her existence. 'Alice, perhaps you could amuse yourself outside for a while?'

Perhaps Alice could not. Being dismissed like a lackey was rude, and how would she know if she was getting the right deal? Her stomach gave a quiet squelch. She wouldn't mind a cup of tea and a date biscuit either.

Mrs Wallace's voice took on a crystal ring. 'I do know what I'm doing.' She flung a hand towards Scarlett. 'Who do you think taught this one all she knows?'

'Then you won't mind if I sit in and learn too.'

For several heartbeats, Mrs Wallace regarded her icily. Then a smile flickered at the edges of her mouth and she nodded. 'A fine idea. Do take a seat.'

An hour later, her van redolent with a mixture of potting mix odour and gin fumes, Alice drove an overly bright-eyed Mrs Wallace back to Levenham and helped her from the van.

'Thank you,' said Alice, meaning it. The old lady not only had negotiated for Scarlett to create a special Show Queen artwork, but the commercial right to print said artwork on fabric and sell any creations until the end of October, provided all profits went into Show Queen coffers. Scarlett also had agreed to prepare the digital files for the printer, saving another hassle. A special reward for Alice for standing up to Mrs Wallace, she'd whispered to Alice on departure.

'You are welcome, Alice. I rather enjoyed myself.'

'Gin before lunchtime will do that.'

'Never fear, you'll also get to enjoy these privileges when you're my age.'

'Not me. I'll probably still be working into my nineties,' sighed Alice, thinking of all the chores she still had to complete that day.

Mrs Wallace patted her shoulder. 'Marry into wealth. That's the answer.' She leaned close, blue eyes sparkling brighter. 'Just make sure he's endowed in other ways as well. A lady does not live on dollars alone. She needs a good jigglestick now and then.'

She strode off, leaving Alice agape and wondering if she'd heard right. Jigglestick? *Jigglestick?*

'You've been talking to Paige!'

'Terrific librarian, your friend,' called back Mrs Wallace. 'Loaned me the most marvellous book, when I popped in the other day. You should read it. Might get your juices flowing.'

MAY SLOSHED INTO JUNE. Alice waited impatiently for a message from Scarlett, but nothing came. When she asked Mrs Wallace about progress, Alice was told in no uncertain terms to leave Scarlett alone. Good art took time, and pestering the temperamental artist might result in her scrapping the whole idea, contract or not.

Everyone's mood was down. Poor Steph Albrecht's golf day was washed out an hour after it started when a nasty storm brewed out of nowhere and lashed the course with freezing rain. Getting wet wasn't the problem – Levenham locals were used to it in winter – but no one was keen on waving mini-lightning rods around when the heavens were rumbling like some hungry god's empty belly.

The weather was equally foul for Alice's pizza-and-bowls night. Only nineteen players turned up, teaching her a valuable lesson. If Alice wanted people to come out on a winter night in Levenham, she needed to make it worth their while, and some. She made a note to include extra attractions at her high tea – assuming she managed to find a replacement venue with adequate facilities that didn't cost a fortune to hire and Kai could manage the catering, as he'd promised.

With the t-shirts in limbo, she focused on the high tea, Paige's book swap and local author night at the library, and Chrissy's idea for a series of open-mike nights, assessing venues and nutting out programs with her friends.

Show Queen meetings were short, uneventful and as poorly attended as everything else. Three competitors quit, citing family reasons or work commitments, but Alice suspected it was more a case of winter lethargy.

Except for Eddie's tally, which was slowly yet steadily climbing thanks to his regular Dare Eddies and perseverance with training-night sausage sizzles and raffles, the rest remained stagnant. The twins, who, much to Alice's dismay were four hundred dollars in front after their hugely successful danceathon, had further progress stalled when flu flattened the pair of them for a solid two weeks, forcing Willow and Chelsea to cancel a couple of small but handy fundraisers.

A meaner person would have been secretly happy. However, having popped around to the Phillips' house bearing ginger ale and the latest editions of *Marie Claire* and *Cosmopolitan*, Alice only felt sympathy. Willow and Chelsea were miserable, both from sickness and devastation at having their Show Queen train slowed.

'This is cute,' said Alice, admiring a gold-crown-wearing stuffed bear tucked among the twins' many get-well cards. The girls were bundled on a couch in front of the television in the Phillips' lounge and the room was stuffy with eucalyptus and a blazing gas heater. Identical penguin onesies made them impossible to separate, until Chelsea helpfully pointed out that she was the one cuddling the plush pink blanket.

'From Eddie,' said Willow.

'He brought butter menthols, too,' added Chelsea before breaking into a horrible bout of coughing that instantly set her sister off.

'He's so nice,' Willow rasped when she'd recovered.

'And cute,' said Chelsea. She took a long drink from her water bottle and sighed. 'Pity he thinks we're too young for him.'

'Does he?' asked Alice. 'How do you know?'

Willow shrugged. 'We can tell.'

'He's already taken, anyway,' said Chelsea.

'Not officially,' argued Willow.

Which earned her a wet snort from Chelsea. 'May as well be.' With a moan, she reached for a tissue and noisily blew her nose, before collapsing back on the sofa and tucking her blanket tightly around her body. 'I hate being sick.'

Eddie and Zoe Robertson were an item now? Alice supposed she shouldn't be surprised. Zoe was very pretty and Eddie ... was Eddie. She swallowed at the sudden dryness of her throat. She hoped she wasn't catching the twins' flu.

Alice chatted for a bit longer, then made her farewell and returned to work, but the nursery held zero appeal. What Alice hankered for was her room, a heater and giant fluffy blanket to snuggle under for the rest of the afternoon while definitely not thinking about a certain oversized farmer and his probable new girlfriend.

As it turned out, Eddie and fundraising proved to be the least of June's worries. Halfway through the month, Chrissy lost her job at Ryan's. She and Nick were devastated. Alice was devastated for them. Chrissy was a tough cookie, however, and immediately hit the phones, marketing her many skills to local wineries and organisations. Alice was convinced someone would take her on, but when July arrived and there were still no takers, Alice's optimism waned. Even super-strong Chrissy began to struggle with her outlook.

Then in a miracle – which had a suspicious whiff of Saint Wallace about it – Chrissy was offered the newly created position of Wine Tourism Officer with the Levenham and District Grapegrower's and Vigneron's Association.

Conflict of interest meant she wouldn't be able to help Alice with her Show Queen efforts. Alice didn't care. Her friend would be staying in Levenham, with a challenging new role and a man who adored her. Alice squealed and cried and couldn't hug her darling friend hard enough.

Even Eddie making the front page of the *Levenham Leader* dressed in a gold jumpsuit with his hair slicked back and singing Elvis's greatest hits on a karaoke machine in the supermarket carpark to an enthusiastic gathering of pension-day shoppers couldn't dampen her spirits.

It might be the dark heart of winter, but it was still game on.

———— ♛ ————

'Holy shit,' said Paige, snatching Alice's phone for a closer look at the artwork Scarlett had sent through.

Alice had called an emergency meeting of the girly brains trust, whose numbers now included Danny's gorgeous saddler girlfriend, Beth, and Harry's beautician girlfriend, Summer. An addition that Alice was certain would annoy Eddie but apparently hadn't.

'It's better on the tablet,' said Alice, setting it on the kitchen table so they could all see.

'Oh wow,' said Summer. 'Those colours are amazing. And the design ... There's so much going on it's hard to know where to look.'

Alice glowed inside. It had taken nearly two months for Scarlett to deliver. With the Show Queen announcement scheduled for September 23rd, the end of July was cutting it fine to sell the amount of merchandise Alice had hoped, but mostly she'd worried that Scarlett wouldn't come through at all. The way things were progressing, she needed her to. Badly.

The high tea had been a great success, as had the library book swap and local author evening, and her darling dad had come on board offering a series of afternoon gardening classes for twenty dollars a pop, with the fee and the profit on any sales going to Alice's Show Queen kitty. Alice had been reluctant to accept his generosity, feeling her dad had done more than enough with the time off he'd allowed, but he'd been insistent. Nepotism wasn't mentioned in the rules and doing things for special daughters was what dads did. To which Alice replied with a choked voice and fierce hug and a heart bulging with love that he was the one who was special.

That every event was successful had stopped Alice from descending into complete hand-wringing anxiety, but she couldn't ignore that Chelsea and Willow's events were just as profitable. Alice and the twins remained neck and neck. With August typically a wet month and September's sports finals hogging the local limelight, fundraising would only get harder. Having seen the artwork and now her friends' reaction to it, however, Alice knew she'd found her edge.

Scarlett had outdone herself. The work was in her style,

except in place of her usual elaborate celebration of the female form, she'd created a festival of crowns. Big crowns, small crowns, simple crowns, fantastical crowns. Crowns of many colours, like Joseph's Biblical coat. Each was luminous in its own way, prompting cries from the girls of, 'I'd wear this one' and 'No, no, this one's better.'

'It's magic,' said Paige, regarding Alice with unusually pink cheeks. 'It practically radiates triumph.'

'I know.' Alice huddled closer to point at the screen. 'But it gets even better. Look at all the secret things she's included. They're hard to see, but if you look closely there are all these tiny hints of the feminine.'

She tweaked her fingers to enlarge the image. A tiny pierced ear emerged from the distinctive swirling background that Scarlett – as Alice had discovered from her research – was becoming much admired for. She enlarged another section. Cleverly hidden among the crowns was a swell of breast and the lace top of a bra. They scoured the rest of the image. A curled tongue was found, a sultry sweep of eyelash, a slender ankle.

Paige, who'd been hunting on Alice's phone, gasped and then sniggered.

'What?' said Alice, her stomach giving an unpleasant lurch. If Scarlett had snuck in something rude ...

Paige found the spot on the tablet screen and grinned. 'She's a cheeky one.'

In the lower left-hand corner, tucked between a small gold crown dotted with rubies and a medium-sized blue one that seemed to be crafted entirely of sapphire, was a tiny extended middle finger.

'Oh dear,' said Alice, covering her mouth. The gesture was certainly rude, but at least it wasn't a vagina and only the most vigilant would discover it.

'I wonder who it's directed at,' mused Beth.

'Not me I hope,' answered Alice.

'Of course it's not for you,' said Paige. 'It's probably a protest against the whole Show Queen competition. An affront against Scarlett's feminist principles or something.'

'I don't see how,' said Summer. 'It's open to anyone. Even dogs and Eddie.'

Alice grinned. She was beginning to like Summer very much.

'Mrs Wallace?' suggested Paige.

'She wouldn't dare,' said Alice, then considered for a moment. Scarlett would dare. Those two liked clashing, and if what she knew of Mrs Wallace was right, the elderly lady would probably get a kick out of the gesture.

'I can't wait to see it for real,' said Beth. 'It'll make amazing t-shirts. How long before we'll have some to sell? They'll look fantastic hung in the saddlery window, and if I get Danny's sister Ebony into a t-shirt, every pony clubber in the district will want one.'

'Not long.' Alice had done her research. Digital printing was incredibly fast. 'We should have them by the poetry slam.'

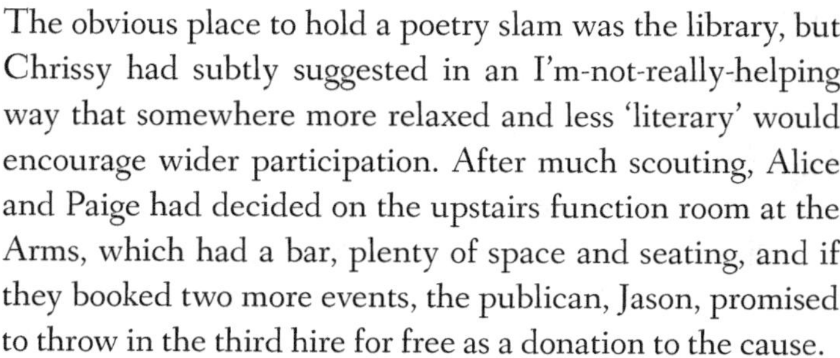

The obvious place to hold a poetry slam was the library, but Chrissy had subtly suggested in an I'm-not-really-helping way that somewhere more relaxed and less 'literary' would encourage wider participation. After much scouting, Alice and Paige had decided on the upstairs function room at the Arms, which had a bar, plenty of space and seating, and if they booked two more events, the publican, Jason, promised to throw in the third hire for free as a donation to the cause.

With the twins' fundraising train back on its usual merry roll, and Eddie being photographed by the *Leader* posing in trunks and a singlet in the front window of McAdams Menswear for yet another silly – and no doubt profitable – dare, Alice needed her slams to work. She also needed venues to sell the two hundred and fifty t-shirts and tote bags she'd ordered, along with the five hundred customised silicone wristbands she'd added in a rush of blood.

'You had a moment, didn't you?' said Paige, laughing as she helped Alice unpack boxes onto the trestle table at the door of the Arms' function room.

It was Saturday night in the third week of August. The slam was due to start in an hour. They had a display and two tills to set up, and VIP judges to coddle. Pre-entries had not been up to expectations and Alice's nerves and voice were as tight as her netball-strained hamstrings.

'We'll sell them,' she said brightly, but not brightly enough to fool her friend.

Paige dumped the t-shirt she was hanging for display and hugged her. '*Of course* we will. They're brilliant. And tonight will be brilliant, too. I had loads of people asking me about it on Friday. They'll come, you just wait.'

'I know.' But Alice couldn't help panicking that she might not cover costs.

'Told you,' said Paige later, nudging her and lifting her head towards the bustling doorway.

Most of the prepaid guests had turned up early and taken seats at the tables nearest the podium, but as the start time neared the trickle of people increased. A queue soon formed. Patrons approached cautiously, clutching notebooks and papers. They paid the entry fee then asked shyly to be put on the competition list. Alice beamed her best smile and thanked them for their support of the Show Queen cause. Warmed by her enthusiasm and the reminder that the slam was for charity, many were enticed by the totes, tees and wristbands. Paige's selling skills did the rest. With the till flush and the merchandise table emptying, Alice finally began to relax a little.

It was minutes to kick-off when the stairwell filled with noise and the door jammed with rowdy men – the Gerrinton Giants and more than a few of the Mount Pitt team, both sides in fine form after wins that afternoon.

What the hell were they doing at a poetry slam?

Alice groaned as Rowan Sanders picked his nose, inspected his finger and flicked whatever was on the end at a teammate. How was she supposed to put on a civilised show with this lot?

'What are you all doing here?' she asked Josh Sinclair, the Giants' captain.

'Eddie. We dared him to write a poem and read it out. Isn't he on your list?' He turned to his men. 'Where's the big sook?'

'Hold onto your nappy, daddy-o, I'm here.' And there was Eddie, looking happy and handsome in a simple chambray shirt with the sleeves rolled up and moleskin jeans. He winked at Alice and her heart gave a bounce. Stupid thing. 'Bet you didn't know I was a poet.'

'Are you going to be like Casanova,' said Paige, 'and treat us to a litany of your conquests?'

'I might if I knew what a litany was.'

Paige's disdainful look might have worked had her mouth not been twitching so much.

Eddie handed Alice his entry fee and door charge, then leaned closer. 'How have you been?' He smelled lightly of beer and Eddie-ness, and his lowered voice drew goosebumps on Alice's back and neck. Her body was such a traitor.

'Good. Busy. You?'

'Same. Lambing. You should come out for a look.'

Alice swallowed back the 'I'd like that' that had formed in her throat. She'd adored lambing when they were together, all the pristine newborns with their cute long tails that they'd wag like excited dogs when they were feeding. The sight made her feel warm and mushy, and Eddie's brazen pride in his flock always made her smile.

'What's your poem about?' she asked instead.

'Secret.' He tapped his nose and winked again. 'You'll have to wait.'

Throughout their conversation, Paige had been shuffling through the t-shirts. 'Ha!' she exclaimed, dragging one from the bottom of the pile and shoving it at Eddie. 'That ought to fit.'

'Hurry up, boghead!' yelled someone from behind.

Eddie ignored him and took his time inspecting the t-shirt, then regarded Alice with a kind of wonder. 'Did you draw this?'

'Not me. A professional artist.'

'It's awesome. Really clever. Right, then. I'd better grab two more for Mum and Dad before they sell out.' He jerked a thumb towards his brother, towering further back in the line. 'Jug-ears can buy his own.' With a final wink, he moved on to let Paige sort out his purchases, leaving Alice strangely hot and breathless and wondering if the heating needed adjustment.

Thankfully, Josh promised to keep the boys under control. There would be no heckling of any of the contestants and no rude behaviour. Violators would face immediate ejection. By Paige.

As Alice had hoped, the range of poets was diverse, enthusiastic and mostly entertaining. The bush poets drew the greatest applause, and an Irish backpacker who usually worked at a rival hotel had the audience in giggles over his borderline bawdy limericks. An elderly man with a beautifully cultured voice recited Alfred, Lord Tennyson's 'The Charge of the Light Brigade' in such a rousing fashion that even the footy boys were left open-mouthed by the end, while a pair of middle-aged ladies amused everyone with a comic duet, riffing off one another like pros.

The star was a young lad who spent his entire reading with his head bowed over the microphone and his long fringe obscuring his face. Many before him had read their own works, but none compared to his stunning ode to Levenham. It wasn't all praise. Although there were biting words about inclusion, tolerance and conservatism, there was also joy in the district's riches and hope in a better future – a future that everyone had a role in creating. Alice blinked back tears and clapped so hard her hands stung. She pegged him as the winner, but it wasn't up to her. Lodged to the room's side, table well stocked with wine, were the judges – Levenham's head librarian Angela Castiglioni, the Mayor Barry McClintoff and, splendid in cobalt silk, Mrs Wallace.

Paige had scheduled Eddie towards the end of the program, using the excuse that it'd force his teammates to stick around, drink more and perhaps be gently persuaded that their mother-sister-grandma-aunt really did need a Show Queen tote bag to match that new Show Queen t-shirt and wristband.

Whoops broke out as Eddie's name was called. Unfazed, he sauntered up to the podium, unfolded his papers and smoothed them out.

Alice's heart began to thump. Eddie had never been great at school, especially with the humanities. Now he was about to read out a poem he'd composed to an audience of not only his footy team, but people who actually knew something about poetry. The potential for an embarrassing farce was huge.

She shouldn't care. She really shouldn't.

But she did.

TEN

EDDIE MIGHT HAVE SAUNTERED up to the microphone like a seasoned rockstar, but the truth was he was
crapping himself.

What if Alice hated his poem? Or the footy boys
laughed and made him look like a numpty in front of her?
Dressing up as Elvis and belting out 'It's Now or Never' to a
bunch of shoppers was just a bit of stupid fun, as was
modelling jocks and socks in McAdams' front window.
This, however, was serious. He'd watched Alice's face as
she'd listened rapt to emo fringe-kid and the urge to create
that same reaction ached like hunger.

He glanced at his poem. Sheep. He'd written about frigging sheep. Great way to impress a girl.

Not.

Eddie took a breath. Too late now. Stupidity or not,
there was nothing to do except get on with it.

'I've never ... Oh, hang on.' Loud bumps sounded as he
adjusted the microphone upwards. 'Better? Good. As I was
saying, I've never been to a poetry slam before. English

wasn't really my forte at school.' He scratched his jaw. 'Not much was, come to think of it.'

He grinned as a few people chuckled. The Giants shuffled, too wary of a prowling, glowering Paige to risk gibes.

'As you probably know, like Alice, who we're all here to support, I'm a challenger for the Wine Show crown, too. One of my fundraisers is to perform dares for money. Usually, it's dumb stuff dreamed up by my footy team, the unstoppable Gerrinton Giants.' He paused as his teammates broke ranks and gave themselves a cheer. 'They're not usually a highbrow lot, but when they heard about tonight the boys figured it for a dare. So here I am.' He lifted his papers. 'I wrote this one myself. It's about sheep. We have a lot of them at our place.

'The ewes waddle to their new home,
From above they look like woolly footstools.
My dog Blue guides them slowly, crouched low, sitting often,
We don't want them spooked,
The lambs inside are precious to us all.

'They have special paddocks,
Hedges of tall wheatgrass for shelter and hidey-holes.
They'll need that when the wind cuts and bites,
That, and good pasture,
Lambing is hungry work.

'The lambs begin to drop,
We don't do much, just let the ewes get on with it.

Sometimes the lambs are breech or positioned wrong,
The ewes strain, weary and distressed, and we step in.
I feel useless when we can't help.

'But most survive,
They're pristine, licked clean by their mothers,
Shrivelled umbilical cords dangle from their bellies like
twine,
And their tails wag as they suckle,
It's impossible not to smile.

'The lambs find their legs,
They canter and cavort, relishing their new existence,
Then curl up and sleep among the safety of the hedges,
And wake to do it all again.
Their mums just eat.

'The lambs grow,
Fat on ewe's milk and good husbandry,
They're a major part of our farm income and we treat
them accordingly.
But in my secret heart I think,
They're a true wonder of nature.'

Eddie set down the paper. For a strange moment, it was as if
the entire room had taken a breath, then uproar broke out.

At first he wasn't sure if it was ridicule, then he realised
they were cheering, even the Mount Pitt boys. His chest
expanded, his heart fat with pride. He searched out Alice

and found her bouncing on her toes, hands above her head as she applauded, smile bright across her gorgeous face.

Not quite her emo fringe-kid expression, but he'd take it.

Eddie lifted a hand in thanks, threw a cheeky thumbs-up at Mrs Wallace, and headed straight for Alice.

'Like it?'

She was fairly jigging with excitement. 'Oh, Eddie, it was wonderful.' Her arms were flapping so enthusiastically that for a second he was sure she was going to throw them around him.

'Really?'

'Truly. I know nothing about poetry, but I know what I like and your poem was lovely. Simple, moving and heart-felt. The whole room felt your passion and that last line ...' She cupped her hands to her chest. 'That was beautiful.'

Eddie's grin broke in full and he had to restrain himself from punching the air. 'Thanks. I was worried it was a bit, you know, personal.'

'It was the personal side that made it special.' She tilted her head. 'You really wrote it yourself?'

'Mum made a few suggestions. Otherwise yeah, I did. Most of it was just stringing together notes I made while doing rounds.'

'Well, you did great. I'm proud of you.'

Eddie stared at her, feeling stupidly dopey, and his smile stuck at high beam. She smiled back, blue eyes luminous.

Proud. She was proud of him. He wanted to yell it to the room, but all he could do was grin while his heart ping-ponged around his chest and his belly tightened with want.

The moment clung. With each ticking second anticipa-tion surged. Alice was flush-cheeked and glowing and looking at him like she used to, in the days when she loved him and he could do no wrong.

This was his chance, he was sure of it.

'Alice,' he said softly, reaching out to touch her.

Before he could make contact, that bum-pinching shit Sanders yelled, 'Hey, ewe-boy!' and the boys responded with laughter.

Alice's gaze shot to the bar. At first, she seemed amused, then her eyes widened and her lips parted, and the glow inside her blinked out, like a lightbulb switching off.

Eddie followed her sightline and spotted Zoe watching them from the edge of the group, sulky-mouthed and arms folded. Cam was nearby, too.

Cam. Eddie had forgotten about him, bugger it. His fingers curled. Surely someone would have said if there was anything going on? He refocused on Alice. Her smile was now forced and brittle, a shattered remnant of her broken inner light.

'I think your teammates want you,' she said.

'They'll keep. I'd rather talk to you anyway.'

She glanced to the bar again and a small furrow dented her brow. 'Thanks, but I need to relieve Paige.'

A fat fib. Having given up terrorising his team, Paige was at the merchandise stand where not a single person was buying anything.

'Well done on your poem, Eddie. You did great. Better stick around, you might even win a prize.'

'Don't go.' He winced inwardly at the desperation in his voice, took a quick breath and lightened his tone. 'I meant it. What I said earlier. About coming to visit the farm.'

'I know you did. I doubt I'll get a chance now spring's so close. The nursery's already getting busy, and with all my Show Queen events and netball finals starting next week ...'

'Try?' He gave her his best pleading puppy look, the one that used to make her laugh and thump him playfully. 'For me?'

His efforts only raised a weak smile. 'I'll see how I go.'

It was a fob-off and he knew it, but the room was quietening as the next poet headed to the podium and Eddie could do nothing other than watch her slip away.

ELEVEN

ALICE WRAPPED her coat tighter against the cold and hurried into the Mechanics' Institute. There was barely a breeze, but the air had a fragile, crystalline feel that nagged of a coming morning frost. She wished it would shut up. Frost made her think of Eddie and his little lambs and brave ewes, and after Sunday's nonstop headache of Eddie-ness Alice was fed up with it.

She liked sheep. She liked Eddie. And that's where this silliness needed to end, but lately when she was near him a pull of want had her hungering to draw closer. Which was the stupidest thing imaginable. He'd been selfish at a time when she'd been wretched with fear and hurt, then deepened her anguish by mutating into Levenham's biggest manwhore. No girl in her right mind would go back there.

Except Alice was feeling far from her right mind, and with each encounter the appeal of a return to Eddie's special brand of warmth and affection grew.

Dumb, so dumb.

The entrance was devoid of the usual echoes of Show Queen meeting noise. Tugging off her scarf, Alice crossed into the hall proper and encountered half-a-dozen faces when there should have been at least ten – Tiffany and Sarah at the front, the twins, Steph Albrecht, and Margot Shulte, who, despite having raised less than a thousand dollars, never missed a meeting. From the way she mooned over him, Alice suspected the cause was Eddie.

Alice took a seat beside the twins in the front row and made a deliberate show of looking around.

'Bit sad, isn't it?' said Willow. Or Chelsea. It was hard to tell without labels.

'Surely we can't have lost that many in the last fortnight?'

Chelsea-Willow shrugged. 'Looks like it.'

Mick arrived with Missy at his heels and an ostentatiously furred Mrs Wallace on his arm. She nodded regally, patted Mick's hand in thanks and strode to her throne from where she regarded the depleted room with satisfaction before narrowing her gaze on Sarah and Tiffany. The two women were huddled behind the Show Queen whiteboard, Sarah scribbling figures as Tiffany read from her tablet.

Sarah paused to purse her lips at the empty seats. 'We'll give it a couple of minutes more.'

Mick had chosen a spot in the second row and was chatting to the twins. Alice shifted onto her hip to join them, only to turn back when Eddie sauntered in and greeted the room with his usual geniality.

'Brass monkeys out there,' he said, rubbing his hands together as he made a beeline for Alice. 'I see you're prepared, Granny B. You been raiding the queen's dress-up box again?'

'Don't be cheeky, Edmond.'

Eddie grinned and plonked himself down, his shoulder pressing against Alice's as if he was homing in for a kiss. Her breath caught, suspended between her ridiculous want and the need to desist, but the kiss didn't come. He settled for a low 'Hey' instead.

A good thing, the non-kiss. Of course it was. Those lips were probably all over Zoe Robertson on Saturday night.

'Hey, yourself.'

'Great night, Saturday. Even the boys thought it was fun.'

'Thanks. Sorry you didn't win.'

'Nah. Emo-boy deserved it. Mum's pretty happy about my highly commended, though.'

She tried not to smile at his description, but it was too perfect. Emo-boy had nearly cried when the mayor announced his name. At least, that was the impression. No one could see under his fringe to confirm.

'Probably don't need this,' said Eddie, shedding his fleece hoodie to reveal a soft flannelette shirt with a t-shirt underneath. Snuggly warmth radiated from his arms and thighs. He smelled newly clean, too, soapy fresh yet outdoorsy. Healthy and comforting, like home.

Her gaze lingered. Eddie had always been gorgeous, uniquely so. No other man had his combination of size, safety and sexiness. She trailed her focus upwards, taking in his broad shoulders, his strong jaw, his delicious lips, and connected with a pair of dark-lashed eyes that were equally intent on hers. The impact was instant. Alice's longing, which had seemed a heavy, dense thing, liquified. A pure rush of heat and sweetness, as though someone had injected warmed honey into her veins and sent it dashing around her body.

She swallowed and broke contact. There was no kidding herself anymore: she had a crush on Eddie. Her heart was going to get one hell of a talking to when she got home.

Finally, Sarah cast a look at the door and fixed a smile. 'Looks like this is it, which will at least make for a quick meeting. First up, thank you for coming. As you can see, we've lost a few more entrants this fortnight. This was always going to be a tough competition and the committee expected some attrition, although perhaps not quite this much. But we cannot commend enough the candidates we have left. You've raised far more than forecast, promoted the Wine Show with integrity and vigour, and captured the imagination of our community in the process.

'Spring is almost upon us. Many of you will soon be busy with sports finals and other events. Organising fundraisers on top might feel like one burden too many and I suspect a few of you have also considered withdrawing. Please don't. You've worked too hard to give up now, and with less than five weeks to go the competition is still wide open. Anyone can win. Why not you?'

'I'm not going anywhere,' said Eddie.

'Or me,' added Alice.

'We're not either,' chorused the twins.

'Or us,' said Mick, to an accompanying bark from Missy.

Alice angled to peer at Steph.

Steph regarded her hands then looked up. 'I'm still in.'

'I am too,' said Margot.

Sarah blinked hard, prompting a sympathetic back rub from Tiffany, and Alice suddenly realised how much pressure they all must be under. Not just with the Show Queen, but the entire Levenham Wine Show. It was their first year and everyone was anxious to make it a success. They had nothing to worry about, though. Alice had every faith in

Tiffany's and Sarah's skills and passion, and with Chrissy well on board the show could only be a success.

'Thank you. You've all been brilliant so far and we know you'll continue to do us proud.' Sarah cleared her throat and indicated her colleague. 'Time for the nuts and bolts.'

'Where to start!' said Tiffany, signalling the change in mood with a clap of her hands. 'Willow and Chelsea, great result on your spelling bee. You'll be pleased to know that we had feedback from two principals that this would be something they'd like to be involved in again. A lovely accolade and fundraiser. Well done.'

The twins beamed as everyone applauded.

Netball training meant Alice had missed the spelling bee. She wondered how much they'd raised and leaned to whisper the question to Eddie. As he bent to listen his breath caught the bare skin of her neck. Nothing more than a fleeting caress, but its touch was enough to shoot shivers cascading over her skin straight to her nipples. Alice gritted her teeth. This crush was unbelievable.

'Alice?' he whispered.

She shook her head to relay it didn't matter. And it didn't. They'd know soon enough from the scores how the twins had fared, and like her, Eddie would have been at training. Which was what her undisciplined nipples needed. Thank God her jumper was thick enough to hide them. Eddie was paying Alice too much attention as it was.

'Steph, nice going with your rock-quiz night. From all accounts it was a hard-fought evening on the dancefloor as well as the trivia.' Tiffany focused on Alice. 'As was your poetry slam, Alice. Who knew Levenham had so many talented poets and orators. Barry McClintoff was most impressed and the *Leader* has promised photos of both events in this week's social pages.' Her smile softened as she addressed Eddie. 'Eddie. What can I say about your latest dares?'

'They were good?'

She laughed. 'Yes, they were. Very good and quite fruitful, too. Which brings us to the leaderboard.'

Everyone craned forward as Sarah wheeled the whiteboard over and flipped it to reveal the latest scores. Alice crossed her fingers then nearly thrust them in the air as she took in the tallies. She'd overtaken the twins. Only by a hundred and twenty dollars, but a lead was still a lead and she had two more open-mike nights to come, merchandise sales to make, and Paige and the girls were bound to come up with more last-minute fundraisers.

She scanned the remaining totals and blinked. Eddie's jokey dares were more serious than Alice had credited, with the last two efforts hauling him to third place, ahead of Steph. Not striking distance – Alice and the twins were still well ahead – but closer than she'd expected.

'You've made it to third,' she said.

'Yeah. Cool, hey?' He grinned and wiggled his eyebrows. 'Better watch out, I'll be snapping at your heels before you know it.'

Alice opened her mouth to reply 'in your dreams', but Mick leaned across to pat Eddie's shoulder and offer a 'well done', leaving the words unsaid.

It was a good reminder of why she was there, though. If Alice wanted to win, she needed to focus. There was no time for Eddie crushes or any other nonsense. The Show Queen was for her mum. For the memories and times never lived, and the futures of others who might benefit from the money raised. This was no joke competition, like it was for some. Alice's drive came straight from the heart.

'On to our upcoming schedule,' said Sarah, when the congratulations had settled. 'Only a few for the coming fortnight, which is understandable this time of year.'

She rattled them off. In addition to Alice's open-mike comedy night at the Arms, the twins were running a 'Night at the Old Levenham Gaol' with a local historian as guest speaker, Steph had a Car Maintenance for Beginners workshop, while Mick and Missy had nothing listed. Mick's tilt at the crown remained reliant on his dog puissance the Sunday after Grand Final day. Total sponsorship had snowballed to fifteen thousand dollars thanks to a multi-national pet-food company's involvement, and the high jump now boasted a first prize of eight thousand dollars. Margot seemed content to drool at Eddie.

'Eddie,' said Tiffany, stepping forward with her tablet. 'We just need to check your next dare. You've called it ...' Colour flooded her cheeks as she paused to read the screen. 'Wax Me Happy?'

'Yeah. Although I'm not sure about the happy bit. More like miserable after a full body wax.'

Mrs Wallace, who until then had been looking bored, perked up.

'Full?' asked Sarah in a high-toned voice.

'Uh-huh. I was hoping I could get away with just my chest, but the boys insisted on full and the money on offer was too good to knock back.'

Stunned silence fell.

Eddie's grin faded as he registered everyone's faces. 'What?'

The twins covered their mouths. Steph bit down hard on her lower lip. Sarah and Tiffany exchanged fretful looks, clearly wondering how they could put a stop to it.

'A full body wax,' said Alice, disbelief dripping off every word.

'Yeees. That's what I said.' Then it clicked. 'No! Not full-full. Jesus, I'm not that much of an idiot and Harry would kill me. So would Summer, come to think of it.' Eddie hurried to calm Sarah and Tiffany. 'Summer's my brother's girlfriend. She's a beautician at Lush Spa and Beauty – you should try going there by the way, she's really good. Anyway, she's agreed to do the waxing as long as I wear trunks. Which is fine by me. Summer and hot wax is a scary enough combo without having both near my ...' He shifted awkwardly. 'Man bits.'

Still the silence hung. Alice suspected everyone was in recovery from the mention of Eddie's 'man bits'. Even Missy seemed subdued.

'Beats the other dare they proposed, even if it won't raise as much.'

'Which was what?' asked Sarah. 'Or perhaps I shouldn't ask?'

'Riding a mountain bike down Rocking Horse Hill's crater.'

'Yes, well, we're very glad you turned that one down.'

So was Alice. Levenham's famous volcanic crater, twelve or so kilometres to the south on the road to Port Andrews, might look benign, but it wasn't without a tragic history.

'Had to, what with footy finals starting. The Giants can't afford to be short a ruckman. Anyway, Mum vetoed that idea straight off, so it was never a runner.' Eddie nodded at Mrs Wallace. 'Didn't seem right either.'

The old lady tilted her head in return, acknowledging the reference to her grandson Digby's fiancée, who'd lost her life at Rocking Horse Hill in terrible circumstances some years before. The fallout had nearly torn the Wallaces apart.

'Good,' said Tiffany. 'I'm glad we've resolved that. Your ...' She blushed again. '... waxing. This will be held where?'

Alice bristled – Tiffany was sounding far too interested in Eddie's dare for her liking, not to mention looking too shapely in a snug yellow-and-purple striped knitted dress – then wanted to smack herself for her jealousy. Her crush was hell enough without adding that to it.

'Giants' clubrooms on Saturday night. There'll be a barbie and the bar'll be open, and Josh, that's our captain, said he'd try to organise some music for later. You're all welcome to come along.'

'We'll be there,' called the twins.

'I'm definitely going,' said a leering Margot.

Eddie gave them a thumbs-up and regarded Alice. 'What about you?' When she didn't answer he pressed closer. 'There'll be a sausage sizzle. Maybe even an Argyle steak or two.'

Alice did not want to think about sausages. Or anything else meaty. It was hard enough getting the idea of Eddie in his trunks out of her head.

He lowered his voice even further. 'Summer has promised pain.'

'In that case, I wouldn't miss it for the world.'

TWELVE

'HAVE you heard about Eddie's latest dare?' said Alice, passing the netball to Paige, who bulleted the ball to Chrissy. As was their normal schedule, all three had arrived early at Wallace Park for extra netball practice and a gossip.

Ten minutes in and Alice's vow to not rush the subject had crumbled. The need to fish for information about Eddie and Zoe had tormented her all day. Several times she'd started messaging Paige only to pull back, wary and uncertain. Things were confusing enough without an interrogation about her feelings, and aside from her rotten, painful crush, Alice didn't know what they truly were. Or what she would do about them.

Stay well away! warned her twice-shy heart.

Gimme! demanded her traitorous body.

Focus on what matters! urged her head.

It was enough to give a girl a walloping headache.

'What's sleazebag up to this time?' asked Paige.

Alice tried not to let the sleazebag comment affect her. It never used to matter – Eddie *was* a skirt-chasing manwhore – but sleazebag made him sound ugly and sordid and

Eddie had never been that, not before and not now. He was *nice*.

And sexy.

And funny.

And kind.

Paige frowned at her. 'Well? What's the dare?'

Alice blinked and rubbed at her brow. She really needed to stop thinking about Eddie. Right now would be helpful. 'Full body wax. Summer's doing it. In the Giants' clubrooms after the game.'

A boing sounded. Chrissy had dropped the ball, along with her jaw.

'Full, as in ...'

Paige wasn't squeamish. 'Back, crack and sack?'

'No, everything else, though.' Alice scooped up the ball and set it on her hip. 'Eddie's too scared of what Summer might inflict on him and I doubt she'd have had agreed to it anyway. I couldn't imagine Harry appreciating it either.'

'Even without the burger and buns,' said Paige, hooting with delight, 'a full body wax is going to hurt like crazy.'

'Yep.'

Chrissy clapped for another pass. Alice shot her the ball, which was immediately flicked to Paige. 'I'm amazed the committee approved it. Even with trunks it's pretty risqué.'

'I doubt Mrs Wallace gave them any choice. She seemed very excited by the idea.'

'She does enjoy her young men,' said Chrissy. 'She practically salivates over Nick. He adores it. Laps it up like a puppy.' She rolled her eyes. 'Men.'

'Word has it she propositioned Harry once,' said Alice. 'Turned him into a gibbering mess.'

That had Paige laughing. 'I bet it did. Which means she's probably tried Eddie. I bet the sleazebag loved it.'

Alice clenched her teeth against that word again and took two breaths for calm. Here was her chance to fish. She forced her tone to sound nonchalant. 'Mrs Wallace would have to get past Zoe Robertson first.'

'Zoe?' Chrissy exchanged a look with Paige. 'He's not seeing her, is he?'

Paige shrugged, but her focus was razored on Alice.

'Looks like it.' Alice addressed Paige. 'You saw her at the poetry slam.'

'Only in passing and she seemed more interested in Cam than Eddie.'

Did she? Alice tried to recall. Zoe and Cam had been standing together when Alice was talking to Eddie, and later in the evening as the event wound down, but every look had held daggers for Alice. Nor did she think Cam would be interested. Zoe was younger than the twins and Cam had a rep for being a steady bloke.

Hope floated inside her before she could squash it, and for the hundredth time since Monday night Alice wanted to smack herself. As her heart kept reminding her, Eddie's track record was hardly good. Even if he wasn't sleeping with Zoe, that didn't mean he didn't have others lined up.

'I wish I could go watch,' said Chrissy.

'Why can't you?'

She bugged her eyes at Alice. '*Giants' clubrooms.*'

'Ah.' Alice had forgotten Nick played for Mount Pitt, the Giants' archenemy.

'Since when should that stop you?' said Paige. 'You're your own woman, aren't you?'

'I know, I know,' said Chrissy, throwing up her hands.

'But you know what men are like when it comes to their football teams.'

Paige spun the ball on her finger. 'And I suppose there's the added controversy of Eddie putting his jigglestick on show.'

'He'll be wearing trunks!' Honestly. Hadn't Alice made that clear?

'Last time I saw a man in trunks they didn't cover much.'

Alice sniffed. 'That was so long ago I'm amazed you still remember.'

'Oh,' said Paige, blasting a pass at Alice's thighs. 'Low blow.'

The girls fell into laughter, then sobered when the coach called the team to order. It was time to get sweaty.

'So,' said Paige as they walked to Alice's car after training. Citing the excuse that Nick had promised to make his mum's legendary beef casserole for dinner, Chrissy had rushed off, prompting Paige and Alice to holler teases about beef and meaty bits in her wake. Teases that ended abruptly with Chrissy's haughty 'Jealousy's a curse' comeback. Cheeky girl. 'I take it we're going to Eddie's dare.'

Alice suppressed a sigh. She should have known better than to believe the subject dead. 'I said I would.'

'Of course you did.'

'I am the one who keeps preaching that we need to support one another.'

'You are.'

'Eddie said there'll be a sausage sizzle and that Josh would try to organise some music.' Alice was aware that she was blathering, but still the words wouldn't stop. 'Could be a good night.'

'Could be.'

Alice spun on her heel and jammed her hands on her hips. 'Okay, what?'

'Not a thing, dear Alice. Not a thing.'

Alice narrowed her eyes.

'Settle, petal. I'm just teasing. It's the night for it.' Then Paige grinned, slung an arm around her shoulders and walked them on. 'Want to make a bet on whether he squeals?'

She knew Paige was lying about the teasing, but Alice was too relieved at the reprieve to press further. 'Fiver?'

'You're on.'

THIRTEEN

OF ALL THE stupid dares Eddie had agreed to this one took the biscuit.

Why the hell he couldn't just stick to sausage sizzles was beyond him. Instead here he was, naked except for a new pair of trunks and flat on his back on Summer's portable massage table in the middle of the Giants' club-room, surrounded by teammates, Giants fans, assorted hangers-on and, most unnerving of all, Alice.

He had no choice, though. Not after Monday night's meeting revealed how far he trailed her and the twins, and not after his early boasts that he could win this thing. Eddie would have to take on every dare offered if he was to fulfil that claim, which had made the Wax Me Happy dare and its twelve-hundred-dollar kitty impossible to refuse.

He should have, regardless. Jesus, this was going to hurt.

The turnout was more than he had expected and great for the Giants' bar takings. As a small country club with grounds and a clubhouse to maintain, it struggled to make a profit most seasons, even with its reliable base of volun-teers. It helped that the Giants had the first week of finals off – their reward for winning the minor premiership, having finished the season top of the ladder. Most of the team had spent the afternoon at Port Andrews watching the third placegetters play fourth in the elimination final, during which beers were consumed and excitement over Eddie's upcoming torture only increased as the day wore on.

Eddie swallowed and eyed Summer as she prepared her kit. His brother's girlfriend looked about as happy as he did. It had taken a lot of persuasion to get her to agree to do the deed, most of it from Harry, who thought a full body wax on his brother was a hell of a lark, provided Summer stayed well away from Eddie's goolies. Jug-ears had even stumped up a hundred to see it happen, the sod.

Though he'd showered, Summer had taken her time wiping stuff over his chest – 'To remove oils,' apparently – and set an electric pot on to heat on a nearby table. A tray laden with pump-pack lotions, wooden spatulas and a giant layer of cloth strips sat beside it, along with a half-drunk bottle of water. Eddie thanked his lucky stars she wasn't on the wine.

He wished he hadn't had so many beers himself, but Eddie had needed the Dutch courage, and thanks to Summer volunteering as designated driver, he and Harry didn't have to worry about getting home. With no food to settle his stomach and his ordeal nearing, the beer was beginning to churn.

Finally, Summer was done. 'Ready?'

'No.'

She patted his leg. 'Do me a favour and try not to scream too loudly. It's not good for business.'

Scream? *Scream?* Was she serious? He'd expected pain, but screaming was a whole other level.

'Or bleed too much. I hate wiping up blood and it makes it hard for the wax to stick.'

Eddie's heart rate hit panic speed. 'Are you taking the piss?'

She smiled and he swore there was evil intent there. 'Gird your loins, Eddie.'

Like he needed the instruction. Eddie's loins were girded so tight his arse was about to punch through the bottom of the table.

'Speaking of loins ...' Summer tossed a towel over his groin. 'Just in case.'

'Of what?'

'Pain turns you on.'

'*What?*' Eddie half lifted then thunked his head against the rest. He closed his eyes as the urge to sob rose in his chest. Pain, blood ... and now the possibility of a hard-on? This was a frigging nightmare. 'You're doing this on purpose.'

'Who, me?'

Definitely evil intent. No wonder Harry fawned over Summer. He was scared stiff.

Summer signalled to Josh, who nodded and threaded his way to Eddie's side. He gripped Eddie's shoulder. 'Right there, big fella?'

'No.'

'Just breathe and you'll be okay.'

That had been Summer's advice, too, which had sounded fine and dandy until she had mentioned scream-ing, blood and potential hard-ons.

'Easy for you to say. You're not getting all your body hair ripped out by the roots.'

Josh laughed and faced the room. The boys had been drinking a while and were restless and rowdy, but such was their respect for their captain, Josh had their attention in seconds.

'Okay, folks, it's the moment you've been waiting for. We have wax, we have our brave beautician, Summer, and now, laid out and quivering in fright for your entertainment, our very own star ruckman and Show Queen entrant, Eddie Argyle.'

'Show King,' muttered Eddie. No queens in on this dare. Chest and leg waxing notwithstanding.

Whoops and whistles bounced around the room.

'First up, any last-minute pledges? No? Let's count it down, then. Ten! Nine! Eight ...'

The crowd joined in. Eddie's stomach gave a foamy lurch as Summer dipped a spatula into the tub and stood over him. He stared at the twirling stick, mesmerised by the globby pink wax, his throat vibrating with the urge to whimper.

Desperate for courage, he rolled his head to the side and hunted for Alice. She was with Paige and a couple of other girls near the window, looking sexy and pretty in a loose fluffy blue jumper and black skinny jeans, and with her long blonde hair styled into messy, beach-girl waves.

His Alice of the wonderland. His strength. His heart. His home.

Their gazes met and she smiled in such a sweet, sympathetic way it was probably a good thing he did have the towel.

It was enough. Summer could cause him agony and Eddie wouldn't so much as squeak.

'... Two! One! Wax time!'

Hoots, wolf-whistles and yells rang out, along with a few calls to start with his balls instead of his chest. Eddie held up his middle finger. No one was going near his precious goolies.

'Sorry,' said Summer, actually sounding it. 'This is going to hurt.'

Eddie expected almost scalding heat, but the wax proved only warm and his shoulders eased a little from their protective hunch. Then Summer began smoothing the wax downwards over the long hairs on his chest and shaping it around his nipple. As she worked the wax began to cool and Eddie felt the strain on his hairs as though they were individual. There were far, far too many.

She dumped the spatula, returned with one of the cloth strips and pressed it firmly on his chest. Suddenly, the room went quiet. Eddie closed his eyes, set his jaw and thought of Alice's smile.

More hairs strained and pinged as Summer pressed on his belly, plucked the bottom edge of the cloth and gripped. Another slow countdown began. Eddie gritted his teeth. Didn't the mongrels realise this was torture enough without dragging it out?

'Three ... two ... one!'

Summer ripped.

He tried, oh how he tried, but there was no stopping the '*gnnnh*' that hissed through Eddie's jammed teeth. Not exactly heroic silence. At least it wasn't a scream.

He lay panting, his chest on fire and sweat beading his forehead. Weirdly, it hadn't hurt that much. It was more the shock of it and the sound, like Velcro being violently separated. He checked his chest. No blood. Just reddening, traumatised skin. Hairless skin.

Breath back, Eddie eased up onto his elbows and grinned triumphantly at his audience. Laughter and beers were held up in his honour, and in a corner, shaking her head but still wearing that smile, was Alice.

Eddie grinned stupidly, heady and high from beer and the endorphin rush. He licked his finger, touched it to the newly slick patch of skin of and made a sizzling noise. He caught Alice cracking up before Paige stuck her scrunched-up face in front of Alice's and regarded him like he was the world's biggest tool.

'Down,' ordered Summer, pushing him back on the table. 'This is going to take long enough without you showing off all night.'

The ordeal took over an hour. At first the boys yelled approval with every ripped strip, however interest soon waned, and their attention returned to sport and the Giants' tilt at the premiership. Eddie tried to listen in, but each rent of hair destroyed his concentration and all he could do was endure. By the time he'd rolled onto his belly, Eddie's front felt like he'd been strapped over a bullants' nest and left there a day. Everything was prickling fire, even his nipples, and they hadn't seen any wax.

Finally, the last strip was wrenched off and Summer smoothed the back of his calf with baby oil. Eddie groaned as he eased gingerly upright.

'Your armpits bled,' she said, giving him a last once-over for wax residue. 'You might want go steady on the deodorant for a day or two. The rest should be fine.'

'Thanks.' He grimaced. 'For the advice, but also for taking this on. I know you didn't want to.'

'If it weren't for charity I wouldn't have. Just don't ask me to do it again, okay?'

'Not a chance.' He regarded her slyly. 'Hey, I'll give you a hundred if you do Harry. The full works.'

'Who said I haven't already?'

Eddie's eyes bulged. '*Really?*'

Summer simply smiled.

Josh hurried over and gave Eddie an up and down. 'Christ, you're red.'

'Yeah,' said Eddie, fingering his sleek chest. It was kind of not bad, if you didn't count the ant fire. Sort of silky. A bit like caressing a really muscular girl. He wondered if Alice would like the new feel. Maybe he could ask her to touch it later. 'Frigging hurts.'

'Beer'll fix that. Best present you first.'

Josh whistled for attention as Eddie stood. The crowd quietened, but there was no stopping the pointing and laughing. Eddie was about to flick them another set of middle fingers then curbed the urge when he spotted Tiff working her way to the front in a lime-green dress. She gave a small wave and thumbs-up and Eddie would have replied in the same way if Josh hadn't grabbed his wrist and hoisted up his arm.

'Three cheers for our newly hairless Show Queen champion!' yelled Josh.

'King,' muttered Eddie, then decided he didn't give a toss as the Giants once more whooped their approval. He'd survived the dare without a scream, squeal, hard-on and minimal blood loss. That deserved some serious celebrating.

Harry thrust a beer at him. Eddie toasted Summer then his teammates and guzzled half the contents. He would have liked to have thrown it over his burning skin but suspected alcohol and hairlessness didn't mix. Besides, he was bloody thirsty.

'Well done,' said Harry. 'Sanders bet me fifty bucks you'd squeal.'

'Bad luck for him, then.' The fairy-arse-pinching shit.

'Close-run thing, though.'

'It was barely a grunt. Bet you don't do it in silence.'

''Course I—' Harry clamped his jaw shut then slurped at his beer in a pathetic attempt at coolness, a state he'd never achieved in his life. Eddie grinned. His brother the kinky bugger. Who'd have guessed? Jug-ears was in for some major sledging now.

'Alice is here,' said Harry.

'Yeah, I saw.'

Harry said nothing for a moment. 'Maybe you should go talk to her.'

Eddie stared at him. His feelings for Alice were hardly a secret at Talanga, but since when did Harry care?

Harry looked at him and shrugged. 'Won't get the girl standing around.'

And this from a bloke who did nothing to get his girl except nearly skittle her horse and stammer like the village idiot. Huh.

Then again, Harry had Summer in his bed every night, which was more than Eddie ever had with Alice.

———— ♛ ————

As it turned out, Eddie had little chance to speak to Alice. The Giants engulfed him like attacking amoeba, slapping congratulations on his smarting back and thrusting beers his way whenever his ran dry.

Despite every intention of pacing himself, triumph and a rocking atmosphere made Eddie reckless. The Gerrinton Giants might be a humble footy club, but eighty-three years of local history made it well loved and supported. Even more so when a premiership looked to be in the offering.

Josh had cranked up a stereo and fed it to the outside speakers, where fires in steel drums kept everyone from hypothermia. Harry put himself in charge of Eddie's fundraiser barbecue and was kept flat out flipping sausages, steaks and grilled onions onto buttered bread and into the grabby hands of starving Giants players, eager to refuel and line their already beery stomachs. Summer even took it on herself to sell raffle tickets on Eddie's behalf.

Several times he caught glimpses of Alice, chatting animatedly with the other wives and girlfriends, and a few of the boys, and once, laughing with Summer and Harry as sauce from the steak sandwich she was eating dribbled on her chin. Fitting his family and friends like she always had.

The star-sequined night turned colder. The fires burned down and the barbecue was packed away. Aware some would be anxious for home, Eddie called everyone inside for the raffle draw then stood sentry at the door to shake hands and thank leavers for their support of him and the club. With plenty remaining, Josh and Harry cleared tables and chairs to the side of the room to make dance space, and doubled the stereo volume.

Eddie was leaning against the trophy cabinet, arms folded and legs crossed at the ankles when Paige settled beside him. Eddie remained silent. He wasn't in the mood for Paige. His skin was sore from the wax and he was greasy from the baby oil Summer had applied. He'd also drunk far too much and eaten too little, and the single sausage he had consumed was making him burp. Not the best state to approach Alice. His stupidity had put him in a snit.

Worse, Cam was doing his hardest to chat up Alice, the slimy bugger.

Paige mirrored his pose, but it was a while before she spoke. 'I thought you'd be pulling moves on Zoe.'

He clenched his jaw.

'Or has someone else caught your interest? Tiffany perhaps? Hard to resist an attractive divorcee.'

Eddie tensed as Cam leaned in to whisper something to Alice. She laughed when he pulled away. Cam had a face like a calf, the idiot, which suddenly soured when the twins bounded from the dancefloor to join them. Sucked in, Cam.

'Everyone knows, Eddie.'

That got his attention. 'Knows what?'

Paige rolled her eyes. 'That you're in love with Alice, dopey.'

Eddie opened his mouth to protest and decided he couldn't be stuffed. Paige knew. So did everyone else, apparently. 'Does Alice?'

'I'm not sure.' The corner of Paige's mouth tucked in as she focused on her friend. 'She's cagey when it comes to you.' She turned to face him properly. Eddie did the same. It'd be hard for Cam to make further moves on Alice with his sisters hovering and this was important. Paige's voice lowered and Eddie had to bend even closer to hear her over the pounding music. 'You hurt her badly, Eddie.'

'I know.' Even if he didn't know how.

'If you hurt her again I will personally rip off your jigglestick and jam it in a blender. Just so you're aware.'

Eddie didn't need to ask what a jigglestick was to get the picture. 'Hurting her isn't part of the plan.'

'What is, then?'

Impressing Alice enough for her to respect him again. Talk. Find out what he did wrong. Make it right, somehow.

Love her like she deserved.

Maybe this was his chance. This was Alice's best friend. If anyone knew how he'd screwed up it would be Paige. 'Fixing it. But I can't if I don't—'

'What are you two talking about?'

Eddie's head jerked around. They'd been so intense neither he nor Paige had noticed Alice's approach. Guilt had them shifting awkwardly.

Alice's gaze kicked between Paige and Eddie, widening with each pass. 'Oh,' she said, flicking her hair, mouth like a ruler. 'Sorry to interrupt.'

'Oh, for God's sake,' said Paige, sounding as pissed off as Alice. 'Are you serious?'

Alice folded her arms and raised her eyebrows.

Eddie stared from Alice to Paige and back again, trying to figure out what his beer-thickened brain had missed. Then it hit like a gut-punch. 'You think I'm coming on to Paige? Your best friend?'

She gave a 'if it walks like a duck' shrug.

Anger rose like scum, muddying his hurt and making it even uglier. This was too much. Jigglesticks in blenders notwithstanding, Eddie wanted to hurt back. Let her see how it felt.

But he couldn't. Not to Alice.

'I need air,' he said. With a shake of his head at Paige, he stomped off.

FOURTEEN

'WANT to explain to me what that was all about?'

Alice had rarely heard Paige sound so coldly furious. Which was fine, because Alice was just as pissed off. She hoisted her nose into the air. 'Wasn't it obvious?'

'Don't play Miss Hoity-toity with me, Alice Eva Lindner.'

'Oh, right. Says she who's hardly standing on a high-moral mountain.'

Paige lifted her gaze to the ceiling and inhaled deeply. 'Sometimes, dear Alice-friend, you are the world's biggest moron. I can't figure out which is dumber. You believing for even a second that Eddie would sleaze on to me, or that you'd think I'd encourage it.' She held up a warning finger to stop Alice's protest, then dug it accusingly into her chest. 'Because clearly you thought I was.'

'Weren't you? You two looked pretty intimate.' Heads almost touching, eyes locked. Looked like a mutual chat-up to Alice.

'We were talking.'

'About what?'

She rolled her eyes. 'What do you reckon? Tolstoy's exploration of the human experience? The US-China trade war? Feed conversion ratios in lactating ewes? You, you silly girl. What else? It's *Eddie*.'

'Yeah, Eddie of the great track record.' But Alice's voice had lost some of its certainty.

'Fine. Eddie's a renowned sleazebag. Or was, which is something else you need to ponder in your bed tonight. What about me, then, huh? Your best friend since primary school? Or am I a sleazebag, too?'

'Don't be ridiculous.'

Paige snorted. 'You're the one being ridiculous, friend.'

Maybe Alice was. She thought back over what she'd seen. Two people with their heads close. Expressions serious instead of flirty. Loud music making it hard to hear. Not a body part touching.

They'd sprung apart like conspiring thieves, shifty-eyed and awkward. But wasn't that what people did when they were caught by the person they were talking about?

A nasty, crawly feeling began to creep over Alice and lodge in her lungs, making her breath hurt.

She'd been a fool. The look Eddie had thrown her wasn't caused by anger at being interrupted, it was from being misjudged. She gnawed the tip of her thumbnail, wondering if she should find Eddie and apologise. She went to ask Paige and winced. Her darling friend's arms were still folded, her expression flinty.

Make that two people she'd hurt and needed to apologise to, and fast.

'Sorry, sorry, sorry. I know I'm a truly terrible friend and you must be so angry with me right now and I know it's not excuse, but when I saw you two together my brain just ...' Alice rubbed her forehead. Damn near exploded with jealousy, is what her brain had done. One glimpse of Eddie chatting up someone else, and instead of thinking 'sleaze-bag', Alice's immediate reaction was to scratch like a feral cat.

'What? Decided I was about to succumb to Eddie's charms? *Please.*'

'Yes. No.' Alice shook her head. This was all so messy. 'I don't know.'

'I'm your best friend. You know better. You know *me* better.' Paige stared at the dancefloor as her barb lodged and dug deep.

Alice regarded her feet, eyes burning with shame. She did know better. It was this crush. It was stealing her sanity. And with the Show Queen tight and close to its end, she needed her sanity desperately right now.

An elbow dug gently into her side. 'Duffer.'

'That's a kind way of putting it,' said Alice, smiling wanly. She and Paige rarely argued, but when they did it never lasted long; Paige wouldn't let it. However, this was different. Alice had stabbed right at Paige's loyalty, and if there was one thing her friend had proven time and time again it was that. 'I'm so sorry. Truly I am. I know it's not much of an excuse, but I'm not myself right now. Stress from the Show Queen, netball finals, feeling like I'm not pulling my weight at work.' Eddie and her rotten crush on him, she didn't add. 'Forgive me?'

Paige pursed her lips and tapped her chin with her fore-finger. 'Hmm.'

'Please?' Alice pressed her hand to her chest and flut-tered her eyelashes.

Paige sighed. 'I guess I'll have to, seeing as I'm your campaign manager. Bloody hard to work with you other-wise.' She broke into a smile. 'Idiot.'

'Yes, I am. A complete idiot. Massive one. And you have permission to remind me nonstop for a week.'

'Three. Your behaviour warrants it.' She shook her head. 'Don't you try to protest. It was appalling and you know it.'

Alice did know it. Three weeks of teasing was a bit much, though. 'Two?'

'I suppose,' answered Paige after a moment's consideration that Alice knew was purely for show. 'But expect it to be a very long two weeks. You have been warned.'

'So,' said Alice, feeling squirmy for asking but unable to let it drop. 'What did he say?'

'What did who say about what?'

'Don't be a smartypants.'

'Who are you calling smartypants, Miss Hoity-toity Jump to Conclusions Lindner? Not much. You interrupted before we could get to anything juicy. Although, I did caution him that I'd liquidise his jigglestick if he ever hurt you again. He went a bit pale over that.'

Alice could imagine it. Eddie loved his jigglestick. So had she. She stiffened as the whole of Paige's comment sank in. 'Hang on ...'

'You should find him,' said Paige before Alice could ask how the 'hurting her' topic had come up. 'Eddie deserves an apology, too. Well?' Paige scolded when Alice didn't move. 'Now is as good a time as any.' She made a shooing motion. 'Go on, get!'

Alice held up her hands. 'Okay, okay. I'm going.' The 'hurting her' conversation would keep until tomorrow, when she could dig at it properly. The Giants' clubhouse wasn't the best venue for the discussion anyway.

Alice circled the club, hunting for Eddie. An enquiry to

Josh yielded a lifted shoulder and a 'don't know', while a hover outside the men's loos earned her only strange looks. She located Harry at the bar, a drowsy-eyed Summer tucked under his arm. Alice couldn't blame her. The poor darling had worked all day in the salon and again tonight. Beauticians' hours were nearly as bad as nurserymen's. A thought that served to remind Alice she had work tomorrow, too.

Harry shrugged at her question. 'No idea.'

'Maybe he went outside,' said Summer. 'I saw him pick up his coat just before.'

Alice thanked her and headed for the door, foregoing her own coat, which she'd dumped on a chair near the window. The thin weave of her loose angora jumper offered little protection, but she didn't plan on being out there long. Find Eddie, get through the embarrassment of her apology then it'd be home to the safety of her bed where the only damage she could do was to herself via her own silly imaginings.

A few smokers and cold-hardy types were huddled close around the fire drums, soaking the last of the warmth from the dying embers. A glimpse revealed none were Eddie. She scanned the pines that formed a windbreak at the rear of the ground, but even with the bright moon and stars, the shadows were too heavy to see if anyone lurked beneath the canopy. Alice switched to the lines of cars, parked nose in to the oval boundary fence in a multi-coloured frill. Again, no hulking figure.

Folding her arms around herself, she headed towards them anyway, only to slow and then stop as she spotted Eddie sitting with his back rested against the rear tyre of a dual-cab ute. The points of his elbows were propped on his bent knees, his face in his hands.

Her heart squeezed. He must be upset to be sitting like that, hiding and alone. And she was the cause.

'I'm sorry,' she whispered.

Eddie looked up then jerked to his feet. 'Alice.'

She stepped closer. 'I'm so sorry for jumping to conclusions. For thinking you were ... you know, sleazing.' Even saying the word made her cringe inside.

Eddie shrugged and shoved his hands in his pockets. 'Doesn't matter.' It did. It showed in the hunch of his shoulders and the way he averted his weary gaze. 'Anyone else would have thought the same. I didn't earn the sleazy tag without reason.'

'I should be better than anyone else.'

His eyes met hers. 'You are. You always have been.'

The soft sincerity of his words shot a shiver across her skin, causing her to cuddle herself tighter in reflex.

'God, Alice, you shouldn't be out her in the cold. Here.' He shrugged out of his fleecy Giants hoodie and wrapped it gently around her shoulders. His fingers brushed her neck as he rearranged the hood and drew the folds together. The jacket was warm from his body and smelled of him. Alice felt a strange urge to cry into it. 'There, that's better.'

'But now you're cold.'

'I'm big enough to take it.' He smiled. 'My skin's still burning from getting waxed anyway. I don't know how you girls get it done all the time. I feel like I've been rolled through a paddock of stinging nettles.'

'You're being kind,' she said. 'And I was horrible to you inside.'

'You weren't horrible. You made a mistake. Shit happens.' His mouth turned down. 'None of us is perfect, least of all me. I just wish stuff didn't stick so hard. I know I don't act like it, but I really hate being known as Sleazy Eddie. I hate more that you think I am.'

'I don't. I mean ...' She grimaced and shook her head. Alice didn't know what she meant. The fact was he *had* been a sleaze. His rampant skirt-chasing had left her bewildered and angry and had intensified the grief of her mother's passing. Yet, like Paige and her cryptic comment about needing to ponder Eddie's reputation, Alice's heart was now nagging her that there could be more to it than she realised.

'It's okay. Can't change the past. Just have to live with it.'

The night hung between them, laced with faint music from the clubhouse and an occasional burst of laughter from the fire huggers. Alice needed to go. Paige would be waiting, so was bed and the busiest day of the week for Lindner's, but her legs refused to move. She was wrapped in Eddie-ness – his coat with its fleecy lining and lovely Eddie smell, the security of his strength and proximity, the tenderness of his gaze – and she didn't want to leave its comfort.

'Tell me something?' she said.

Eddie's eyes shifted warily. 'Sure.'

'Why did you sleep with all those girls?'

He stepped away, shoved his hands back into his pockets and tipped his head to stare at the stars. His chest fell as he took in a long breath, then rose as he let it out in a steamy plume. 'Because I was in pain and stupid and thought I might find another you. I missed you so much it was like a sinkhole had opened inside me. One that kept collapsing no matter how many Alice substitutes I tried to stuff into it. Trouble was no one came close to filling that hole. No one was you. Eventually, I gave up trying. No one noticed.' He shook his head, his eyes shiny in the moonlight. 'How's that for irony? I haven't been with a girl in over a year, yet I'm still Sleazy Eddie. And because I'm an idiot, I laugh and play along and pretend I don't care.' His voice quietened. 'But I do.'

Alice's heart throbbed as she fought for calm. He'd missed her? It was hard to believe that after the way he'd acted, but every word he'd just uttered rang with truth. And remorse. Eddie genuinely regretted his behaviour.

He caught her expression and rubbed his jaw. 'Sorry. Bit much. Too many beers. Forget I said it.'

'How can I forget that?'

'I don't know. Try?'

'But ...' She frowned, still navigating his admission. 'What about Zoe?'

'Zoe? Robbo's sister? Nothing there. Never was, never will be.'

'But I saw you at the Arms, and at the poetry slam. You looked, I don't know, together.'

'She wants to be. I don't, but she's my teammate's sister and a nice girl, and I don't want to hurt her.'

'Oh. Right.' Alice crossed her arms and hugged herself. 'I've jumped to conclusions again. Sorry.' She winced. 'Again.'

'Don't worry about it.'

But Alice would. She'd worry all night over this moment, over all her assumptions. Over Eddie and his feelings. Over her own more tangled ones.

He smiled. 'You're cold. You should be inside.'

'What about you?'

'I'm a tough farm boy. I'll be fine.' His focus slid to the clubrooms and he gave a small laugh. 'Uh-oh. Your bodyguard is looking for you. Or more likely me, to blitz my jigglestick. Where did that name come from anyway? It's nuts.'

'Not quite nuts, but in the region. Paige discovered it in an old romance novel.'

'Huh. I'd never picked her as a romance reader.' He leaned down and kissed her cheek. 'Thanks for coming tonight. Appreciate it.'

'You'd have done it for me. All to support the cause.'

'Nothing to do with seeing me tortured?'

'Well, I suppose there was that.'

They shared a smile that made Alice's heart flip-flop, and the urge to linger grew even stronger. She made herself move. Paige was waiting and Alice had a lot to think about.

She was only a few cars away when he called her name.

'Those lambs are still waiting. You should see them. They're a true wonder of nature.'

Alice was sure they were, but now she was beginning to believe that Eddie just might be too.

FIFTEEN

ALICE ROLLED LEFT, rolled right, laid on her back, laid on her belly. She humphed and moaned and slammed her pillow on her face to silence a howl of annoyance. She needed sleep, but her mind was too thick with Eddie.

Tonight, her assumption that he'd carried on fine without her after they'd broken up had been shattered. Alice had thought he hadn't cared, that his behaviour was proof of how little she'd mattered, yet tonight he'd spoken of a sinkhole opening inside him, one he couldn't fill. Of missing her.

He made it sound like heartbreak.

Like love.

That period of her life had been loaded with confusion and powerlessness. She'd had to stand back helpless while her mum had faded and then passed. She'd had to endure her own grief as well as that of everyone who'd loved Kate Lindner. The endless condolences. The platitudes of her being in a 'better' place. The staying strong for her dad and brothers, who as men felt bound to keep their agony bottled, even when doing so was dangerous. It had left her an emotional wreck, her thinking a mess.

Not in a state to judge anything with rationality.

Alice glanced at the glowing numbers of her clock. Two-fifteen am. Across the room, silvery streaks laddered the carpet where light from the moon and stars filtered through the not-quite-closed vertical blinds. They seemed to point to Eddie's hoodie, folded neatly on the dresser opposite the bed.

She raised her eyes ceilingward. Even nature was against her tonight.

It was no good. She couldn't resist. With a huff, she retrieved the jumper and sank back into bed. The fabric was soft and strangely warm, as if it still held Eddie's body heat. She cuddled it closer and was rewarded with the scent of him, that lovely smell of outdoors and essence of Eddie-ness.

Alice hadn't realised she'd been still wearing the hoodie until she'd fetched her own coat from the Giants' club-house, but when she went to hand it back to Eddie on her way out he'd disappeared once more. She hadn't worried. She could return it Monday week at the Show Queen meeting or drop it out to Talanga if he needed it urgently, finally see those lambs he kept reminding her about.

For now she was glad she had it.

She cuddled the hoodie closer, breathing him in. Memories flooded. Eddie and her together, in the days when Alice was still alight with love. When being with him was the only thing that mattered. Being young, they had few places to be alone, but Eddie always found somewhere nice. A friend's beach shack. An isolated hay shed. A sheltered bit of scrub. His ute. Too many times to remember in his ute. Their endless jokes about stiff gear sticks before joking was trumped by passion.

She smiled, only to sober when her mind skewed to where he'd taken the other girls. Eddie must have looked after them. None had a bad word to say, except perhaps disappointment at the brevity of the relationship. Not that Alice had asked, but she'd heard. It was impossible not to in a place the size of Levenham. The sleazy teases had come from his mates, not the girls he'd been with.

Why hadn't she realised how much he hated being called sleazy? Eddie wasn't like that. The Argyle boys were brought up to respect women – neither Melanie nor Warren would tolerate anything else. So why had Alice thought he'd behave that way?

And if she was wrong about that, could she be wrong about everything else?

The possibility seemed more than real given his admission that all those girls were about trying to find another her. Eddie had made it sound like he'd really loved her. That their relationship hadn't descended into a farce of sex in diverse places. Alice had enjoyed it at the time, only to be flattened by guilt on her return home. How dare she enjoy such pleasure when her mum was dying, her family shattering? Blaming Eddie had been easy. He'd initiated the sex, after all. At least, that's what she'd kidded herself.

Now, looking back with honesty, perhaps the blame wasn't all with Eddie. She'd been a tangled mess of emotion during that period, swinging from grief to anger to guilt and a hundred feelings in between, her thoughts unreliable.

Could they have also been unreasonable?

Saturday's clear night broke to a gorgeous Sunday that brought out Sunday excursioners and garden junkies keen to get a head start on spring. The nursery was mayhem. Alice was kept running from the moment the doors opened, with little time to check her phone, let alone message Paige to probe about her supposedly nothing conversation with Eddie. By day's end, exhaustion had set in and even Alice had trouble plastering on a cheerful smile when stragglers made them late finishing up.

She and her dad trudged up Evermore's darkened laneway, too tired to talk much. Even a long shower didn't revive Alice, and dinner was a scraped-together affair, although that didn't stop her dad pouring them each a glass of wine. Alice accepted hers gratefully. It'd help her sleep, and with another busy week of work, netball and show-queening she couldn't afford another night like last night.

As she'd hoped, the reheated leftovers and wine did their job. Too much so. Alice had a mind to call Paige, but the yawns started as she was packing the dishwasher and refused to stop. Tomorrow. She'd get onto it then, once she'd dealt with all the other chores on her list. It wasn't even nine pm when she kissed her dad goodnight and snuggled into bed with Eddie's hoodie. Within minutes, she was adrift on its softness and lovely Eddie smell.

Between the swamp of Alice's work and Paige being holed up in library meetings, it was mid-afternoon Monday before they finally caught up, and then only via messaging. The answer to Alice's burning question was brief and disap- pointing. Paige and Eddie's 'hurting her' conversation related to Alice's chances in the Show Queen competition, which sounded a little at odds with how Eddie had put it but far more Paige-like.

The news freed Alice to concentrate on other matters,

like Saturday night's comedy club at the Arms and its mate the singer-songwriter open-mike night. Neither eased Eddie fully from her head. He'd lodged himself like a good-looking squatter with an eye on permanent residence.

Alice knuckled down to business, but every night she sought solace in Eddie's hoodie. If her father knew of his daughter's hoodie-hugging addiction he didn't let on. He did make a point of showing off Thursday's *Levenham Leader*, which featured yet another photo of Eddie, this time launching himself off the end of Port Andrews' jetty while wearing a black-and-white, boggle-eyed sheep costume and, according to the caption, belting out 'Baa-baa Black Sheep' in a 'fine tenor' voice. A second photo showed him emerging from the sea with the sheep's comic head held up in victory and looking disturbingly sexy for a man dressed as an adored children's television character.

By the time Sunday arrived, the hoodie smelled more of Alice than Eddie. Alice reluctantly washed it and hung it out to dry, then, even though she was bone tired from work, netball and the previous night's comedy club, she gave it a quick iron in readiness for Monday's second-last Show Queen meeting.

Like a recalcitrant turtle, the newborn spring that had treated Levenham to gorgeous, if feeble, sunshine most of the week had sunk its head back into its shell. Alice hurried into the Mechanics' Institute with Eddie's hoodie tucked under her arm and rain pattering her head. Her heart gave a girlish skip as she spotted Eddie, chatting with Chrissy and the twins, then did a full-on tumble-turn when he beamed at her in welcome.

'Thanks,' she said, passing over the hoodie once she'd greeted the others and Eddie had kissed her hello. He smelled weirdly of lavender. 'How's Harry?'

Poor Harry had been knocked unconscious during the Giants' hyper-charged and rivalry-fuelled semi-final against Mount Pitt and carted off to hospital as a precaution. His departure had rattled the Giants and led to an unexpected loss, which meant instead of a straight Grand Final berth, they'd now have to take the hard road for their shot at the flag and first win their way through a preliminary final.

'Fine. They let him out yesterday morning. Mum and Summer are fighting over who's nurse. Harry's playing it for all it's worth, the sook. Sorry I missed Saturday night. I should have been there, looking out for you.'

'I can look out for myself and you had family to be with. Anyway, Nick and Danny took care of things.'

'They did,' agreed Chrissy. 'Nick's still crowing about it. He's very full of himself right now after Mount Pitt's win. Booting Connor and Todd out was cream on top of a good day. He spent most of yesterday strutting around like a puffed-up turkey, patting his chest and going "Who da man!"' She shook her head and sighed, but there was love in her expression. 'Footballers. Breed of their own.'

The comedy club had been progressing well until Connor Viccary and his idiot mate Todd Leppington started heckling, triggering an argument with the other patrons who were having a good time and wanted to listen and laugh. The argument might have descended into a brawl if not for the Burroughs boys. Danny, who'd been attending the bar, pulled rank, while Nick, who'd had his own run-ins with the pair, immediately stepped in as backup. The two gladly escorted the troublemakers downstairs and outside, where the publican, also gladly, advised Connor and Todd they were banned from the premises for three months.

Though the incident was short-lived, it put a downer on

what was, until then, an enjoyable evening, and left Alice fretting over the following week's open-mike night and whether she'd need to fork out for proper security.

'Still should have been there,' said Eddie, sounding unhappy, then the subject was dropped as Mrs Wallace strode in, resplendent in a crimson wool coat and matching fedora, and Sarah summoned them to attention.

'Duty calls,' said Chrissy, ducking off to escort Mrs Wallace to her throne.

Alice sat in the front row, with Eddie on one side and the twins and Steph on the other. Mick and Missy slid in behind them with Margot joining Mick alongside.

The meeting coasted through its usual agenda, with praise for their fundraising efforts and media coverage. Every now and then, Eddie would lean down to scratch an ankle, sending a waft of lavender Alice's way. She frowned, puzzled by the smell and missing his normal outdoorsy freshness.

As Sarah took over from Tiffany, Eddie gave his leg another vigorous scratch.

Mick leaned in from behind. 'Need some flea powder there, lad?'

'Nah. Hairs are growing back and it's as itchy as buggery.' Eddie shrugged. 'Summer gave me some soothing lavender cream, but it doesn't seem to be doing much good.'

'You could try aloe vera,' suggested Alice.

'I find calendula salve good,' said Steph, leaning across the twins.

'Use a sea sponge loofah and an almond shower gel,' added Tiffany.

'Is this relevant?' asked Mrs Wallace, causing everyone to look guiltily at their feet. She sniffed. 'Personally, I find a cigar and a good three fingers of scotch works wonders. Keeps one's hands busy.'

'Sounds like a plan,' said Eddie, winking at her. 'Can we make it a date?'

'Only if we can have sex afterwards,' replied the old lady, causing an eruption of bulging eyes and splutters to echo around the institute. 'I've never had a waxed man before. One needs these adventures when one gets old.'

'Right, then,' said Tiffany with a loud clear of her throat. 'Moving on to the tallies.'

Mrs Wallace folded her hands on her lap and regarded the flabbergasted room serenely, as if the social grenade she'd tossed was nothing untoward. Chrissy hid her mouth with her notebook, her eyes sparkling with mirth and her feet tapping out a little dance. Eddie wasn't much better, vibrating with suppressed laughter.

He glanced at Alice and leaned close. 'She's amazing.'

'She's naughty, is what she is.'

Eddie's lips twitched. 'Is that jealousy I hear?'

It was, not that Alice was about to admit such a ridiculous thing. She knew Eddie and Mrs Wallace were having fun with them, yet the thought of Eddie having sex with anyone other than herself – even Mrs Wallace – had discombobulated Alice completely.

She gave him a look. Eddie returned fire with a grin so knowing and sexy her insides fluttered and heat bloomed over her upper chest.

Thankfully, Tiffany recaptured everyone's attention by wheeling out the whiteboard. It would be the last time they'd see each other's totals. Alice straightened. The twins would be pulling out all the stops in the final weeks and she'd need all the intelligence she could gather to keep ahead.

'Tada!' said Tiffany, flipping over the board to show their tallies.

Alice breathed out. She was still in the lead. In fact, thanks to the comedy night she'd increased the margin to over seven hundred dollars. Not safe by any means, but breathing space.

'Congratulations,' said Eddie.

'Thanks.' She indicated the board and Eddie's remarkable total. 'Looks like Wax Me Happy paid dividends.'

'Yeah,' he said, scratching the underside of his knee. 'Glad some good came from it.'

Tiffany recapped their events, offering, Alice noted, special praise again for Eddie and his 'brave' waxing. Then the agenda turned to the eighteen fundraising days they had left. 'All set for the puissance, Mick?'

'Seem to be. Sponsorship's now at fifteen grand and we've set prize money for the main event at eight. Young Missy here's in prime condition for a win.' A claim Missy backed up with a woof.

With all that had been going on, Alice had completely forgotten about Mick and Missy. Their fundraising events had been few and brought in only modest amounts. She did a quick mental calculation, then twisted around to offer Mick her condolences. With the high jump scheduled for the final Sunday of the competition, there was no way Mick could make up the numbers, even if Missy won.

Margot got in first. 'You can't win the crown.'

'Never thought we would. Didn't enter for that anyway. Too old for crowns, aren't we, Missy?' He stroked the dog's head, then directed a nod at Alice. 'Like young Alice keeps saying, it's the money we raise that matters.'

It was; still Alice couldn't help feeling bad for him. 'I'm sorry.'

'Don't be. We've had a wonderful time. Gave me a whole new lease on life, being with you young things.'

'Which leaves us with what's coming up.' Tiffany consulted her tablet. 'Eddie, you have your raffles. Any chance of another dare?'

He shook his head. 'Got to concentrate on footy.'

'What a shame. Alice, you have another open-mike night. Anything else?'

'A few ideas on the brew, but nothing firm at this point.' Other than selling the remaining tote bags and t-shirts. After the initial flurry sales had slowed, leaving her with an uncomfortable amount of stock.

'Just make sure to send in any proposals for approval first.' She regarded the others sternly. 'That goes for all of you. We'll do our bit and yay or nay events as fast as we can, however we can't do that if you don't submit your proposals.' Her face lightened. 'If you can make them fabulous, even better. This competition is far from over. The tougher and tighter the competition, the more publicity we'll generate.'

The twins didn't seem to have anything big planned, but Alice was wary nonetheless. One smart fundraiser and Willow and Chelsea could easily leapfrog her total.

The meeting closed with calls of 'good luck' and promises to attend each other's events whenever possible.

Eddie rose with Alice. Neither made a move towards the door. Alice watched Missy perform a trick for the twins as she scoured her brain for something to say. The only thing that came to mind was an offer to soothe Eddie's itches.

'They're still there,' said Eddie.

Alice blinked. 'Pardon?'

'The wonders of nature. Getting big, though. More like

little roasts on legs.' He scratched his ribs. 'And no more cute tails wagging.'

'Poor things. Mind you, I could say the same for you with that itch.'

'Yeah, it's not much fun.'

'Don't worry, it'll go away soon. If things get desperate you could always try Mrs Wallace's remedy.'

Eddie glanced in Mrs Wallace's direction and grinned. 'Three fingers of scotch and a cigar? I doubt I have the constitution for that kind of abuse.'

'And there I was thinking you were tough.'

He laughed, giving Alice a wonderful attack of the warm fuzzies, then lifted his ankle to attend an itch. 'Suppose I'd better go. I didn't get a chance to eat dinner before I left and I want to check the supermarket for aloe vera.'

'I should head home, too.'

Neither moved.

Then they both stepped forward and almost collided.

'Sorry,' said Eddie, steadying her with a strong hand.

'My fault,' said Alice. She smiled her thanks and with a final wave to the others headed for the exit, her tread slow. Eddie kept pace alongside. 'No dares scheduled for this week? Sheep dips, Elvis recitals?'

'Nah. I'm sure the boys will find something, don't worry. Something painful or embarrassing, or both. Wish I knew who was coming up with this stuff.'

'I thought your teammates did.'

Eddie shook his head. 'They ran out of ideas ages ago. Someone using the address longstaff@gmail.com emails them to Josh and he passes them on to the boys.'

Longstaff?

Alice's eyes narrowed at the name, but she was saved from further comment by Chrissy's arrival.

'I'd wish you luck for Saturday's preliminary final,' Chrissy said to Eddie, 'but that would be disloyal.'

'Luck? That's for sooks. The Giants will win on talent alone.'

She rolled her eyes. 'You men and football. Which is nothing like us girls and netball.'

'Professionals,' said Alice.

'Total,' agreed Chrissy, then hooked her arm in Alice's. 'Want to sneak off to the pub? Beth will be there.'

'I'd love to, except I just remembered I have something I need to take care of.'

Namely strangling her best friend.

———— ♛ ————

'Why?' said Alice.

For a second Paige didn't answer, forcing Alice to check if her phone had dropped out. She was driving home, using hands-free. Alice had wanted to call the moment she strode from the institute and again when she sat in her car, but she didn't want anyone listening in or banging on her window to ask if she was all right. The discussion was too important for interruptions and Alice needed a little bit of calm time before going on the attack.

'Why what?'

'You know very well what, *Ms Longstaff at gmail dot com.*'

'Ah.'

'Yes, ah.'

'What can I say? All's fair in love and show-queening.'

'All's fair? For God's sake, Paige, you've been helping him!'

Paige remained unrepentant. 'Hardly. I'd describe it

more as a form of mild torture than helping, and Eddie was never going to win. What's he at now? Well?'

'Just over thirteen thousand,' muttered Alice.

'Exactly. Besides,' said Paige, her voice taking on a superior lilt, 'I thought raising money was the point.'

It was. But that didn't excuse her best friend from playing turncoat.

'That does not make your betrayal okay.'

'Makes us kind of even though, doesn't it, person who accused me of encouraging Eddie's attentions.'

Alice had to grudgingly concede that one.

'Perhaps,' said Paige, 'instead of thinking about me, you should concentrate your mind on why Eddie entered the Show Queen in the first place.'

'Because I dared him to.'

'Why would Eddie, the ex-boyfriend you've barely spoken to for four years, care about a dare from you?'

'I don't know!'

'I think you do. You just don't want to face it because then you'd have to face your own feelings.'

Alice didn't have an answer for that because it was the truth. She didn't want to face it. Not Eddie's feelings, not her own, because then she'd have to acknowledge that she might have screwed up the most wonderful thing in her life for a reason that never existed.

The edge of Lindner's appeared in the headlights. She passed the nursery entrance then slowed and indicated for the laneway. As Alice turned into it, her lights illuminated the small white sign nailed to the top of the open timber gate.

'Evermore'
R. & K. Lindner.

Alice braked hard, her tyres skidding a little on the

gravel. An ache gripped her chest. She rubbed at it, focus locked on the tragic irony of the name they'd chosen. The evermore that had never happened.

'Alice?' Worry lined her friend's voice. 'Are you still there? I'm sorry if that sounded harsh. I just want—'

'I can't think about this right now, Paige.' She swallowed, her throat as gravelly as the driveway. 'It's too much.'

'You're going to have to face what's between you two one day.'

'I will. I promise.' Her gaze returned to the sign. 'After I win the Show Queen.'

SIXTEEN

EDDIE DIDN'T KNOW how the argument started. Fights between Harry and him never needed a reason, they just happened. A sneer here, a 'who's bigger' shove there, and it was on.

They were rarely serious. Just brothers being brothers, testing their strength, enjoying a playful wrestle. Most of the time they ended up laughing.

But not today.

Not after Alice was witness to his humiliation.

They were in the back yard, having wandered in from the paddocks for morning tea. Mum's order to shift the hose so she could mow had resulted in a 'you do it – no, you do it' argument between Eddie and Harry that, naturally, had progressed into a scuffle, then a full-blown wrestle that ended up including the hose they were fighting over. And Eddie had lost.

Harry was throwing a last loop of hose around Eddie's ankles when a green Lindner's van trundled into the drive. Eddie took one look at it and flopped his head back on the lawn with a groan.

Why now?

'This is going to cost you blood, brother,' he said to Harry. 'A whole lot of blood.'

Harry stretched the bright-blue hose tight and wedged the end between Eddie's lashed-together boots, using the brass connector as a stopper to lock the hose in place. He stood, dusted off his hands and grinned at his handiwork. Eddie was tightly cocooned from shoulders to ankle like an oversized chrysalis. 'In your dreams, shortarse.'

Eddie's eyes narrowed. A quarter of a frigging inch difference and he gets labelled shortarse. There was going to be pain, blood, and at least a week's worth of jug-ears and kinky-wax-weirdo sledges as payback for that comment. Once he got out of this mess.

Their mum bustled from the house, a tea-towel in hand. Spotting Eddie and Harry, she set her fists to her hips. 'What the heck are you playing at, Eddie? You know your brother's still recovering from concussion.'

Recovering? Harry? Like hell. Harry wasn't the one trussed up like a roast chook. Concussion hadn't hurt Harry a scrap, which just proved Eddie's theory about his brother's thickheadedness.

Her disgust made known, his mum smiled widely at Alice and hurried over to hug her.

'Hello, Alice darling. Wonderful timing. I've just made a date-and-walnut loaf. You'll stay for a cuppa, of course.' Not waiting for an answer, she snapped her fingers at Harry. 'Come along, Harry. You can unload.'

'I can do it,' said Alice. 'It's just a few bags.'

'No, no. Leave it to us. I'm sure you and Eddie,' she flapped a hand towards her prone son, 'have Show Queen business to discuss.'

'Not really ...'

But Melanie Argyle was already on her way to the back of the van. Having kissed Alice hello, Harry sauntered past to join his mum, stupid grin still in place.

Eddie could only wait on the lawn like a slug, cursing inwardly.

Alice strolled over, arms folded as she inspected him. She was looking cute in her Lindner's uniform and her long hair held back by a ponytail and red headband. 'I suppose you'd like me to untie you?'

'Yeah, if you have a minute.'

She smiled and crouched to tug at the hose end. 'Harry still getting the better of you, huh?'

'No.'

Alice regarded him with a single raised eyebrow.

'He cheated. Caught me when I wasn't looking.'

'Uh-huh. Like that time when he got you with the clippers?'

Eddie winced as the loosened hose shot feeling back into his ankles.

'Or when he got you in the dam?'

'Shut up,' Eddie muttered.

Alice grinned.

Finally free, Eddie clambered upright, trying not to groan at the muscle he'd twinged or rub at his wrists where the hose had chafed. Of all the humiliating situations Alice could have found him in, this had to be the worst.

'So,' he said. 'You came.'

'Yes.' A sweet flush climbed her neck and cheeks. 'Your mum rang yesterday and asked if we could put some rose fertiliser aside for her. I thought I'd save her a trip.'

Talanga was nineteen kilometres from Levenham and Lindner's was on the opposite side of town. Alice made

dropping off a delivery sound casual, but it was far from that. Eddie's pulse began to quicken.

'That and your "wonders of nature".' She slid her hands into her back pockets and squinted at the surrounding paddocks. Warmer weather, rain and good management had led to a surge of new growth that left the land blanketed in vibrant greens. 'I can't stay long.'

Long, short, it didn't matter. Alice was here. Eddie wanted to whoop.

'Farm's looking good,' she remarked, then smiled in delight when Blue trotted over and shoved his wet nose right into her crutch. 'Oh, hello, sweetheart.' She squatted to give Blue a kiss and chin tickle.

Eddie gave the dog a look of annoyance. It was all right for some. If Eddie had shoved his nose where Blue just did, he'd lose not only his snout but his goolies with it.

'Better go look at these wonders, then,' he said.

They took the old farm ute. Eddie was tempted to take the quad, imagining Alice tucked behind him, her warm body pressed against his back. However, Tuesday's down-pour had left Talanga's tracks soggy, and unlike his old jeans and jumper, her work uniform was clean.

Eddie took the long way around to the lambs, pointing out improvements as he drove. The new cattle yards, the replaced fences, renovated pastures, and the area of remnant native vegetation they'd fenced off to act as a wildlife refuge and corridor. Shiny-coated black Angus cattle grazed lush grass, trailed by birds picking off the insects they disturbed. The calves that had been born in May and June had lost their gangly charm, not that Alice seemed to mind. She wound down the window and rested her arm on the edge, smiling as they eyed her back with bovine curiosity.

Thank God they were only tooling around paddocks. Eddie couldn't have concentrated on a road or dealt with traffic. Alice was too big in his mind. Too close. Too gorgeous. Too here. With him.

His Alice of the wonderland.

A bloke would gush a sigh if it didn't make him sound like a lovesick twit.

Which Eddie was. But still. Being caught trussed up with a garden hose was enough humiliation for one day.

He couldn't stop staring at her. There was no question that things had been changing between them, and after Monday's Show Queen meeting his hopes had risen further. Eddie's eager glances at the road to the farm had been missed by no one, especially his mum. Then Tuesday had slipped into this morning and Eddie's confidence had begun to flag. Alice had a glut of reasons not to visit. It was spring, Lindner's busiest time. She had Show Queen events to organise. Netball training. The lambs would have grown too much, no longer tail-wagging cute. She hated him still.

He'd woken this morning sure she wouldn't come and now she was here, her visit probably orchestrated by his mum, but Eddie wasn't about to complain.

To keep from sighing or saying anything stupid, Eddie blathered on about the new chicory variety they'd included in their perennial pasture mix this year, then quickly shut up when Alice's mouth lifted in one corner. So much for not saying stupid things.

'Sorry,' he said.

'Don't be. It's interesting.'

He was sure it wasn't, but when she asked about bloat risk and followed it up with another question about the plant's persistence he was too delighted not to answer. It brought back memories of when she first had started coming

to the farm and the questions she'd bombarded him with. Alice had always been curious, and with her horticultural background she was as fascinated with plant production as he was. It was another thing that had made them so perfect together.

Eddie pulled up at a paddock striped with tall wheatgrass hedges and indicated for Alice to alight.

'We won't go in,' he said, leaning on the ute's bullbar and feeling smug at her wide-eyed wonder. Nothing like baby lambs to please a girl. 'Better if they're not disturbed too much.'

'They're so cute! Are they all twins?'

'And triplets.'

'There are so many!'

'We scan for them, then separate the ewes into singles, doubles and triples at lambing. It keeps the mob sizes down and helps with feed management.'

Alice hoisted herself up on the bullbar, slim legs dangling. The extra height put them almost at face level. 'And the hedges?'

'Tall wheatgrass. Remember EverGraze, the perennial plant research project with the big proof site at Hamilton?' He went on when she shook her head. 'They published a bunch of case studies looking at hedges for lambing shelter. The results were so impressive we thought we'd give it a try. First year it cut our lambing losses from exposure by forty percent.'

'Wow.' She tilted her head and studied the sheep. A few of the late lambs were tucked in the hedges, snoozing. The others picked at grass or suckled while their hungry mothers stuffed themselves. 'I always thought it was mean to drop lambs in late winter, when the weather is at its worst.'

Eddie shrugged. 'It's when we have the most feed.

Takes a lot of energy to produce milk for doubles and triples. The lambs need extra pasture as they grow, too. When the spring flush arrives they'll have it.'

They were silent a moment, content in the mild sun and, Eddie hoped, each other. Alice bounced her legs back and forth, her face alight as she watched a set of cavorting triplets. Eddie tried to remember the last time he was this happy. Just having her near him made the world feel right.

Except it wasn't right. He'd hurt her, and no cavorting lambs or spring days were going to fix it. Only Eddie himself could do that.

'We used to have fun, didn't we?' he said. 'When we were together.'

'We did.'

He hauled in a breath. It was now or never. 'What went wrong? I never understood.'

She shook her head and kept it turned away. 'Don't spoil it, Eddie. Please.'

'I'm not trying to. I just want to know.' He softened his tone. 'I hurt you. I don't know how but I did, and that matters. Maybe not to you anymore, but it does to me.'

Alice slid off her perch. 'I should get back. I've been gone too long as it is.'

Dismay washed through Eddie like a cold change. They needed to talk about this, yet one mention and she closed down. He reached out, then stopped when she locked her arms around herself. He swallowed at how rough that made him feel, how small. 'Is it that painful?'

'Yes. No.' She blew out a breath. 'I shouldn't have come, that's all. I promised myself I wouldn't, then your mum rang and I figured it'd be fine. A quick visit. Nothing more.' She bit her bottom lip as she gazed across the paddocks. 'This place, though ...'

Eddie frowned. 'You used to love the farm.'

'I know. I did. I still do. I just can't do this right now.'

Now he was really lost. 'Why not?'

'Because I *can't*.' She pressed her hands to her head. 'My head feels like it's going to explode with all the thoughts running around in it. There's the Show Queen and work and everything else going on. And I'm just so confused.'

'About what?'

'Us!'

Frustration made his tone bitter. '*You're* confused? How do you think I feel? You dumped me. Me!' Eddie thumped his chest. 'The man who loved you stupid, who treated you like a princess and dreamed of building you a castle and living happily ever after in it together. Who would have made you *his* queen, not some stupid wine-show version, and you couldn't even give me the courtesy of a why. You wouldn't even look at me let alone talk, and now, just when I think I might have a chance again, you're telling me it doesn't matter?'

She stared at him with wide, unblinking eyes, although there was no missing the shine of impending tears.

Shit.

Eddie stepped closer, wanting to apologise, only for Alice to skitter away.

This was all going down the toilet. He was never going to get any answers or have a hope in hell of winning her back, if he kept screwing up like this.

Eddie breathed deeply and channelled some calm. 'I know it was a bad time, with your mum and everything, but I thought we were doing okay.'

'No, Eddie. *You* were doing okay. I wasn't.'

'I know that, but—'

'No, you don't know.' Alice's hand went to her chest. 'My mum was *dying*, Eddie. My precious, beautiful mum. The woman who brought me into this world and nurtured me through childhood and was meant to be there for me when I brought children into the world. It wasn't just a *bad time*.' She made air quotes around the two words. 'It was wrong on an elemental scale. And what were we doing through all this? Having sex, that's what. All. The. Time.' Her body slumped. 'It made me feel like it was all you cared about.'

What the hell? Eddie blinked, too stunned to speak.

'All I wanted was comfort. Someone to hold me and tell me it'd be all right. That we'd get through this. Not ...' She sucked on her bottom lip. 'Not that. I guess I just expected more.'

The unfairness was unbelievable. What little composure Eddie had left disintegrated.

'More? Jesus, Alice.' He spread his arms. 'I wasn't even twenty when your mum got sick! I had no idea how to handle what you were going through. When I asked Mum what to do, she told me to be patient and kind, and I thought I was. I thought I gave you that in droves. Yeah, we ended up having sex most of the time, but I just wanted to make you feel nice, give you an escape from your worry and fear. Show you how much I loved you. If I'd thought for one second ...' Eddie stopped as his voice cracked. He shook his head. 'I wish you'd said. I would have stopped. I would have done anything if it meant us staying together.'

Alice stared at him as though frozen.

'Shit.' He scraped his hand back and forth over his hair. Eddie had no idea what to do, what to say. It was all so long ago. He dropped his arm and gazed at her. 'I'm sorry. I should have been a better man. I should have known, somehow.'

She sniffed and rubbed a sleeve across her face. 'I'm sorry too.'

'For what?'

'Getting it so wrong. For not saying anything, but I didn't know how and I was so mixed up. And you were right. It *was* nice. You know ...' Her cheeks pinked. 'Being with you.'

That was something, at least. Not that it made Eddie feel any better. What he'd thought were some of the best experiences of his life – of both their lives – were now tainted, and the loss made his heart ache. Even worse was the realisation of what their immaturity had cost them. A few words on Alice's part, a bit more awareness on his, and they could have made it through.

Now, here they were, facing one another in an isolated paddock with all their hurt laid bare, and neither of them seemed to know what to do. Again.

Eddie sighed. 'So where does that leave us?'

'I don't know. Friends?'

'I was never not your friend, Alice.'

She looked at the ground, cuddling herself. Eddie wished he was confident enough to wrap her in his arms, but he had no idea where he stood.

The atmosphere clotted, bogging them in indecision. Alice stared at the ground, at the lambs, at the sky, at anywhere but Eddie, her mouth closed and turned down. All Eddie could do was watch, wretched and useless. Afraid.

He sighed. 'I'd better take you back.'

Alice sniffed and nodded.

They barely spoke on the return journey. Neither of

their hearts were in it and his was sore from the bruising it had taken. For Alice to believe such a thing about him seemed unfathomable. She knew him, knew his family. She'd been a part of it, welcomed like a daughter because Eddie loved her. Nothing he'd done should have led her to believe he didn't care, that his motivation was purely sex.

Yeah, Eddie loved sex. But he loved Alice more.

The house appeared, the Lindner's van's bright-green livery shiny in the sun. Eddie swallowed. For all his bruises, he didn't want her to go.

He reached across for her hand, half expecting her to jerk it away, but she took it willingly. It was soft and small and warm in his. 'Are you okay?'

'I don't know. Maybe. I think I just need time to process things.' She glanced at him and Eddie was relieved to see her tearstains had faded. 'Are you?'

He smiled and squeezed her fingers. 'I'll live.' He pulled up next to the van, relieved that Harry and his mum were nowhere around. 'Can I offer you a cuppa or anything before you head back?'

'Thanks, but I'm fine.'

They sat in the ute, anchored by something stronger than their joined hands.

'Maybe ...' Eddie glanced at their hands and back up, his heart rate increasing. 'Maybe you and I could do something together one night, like dinner or ...' His brow furrowed as he tried to think of what else they could do at night. Between work, sport and the Show Queen, neither had much spare time.

It was long seconds before she answered and then her voice was unusually shy and uncertain. 'Dinner would be nice. If you're sure.'

'I'm sure,' said Eddie, then grinned like an idiot. 'Couldn't be surer. When?'

Alice laughed and loosened her hand from his. She slid out of the car and faced him. 'Why don't we get through the Show Queen first, then see how we go?'

Eddie did his best to hide his disappointment. The Show Queen had two weeks to run. He didn't want to wait a day. 'Sure. Okay. Whatever you want.'

At the van he tenderly kissed her cheek and forced himself to step back. They looked at one another, hovering between farewell and the desire to stay. The air between them buzzed with all the words they'd yet to say and the charge of something else. The memory of what they'd had, what they'd broken, and the fear that they might not be strong enough to repair it.

The words 'We'll be okay' were forming in his head when Alice's mouth suddenly crumpled and she launched herself at him like a little rocket. Eddie stumbled then quickly steadied. He regarded her with bemusement. Alice's arms were pincered around his waist, her face buried in his jumper. He hovered his hands over her body. Was this bad? Should he touch her?

'I'm so sorry, Eddie. I got it wrong. Really, really badly wrong and I hurt you and treated you so awfully and I feel guilty and horrible, and now I don't know what else to do except say sorry a million times, which only makes me sound needy and pathetic and it's not enough anyway.'

'Hey, it's okay. We both stuffed up.' He kissed her silky hair and laid his cheek against it as he closed his arms around her. She was tiny and sweet and perfect in his hold. The urge to soppy-sigh whacked him in the chest like a flung wet sponge. God, he'd missed the feel of her. 'We were young, you were going through hell. I wasn't smart enough to read how you were feeling. What matters now is putting it behind us and moving forward.'

Alice lifted her head. 'I can't believe how forgiving you're being.'

'You know me, easygoing Eddie.' He stroked the length of her ponytail. 'And I've always been a sucker for cute blondes.'

She laughed, and for the first time since the lamb paddock Eddie felt the return of real hope.

He watched until the van was a speck on the gravel road, so lost in a daydream he nearly shot out of his skin when Harry lobbed a pine cone at his head.

'Hey, shortarse, quit mooning and get back to work.'

The drippy smile disappeared. Eddie's gaze narrowed. Things might have turned out okay between Alice and him, but that didn't change the fact that Harry had humiliated him in front of her.

'Jug-ears,' he growled, scooping up the pine cone and stalking after his brother, 'prepare to feel pain.'

SEVENTEEN

GUILT WAS LIKE A WET BLANKET: heavy, unpleasant and hard to shrug off. Alice wished she had more time for it. Eddie's revelations deserved an evening of solid brooding, preferably with lots of wine and chocolate and good friends to mop up her tears and tell her it wasn't her fault.

Except Eddie's hurt *was* Alice's fault, and no amount of wine, chocolate or girlfriend spin would change that. As with his Wax Me Happy night confession, Alice's only solace was that it had been a traumatic time. Anyone would have been hard-pressed to be rational.

What astounded her was his easy forgiveness. There'd been a small show of anger – anger he had every right to feel – followed by only kindness and understanding, and regret for what could have been.

It was so Eddie, so the man she'd loved. No wonder Alice's heart was full of him. And, it seemed, his heart was full of her, too. If they could get past this, what might the future hold?

The potential made her want to waltz around her

bedroom clutching his hoodie to her chest. Having returned it to Eddie, Alice made do with a soft toy rabbit that Paige had given her one Easter. If this kept up she'd have to invest in a toy sheep, or forsake her self-imposed ban on starting anything until after the Show Queen and dance with Eddie instead.

Preferably horizontally.

Alice's happy mood lasted one day. Paige arrived at Thursday's netball training with the news that the Phillips twins were hosting a Grand Final weekend online e-sport tournament. Scrabble for word nerds, a soccer game for armchair sporties, and a swashbuckling fantasy quest for those who liked adventure. There were no prizes, only kudos for winning and the slim chance of scoring a photo in the *Leader*. With Levenham in the grip of finals madness, it was perfectly timed to attract the less athletically inclined and those that had simply had enough of the hype.

'Clever,' said Alice, resting her foot on a rail and tightening her shoelace.

'Very.'

'How much is it to enter?'

'Twenty dollars.'

Alice whistled. 'That's a lot for no prize money.'

'You clearly haven't met anyone from the e-sport community. It's not about the money. It's about pride. They're bonkers for it. Willow said they've already had forty-two sign-ups.'

Forty-two? Alice did the maths and regarded Paige with her mouth open. 'But didn't you say they only announced it yesterday?'

'I did. If you recall, I also mentioned bonkers. Especially the Scrabble people. The library's Scrabble club is literally frothing at the mouth.'

Alice stared across the courts. The twins were always going to be tough competition, but after the previous Show Queen meeting Alice had been confident she could hold them off. Now, with one simple idea, they'd leapfrogged her. Grand Final weekend was eight days away. What would their total be by then? 'This is *not* good news.'

'I wouldn't worry. Your open-mike night is going to be huge.'

Alice could only hope so, but it rattled her into having to push her Show Queen totes, tees and wristbands harder on Lindner's unsuspecting customers. Success wasn't easy to come by. Regulars had already purchased their items and the remainder weren't interested or said they'd contributed in other ways, which only made Alice fretful that the much-dreaded fundraising fatigue had set in.

On Saturday afternoon, the Rebels played South Levenham for a berth in the Grand Final. It wasn't the Rebels' day. A dislocated finger in the first quarter left their goal shooter struggling with her accuracy and their wing defence had to be helped off in the second quarter when a heavy landing resulted in an ankle injury that saw her side-lined for the remainder of the game.

At half-time, the Rebels had held their game together enough to be only three goals down. Alice, Paige and Chrissy made a pact to play like their lives depended on the win, but even their herculean efforts weren't enough and the Rebels lost by six.

As much as she wanted to, Alice couldn't stick around for team commiserations. After thanking her teammates and coach for a wonderful season, she and Paige zipped home for quick showers before heading to the Arms to set up for the evening. Chrissy had already bolted to join Nick in enemy territory at Gerrinton for the remaining minutes of the Giants versus Port Andrews game, to see who Mount Pitt would play in the Grand Final.

Alice wished she could go with her. With Harry ruled out for play due to his concussion, Eddie would have to cover most of the Giants' ruck work, a tiring task that would leave him open to injury. All she could do was hope he'd be okay.

To Paige's and her delight, the Arms' function room filled quickly, the atmosphere abuzz as nervous performers chatted with supporters, and music lovers anticipated a good night's entertainment. Alice and Paige had set out the tables like an intimate club, with black tablecloths strewn with music-themed silver-and-gold confetti and clef-shaped candle holders that Alice had bought cheaply online. The lighting was low and focused on the small stage where a microphone and stool were set up, and reminded patrons that the evening was all about the performers.

Twenty-three had registered. Alice had hoped to give each singer three songs, but when five walk-ins turned up asking if there were still slots, she took their money and cut it back to two. That earned her a few grumbles when she announced it to the warm-up room.

Alice returned fire with her brightest smile. 'Thank you for your generous support of this charity event. Allowing more performers will help us raise even more money.'

'Good girl,' said Paige. 'Nothing like guilting people into compliance. Less painful for our ears, too. Some of that lot look as musically talented as I am.'

Judging by the cacophony in the warm-up room, there were a few of dubious talent, but the night was for anyone who stumped up the fee, even the caterwaulers.

Eddie arrived half an hour after the start, dragging Harry and Summer and a couple of teammates behind him.

He planted a lingering kiss on Alice's cheek that made a kaleidoscope of butterflies launch inside her.

'Congratulations,' she said. Chrissy had already phoned to say the Giants had won, and that Eddie had been awarded another best-on-ground. 'On both counts.'

'Thanks. The boys all put in. What happened with the Rebels?'

'Injuries put us behind and we never managed to make it up.' She glanced at the stage and touched Eddie's arm. Even touching him through his clothes made her fingers tingle. 'I'll be right back.'

Alice introduced the next act, a singer from across the Victorian border who'd come prepared with an iPad and keyboard. Fortunately, she'd also brought a helper and was quickly organised. Good. Alice wanted to get back to Eddie. He was looking delicious in well-fitting jeans and a collared fine merino jumper that showed off every muscle.

The singer, a beautiful dark-haired girl, began to play, quickly proving herself to be one of the professionals. The music was gorgeous, the keyboard's piano tones astonishingly clear. Satisfied all was well, Alice hurried towards Eddie only for Paige to intercept her at the back of the room.

'You forgot to mention the tees and totes. And the collection tins.' Paige gave hers a light rattle for emphasis.

Alice winced. 'I shouldn't labour them too much. People will get tired of it.'

'Yes, you should. Charity, remember? I know your lady parts are jingling for the jigglesticker.' She tapped Alice's head. 'But *Show Queen*.'

'Sorry,' Alice muttered.

'You're not, you know.'

'I am. Truly.'

'Not.'

'What do you expect me to do? I can't just ignore him.' She looked at Eddie, who smiled sexily and winked, causing Alice to fizz like sherbet and emit a childlike *teehee*.

Paige regarded her with pantomime horror. 'Did you just *titter*?'

'Might have,' mumbled Alice.

'That is unspeakably uncool.' Paige scowled at Eddie. He answered with an eyebrow wiggle. Paige's response was to rub the side of her nose with her extended middle finger and tut. Luckily, they were well behind the audience. 'You two are like teenagers.'

'Are not.'

'Totally *are*.'

Alice sighed. 'I know. I also know I don't have time for this.'

'You're dead right you don't.' Paige softened. 'No one ever said love was convenient.'

'That's the thing. I don't know if it's love or lust, or if I'm trying to make up for my guilt by being nice.'

Paige folded her arms. 'Do you really believe that?'

Alice glanced at Eddie and quickly away. 'No.'

'There you go.'

She was quiet for a moment. The singer's husky voice was the perfect tone for her inner turmoil. 'I don't want to hurt him again, Paige.'

'You won't. Times have changed. You've both grown up. You've learned how to talk.'

They had. Probably not as much as they needed to, but it was a start. Whether they could mend the emotional damage remained to be seen. One thing Alice was confident of, sexual attraction wasn't an issue.

'I hope you're right.'

'Of course I'm right.' Paige grinned and slung her arm around Alice's shoulders. 'Stop looking so wretched. A certain birdie once told me that you advocated, quite strongly I might add, that it was perfectly okay to fall in love.'

'Chrissy's a telltale.'

'That she is. But only with things that matter.' Paige released her. 'Perk up, Your Majesty.' She bopped Alice lightly with her collection tin. 'You have a tin to rattle.'

EIGHTEEN

LEVENHAM COULDN'T HAVE PUT on a more glorious spring day for the puissance if it tried. Not a cloud graced the sky and locals had taken the fine day as a cue to don some colour. Between the bright clothes, bunting, signs, and food and drink stalls, Civic Park was like an ever-moving rainbow.

Despite his mild hangover, Eddie felt like the weather – warm and sunny. The Giants were premiers. Eddie had played a blinder and won the Ethan Grey medal for best-on-ground in the Grand Final. And last night he'd kissed Alice.

Not a proper kiss. That would have been tricky with Paige hovering and projecting if not disapproving 'goolies in a blender' vibes, then certainly 'don't take forever' ones. Which was fair enough. As she had reminded him several times that evening, Alice had work in the morning. The clubroom carpark wasn't the most romantic venue either. But a lingering goodnight kiss on the mouth was still a lingering kiss on the mouth, and there was enough promise in it to signal this was only the beginning.

Eddie crouched to dog height and gave Blue a good neck scruff. 'You're going to be a champion, aren't you, mate?'

Blue gave him a look. Yeah, even the dog didn't believe that.

Eddie treated him to a last ear fondle and straightened. Chrissy had phoned on Thursday evening to ask if he and Blue would mind making up numbers. While the Dogs Under 50 cm class was full to bursting, there'd been an unexpected number of withdrawals in the Over 50 cm class, leaving the premier event at risk of ending up more Missy demonstration than competition. Eddie didn't hesitate. Although Blue stood no chance of winning, the dog had a good leap and a big heart, and, being a bit of a show-off, he would love the attention. Plus, entering might earn Eddie extra brownie points with Alice.

The lead-up events were fat with dogs of every breed, along with a few animals that looked like they had every breed in them. The agility program had been a huge hit, especially the kids' classes, which saw dogs racing off every-where except the jumps and tunnels and turns of their designated course. The costume contest caused great hilar-ity, as did the Strut Your Mutt parade and the Pet Look-a-like contest.

Eddie scanned the crowd yet again for Alice and spotted Paige.

'Having fun?' he asked.

'I am.' She squatted to pat Blue, then held the dog's chin and compared Blue's face with Eddie's. 'Not much resem-blance there.'

'We wouldn't have stood a chance against Brenda and Brunhilda anyway.'

Brunhilda was a pure white Samoyed of too-large

proportions, with dark-brown eyes, a self-important walk, and ridiculously fluffed-up hair. In a voluminous white dress with her own silver locks teased to scary heights, Brenda was identical.

Paige laughed. 'That was amazing, wasn't it? Although, that bloke with the basset put up a good fight. Alice is on her way, in case you're wondering.'

'Good.' He rubbed at his jaw. Other than a few short conversations last night, and most of those were warnings, he hadn't had a chance to talk to Paige properly until now. 'I'm guessing she told you all about the other day, at the farm.'

'She did.'

Eddie gave her a hopeful look. If anyone knew how Alice truly felt it'd be Paige. He could guess the answer, though it never hurt to double-check. Especially given Alice's and his history. They weren't dating, but they had something. Eddie hungered to know what it was.

'Don't give me those puppy-dog eyes, Eddie Argyle, they won't work.'

'Not even a hint?'

'No.'

He sighed. *Women.*

Paige pointed to the high-jump arena where Chrissy was herding competitors and ticking them off her list. 'You'd better get over there. Chrissy's stressed enough to explode as it is. Oh, and Eddie?'

'Yeah?'

'Good luck. But not too much.'

He laughed and went off to hunt for Harry, who'd agreed to act as his second.

'Oh, thank God,' said Chrissy, looking relieved and stricken at the same time. A tiny sheen of sweat glistened

above her lip and teeth marks pocked the end of her pencil. 'I had another pull-out this morning. At this rate there'll be no competition at all.'

'It'll be fine, you'll see.'

'I hope so. This is meant to be the main event and we're down to fifteen dogs, and one of those is the fattest labrador you've ever seen.'

'Wave a sausage and it'll jump. The crowd will go nuts.'

'Yeah,' said Harry. 'Everyone loves a sausage dog.'

Eddie did a double take. Had his twit of a brother just made a joke? He'd have to have a word with Summer. She was giving Harry far too much confidence these days, and Eddie still hadn't got him back properly for the hose incident.

With a pat of Chrissy's shoulder, they wandered into the arena to greet Mick and Missy, who introduced Eddie, Harry and Blue to the other dogs and their handlers. There were multiple bright-eyed kelpies and border collies, along with the fat lab, a few mixed breeds and a scarily tall Irish wolfhound whose male owner grinned at Eddie's astonishment and shook his head. 'Don't be fooled by his size. Laziest dog God ever put breath into.'

Eddie wasn't convinced. The dog was so tall it could step over the jump. He turned back to Mick. 'How's Missy feeling?'

'Good, good,' said Mick. 'Blue?'

Eddie shrugged. 'Seems happy enough.' He indicated the lab. 'Bit worried about that one. I reckon the owner is trying to lull us into a false sense of security.'

The inappropriately named Titan was flopped on its belly with its head on its paws and a doleful expression on its face.

Mick chuckled and tipped his head towards a dark-brown kelpie with tan eyebrows. 'I'd watch Elf. He came third to Missy at the muster a couple of years back, and that tri-coloured collie put on a good performance at the Colac Show last November.'

That was serious competition. Chrissy might be in for a contest after all.

The high jump consisted of stacks of wooden boards added layer by layer as the contest progressed, with each dog allowed three attempts to clear the wall. Fake grass had been laid over the run-up area, and large square hay bales winged the jump to help prevent the dogs from running out. Harry would lead Blue to a point at least three metres from the jump and let him loose, while Eddie stood on a platform above the jump, calling his dog on. Handlers would stand close by, ready to catch any dogs that might fall.

As the crowd swelled, Eddie's insides began to rattle with nerves. Missy's best was over 2.8 metres. That was a long way for a dog to fall, even an agile, clever kelpie like Blue. If his mate suffered an injury because of this event, Eddie would never forgive himself.

He checked out the opposition. No one else seemed fussed; even Titan's owner appeared relaxed. With super-stars like Elf and Missy contesting, they probably thought they had no chance and were in it for laughs. Eddie sidled over to Mick anyway.

'Those handlers.' He nodded at the men attending the jump.

Mick eyed him. 'They do the Muster. They know what they're doing. Blue will be fine.'

'Good,' said Eddie. 'Good.'

That didn't stop him feeling sick. Maybe it was wrong to make Blue do this. He glanced down. Blue looked up, his eyebrows raised as if to say, 'What's your problem?'

He stroked Blue's soft head. 'You okay with this? That jump's going to get pretty big.'

Blue yawned.

Eddie gave him another pat and searched the crowd for the one person who'd raise his spirits. His heart swelled. Alice was pressed up against the rope barrier, near the end of the right-hand hay-bale wing. She was still in her work shorts and safety boots, but had changed into one of her Show Queen t-shirts. Her blonde hair was piled into some sort of loose bun and Show Queen wristbands in every colour decorated her right arm. Eddie grinned and waved, winning a broad smile in return. Then Alice pointed to Blue and blew a kiss at him.

A kiss for him last night. A kiss for his dog today. Good signs. Good signs for sure. Maybe after the high jump he'd get to kiss her properly.

The first jump was set to only a metre high and every dog cleared it easily, even the lab, who hauled himself up with a loud, martyred groan and earned a huge cheer from the crowd for his effort. As predicted, the wolfhound barely had to leap.

The wooden planks were layered on. After two attempts at 1.2 metres, Titan dug his paws in, flopped down with exhaustion at the bottom of the jump and refused to rise until Chrissy coaxed him upright with a pig's ear chew treat. His owner shrugged, clipped on the dog's lead and waddled Titan away to *awws* and chuckles from his fans.

'Should've waved a sausage,' said Harry.

'Don't think it would have helped,' replied Eddie. 'I still can't figure out how he made it past the first one.'

'That dog's so fat inertia probably carried him over.'

One by one, the planks were added and with each round more dogs dropped by the wayside. Living up to its owner's prediction, the wolfhound bowed out at 1.8 metres. To Eddie's, and he suspected Mick's, surprise, Blue continued to clear each fence without fuss. After just scrambling over 1.9 metres on her third attempt, one of the collies decided in the following round that she'd had enough and, instead of shooting for the heightened jump, dashed off sideways under the rope and into the crowd. Her red-faced owner coaxed her back only for the collie to repeat her offence and the owner signalled her retirement.

Another dog dropped out at the same height, with two more gone at 2.1 metres. At 2.2 metres only Blue, Elf, Missy and the tri-coloured collie remained in contention. All four dogs seemed happy enough, facing the timber wall with bright eyes and pricked ears, treating the jump as a game. Eddie fretted that Blue might be getting tired, but Harry told him to stop being such a sook. Blue was fine. Eddie only had to look at him to see that.

At 2.4 metres, to an explosion of gasps from spectators, Missy failed her first attempt, then made the second. Mick shrugged, apparently unfazed. Eddie could only suppose these things happened. Blue made it up on his first try, landing in Eddie's arms at the top and plastering his master's face with gleeful licks. Elf wasn't so lucky and missed each of his three attempts, as did the collie.

'Must be having a bad day,' said Eddie, stunned.

'Not fit enough,' said Mick.

Eddie swallowed as the attendants added another wooden board. As a working dog Blue was fit, no problem, but at 2.5 metres that timber wall was bloody high. How any dog was meant to make it up and over was beyond him. That Blue had made it this far was testament to his courage and eagerness to please his master. Eddie swallowed again, this time to ease the lump that had formed in his throat. Win or lose, his dog was a star.

Word had spread that the competition was going down to the wire, and the crowd was swollen and animated. People jostled for position. Parents lifted their children onto shoulders or snuck them under the rope barrier to sit at the fake lawn edge. In the designated media zone, the *Levenham Leader*'s photographer was arguing with a television cameraman over who had primary position. Even Granny B had come in for a stickybeak, her jaunty trilby decorated with peacock feathers to match her green-and-blue trouser suit.

Eddie locked gazes with Alice. Unlike everyone else, she was looking as ill as Eddie felt. Paige was strangely sober, too. Worried about Blue, Eddie supposed. He couldn't blame them.

Missy was first to go at the new height. Again, she missed her first try.

'One down,' said Harry below his breath. 'Two to go.'

Missy failed on her second attempt, too. Mick led her back to the line and crouched to murmur in her ear. Missy was so perfectly trained Mick didn't need anyone to act as his second, like Harry was for Eddie, or to climb on the platform. He simply pointed the dog at the jump and gave the signal. Except this time, when he'd finished his dog whispering, Mick broke routine and headed for the platform, leaving Missy at the line restlessly lifting her paws.

Harry nudged Eddie. 'Must be worried.'

It certainly seemed like it, but Missy was a good dog and Mick an expert trainer, and it was inconceivable they could fail three times at only 2.5 metres when Missy had cleared another foot just the year before.

The crowd hushed. Eddie looked at Alice, his heart

hammering. Her eyes were enormous and both hands were folded in front of her face, as if she was praying. Paige was giving him a stare that was clearly meant to mean something but was beyond Eddie's understanding.

Mick signalled to Missy.

She galloped at the wall and leaped. It was a solid jump, her hind paws catching a plank with enough force to leapfrog Missy upwards to the top rail. She caught it with barely a claw on her right foot, the other falling just short. The crowd roared. Mick hunched over the edge, calling his champion dog on. Spectators yelled their encouragement. Missy's back legs scrabbled, desperate for the smallest purchase, but with momentum lost, and her hold on the top rail too weak, gravity took over. Missy tumbled down into the arms of a handler, who set her safely on the grass.

The crowd was silent.

'Oh shit,' said Eddie, loud enough for those near him to hear and laugh. If Missy couldn't make it, what chance did Blue have?

'Cut it out,' said Harry. 'Blue'll do it easy. Now get up there and let's get this done.'

Eddie passed Mick on his way to the platform. All he could think of to say as he shook Mick's hand was, 'Sorry.'

'Don't be. It wasn't Missy's day.' Mick nodded towards Blue. 'That's a good dog you've got there.'

'Yeah, he's a beauty.'

He bloody was too. Blue was only meant to make up the numbers, but here he was with a chance to win, and suddenly Eddie really wanted him to. The competition didn't have a countback and they'd come too far to walk away with a draw.

Eddie climbed the platform, leaned his hands on his thighs and looked down at Blue. The kelpie strained at

Harry's hold on his collar, his body quivering, his toes scrabbling at the grass.

He grinned at his dog. Blue gave a doggy grin back. Oh yeah, they were going to murder this sucker.

Civic Park was once more reduced to silence.

'Go!' yelled Eddie.

Blue shot from Harry's grip and hurled himself at the jump. Using his claws and the power in his hind legs, he bounced off a lower rail and shot his front paws to the top. They caught and stayed, Blue's shoulder muscles bulging from the effort.

'Come on, Blue-baby. You can do it.'

Blue locked his jaw, and with a mighty heave and a roar from Eddie he was over.

Eddie collapsed onto his back, laughing as he cuddled and kissed a wriggling, ecstatic Blue. After a prod from an attendant, Eddie clambered to his feet, his heroic dog still clutched to his chest. Grinning wider than he ever had in his life, Eddie shot a fist skywards. The crowed bellowed its approval.

He carried Blue down from the platform and set him on the ground with a proud ear fondle. Blue would be dining on Argyle steaks for a week after this effort.

Harry rushed up to hug and thump Eddie soundly on the back before fussing over Blue. Wanting to share his triumph with the girl he loved, Eddie hunted for Alice and found her not bouncing up and down with excitement at the rope's edge, but slipping backwards into the crowd.

Her face was the colour of curdled cream. Paige's was not much better. Both were staring at him with what he could only interpret as horror. Then Alice buried her face in her hands and swung away. In a heartbeat, they were swallowed by a swarm of Levenham locals.

'What the …?'

Eddie strode for the rope, but Chrissy grabbed his sleeve and wrenched him back.

'You're not going anywhere, mister.'

Eddie barely glanced at her. He was too busy searching for a blonde head. Where had they disappeared to? And why was Alice so upset?

Chrissy yanked again. 'Eddie!'

'What?'

She held up a finger. 'Listen!'

Eddie didn't want to listen. He wanted to follow Alice. Gritting his teeth, he did as he was told.

A chant was ringing through the air. 'More! More! More!'

He shook his head. More? What did they want, for him to sing?

'They want Blue to go for the next height.'

Two-point-six metres? Not a frigging chance.

'No. Blue's had enough.' His brave dog had worked his guts out today. Eddie wasn't going to ask him to do any more. 'I mean it. That's it.'

Chrissy opened her mouth to protest then relented with a sigh. 'Okay.' She glanced at her watch. 'It's getting late anyway.'

'Thanks.' This time it was Eddie's turn to stop her from hurrying off. 'Do you know where Alice has gone? She was fine a minute ago then she rushed off. I thought she'd at least stick around to congratulate Blue.' He scanned the crowd again. 'I thought we could maybe go for a drink to celebrate.'

Chrissy regarded him like he was insane. 'Not going to happen.'

'Why not?'

'Why not? Eddie, you've just won eight grand for your Show Queen account.' Her expression narrowed. 'You *are* going to donate the money to the Show Queen cause.'

'I suppose. But what's that got to do with anything?'

'What's that ...' She stroked her fingertips across her forehead. 'Because it means you've won, that's what.'

He scratched the back of his neck, feeling thicker than the high-jump planks. 'Yeah ...'

'Eddie,' said Chrissy, exasperated. 'Do you have any idea what winning the Show Queen title means to Alice?'

'About as much as it does me.' At her dropped jaw he carried on. 'Come on, Chrissy, it's just a dumb contest. The main thing is to raise as much money as possible. Alice herself said that to me. She said it to all the entrants.'

Chrissy closed her eyes for a second as though mining for strength. 'Yes, the money's important, but Alice entered for more than that. She's doing it to honour her mum. Winning means *everything*.'

And with one jump from Blue, Eddie had beaten her.

Shit, shit, *shit*.

'I'll keep the money. No, I'll hand it back. Or how 'bout I donate it to something else? Yeah, that'll do. I'll donate it straight to the hospital.'

'You can't do that!'

'Why not?'

She spoke slowly, as if to a child. 'Because this was always earmarked as Show Queen money. Donating it was what Mick would have done, had Missy won. It's what you're going to do. It's *expected*.'

'But ...' He searched for a way to stop his rising panic.

'Christina is right,' said Granny B, who'd sidled up without anyone noticing with Blue obediently at her heels. 'You must donate the money.'

'I can't.'

'You must, and you will,' said Chrissy.

Eddie felt everything slipping away. 'What about Alice? What about ...' He stared at the point where he'd last seen her, swallowing at the growing thickness that threatened to close off his throat.

'Oh, I'm sure she'll forgive you one day,' said Granny B, patting his arm. 'Just don't expect it in this lifetime.'

NINETEEN

HANDS over her mouth and her breath frozen, Alice stared at Eddie as he joyfully cuddled Blue, then punched the sky in victory. His grin was as brilliant as her despair was dark. Her dream, all she'd worked for, was gone. With one brave leap from Blue, Eddie had won the Show Queen.

'Drink. Now,' ordered Paige, anchoring Alice to her side and ploughing an escape channel through the milling locals. Too stunned to resist, Alice allowed herself to be led.

The Arms was thankfully quiet. Alice collapsed onto a chair in the back bar and stared at nothing as she breathed shallowly and tried to hold herself together. It didn't work. Heat kept stinging her eyes and her hands wrestled in her lap. Even a firm bite of her bottom lip couldn't stop Alice's mouth developing a giveaway wobble.

Paige's gaze narrowed and her voice came low and growly. 'The world hasn't ended yet, my friend.'

Alice shook her head. 'I'll never catch Eddie now.'

'You can, and you will. We'll find a way.'

Alice loved Paige for her never-say-die attitude, but by

Alice's calculations, with eight thousand dollars hitting his fund and the competition officially closing at five pm this coming Friday, Eddie's lead was unassailable.

She stared at her hands, calloused and permanently stained from the nursery. Funny that Eddie's had similar wear. She'd loved that they were alike in this way, happier outdoors than in. Except for now, when the idea of locking herself away in a dark room for a good, long pity-party held infinite appeal.

Eddie, Eddie, Eddie. He'd stolen back her heart without her wanting him to, and now he'd stolen her crown.

She half sobbed, half laughed. What a gargantuan screw-up. And she only had herself to blame.

Paige touched her forearm.

Alice looked up and smiled wanly. 'That'll teach me for being a smartypants, hey?'

'Like I said, we're not dead yet. Now stay there while I fetch medicine.' Paige strode for the bar, mutterings of 'jigglestick' and 'blender' wafting in her wake.

Locals began to pile in from Civic Park, ruddy-faced from the walk and rapidly cooling evening, thirsty for drinks and an easy Sunday-evening meal at the bistro. Though she half expected it, Eddie wasn't with any of them. Alice couldn't decide if she was relieved or not. Part of her wanted to hug him in delight for Blue's incredible win. The rest of her wanted to pound her fists against his big chest at the unfairness of it all.

The problem was none of this was Eddie's fault. Alice was the one who'd goaded him into entering the Show Queen. How could she then complain when he won? The money the competition had raised for local charities exceeded all expectations and they had gained valuable publicity for the district's first Wine Show. Surely that mattered more than her foolish ego?

It did. Of course it did. But that didn't mean losing didn't hurt.

Having just ended a call from Chrissy, Alice was hurriedly sniffing and wiping her damp eyes when Paige returned with their drinks. As the person responsible for Eddie's puissance entry, Chrissy blamed herself for the day's disaster and felt terrible. Alice told her not to be so silly. She'd been doing her job and Alice wouldn't expect any less. In fact, she'd be appalled if Chrissy held back on her professional performance because of their friendship. Besides, no one had thought for a second that Missy would lose, and more astonishingly, lose to Blue.

Her friend still had work to complete, but as soon as Chrissy was free she'd join them for a drink and to plan their next assault.

'To hell with impartiality,' said Chrissy when Alice questioned her involvement. 'This is a crisis.' A kindness that triggered sniffles of gratitude from Alice. Her friends were incredible – loyal, supportive and strong. She made a mental note to do something special for them in return when this was over.

'Those had better be happy tears,' said Paige, handing her a glass of red wine.

'They are. Chrissy's coming down later for a debrief.'

Her phone pinged. Chrissy sending her a warrior-princess gif with a *'You can do this!'* caption. Alice grinned, replying with, *Thank you, gorgeous person* followed by a set of flexed biceps and emoticons blowing kisses. Seconds later the phone vibrated again, this time with a call.

Eddie.

Alice let it ring. She wasn't ready. Not enough wine, not enough calm. Not enough time to reconcile her emotions with her defeat.

'Want me to answer?' Paige gave a crocodile smile. 'I'll be good. Cross my heart.'

Alice shook her head. 'I'll deal with him later.'

Eddie called five more times before resorting to texting. Alice relented only after Eddie sent a wonky selfie of Blue and him, looking forlorn and holding up a 'We're sorry' sign. Even Paige agreed she couldn't ignore that.

Alice breathed in deeply and typed back, *It's okay*.

His reply was immediate. *Talk to me?*

She showed Paige, who rubbed her shoulder in sympathy. 'You're going to have to talk to him at some point. He does sound truly sorry.'

'I know.'

The phone pinged again. *Please?*

Alice hesitated. Eddie was a good man, a kind one, and he deserved better than another cold shoulder. She'd caused enough hurt with that treatment for one lifetime.

Tomorrow, she typed back. The back bar of the Arms wasn't the place to have any sort of conversation. Not when she was feeling so raw. *See u at the meeting.*

He didn't reply for a while. Finally an *OK* appeared. Then, *I'll figure something out.*

'What do you suppose he means by that?' Alice asked Paige.

'I guess he wants to help you win.'

'How? I have five grand to make up in five days!'

'Nope. Less.' Paige leaned forward and tapped the table. 'By my calculations, you were at least eight hundred dollars in front of the twins before this afternoon, and around four K in front of Eddie. That leaves only a bit over four K to make up.'

'Hang on, I thought I was behind the twins, even after last night. I have to be. You said yourself that their e-sport thing was huge.'

'Not anymore. I got chatting to Mal Cavanagh's wife at the bar just then – Mal's the hairy bloke from ByteMe, where I bought my laptop – and she said they had some sort of computer failure this morning and lost all the tournament data. Mal's working his butt off to retrieve it, but it's not looking good. If he can't, Willow and Chelsea will have to refund all the players. They're devastated.'

Which made three of them.

'So, like I said, only a bit over four K to make up.'

'Only,' said Alice, slumping and taking a slug of wine.

'It's doable.'

Alice rolled her eyes. 'How?'

'Don't you roll your eyes at me, little Miss White-flag Waver. Queens don't surrender. Not our kind. There'll be a way. We just have to find it.'

Even with Chrissy's expertise, they could only think up small last-minute activities. Things like panhandling and doorknocking that Alice and Paige would somehow have to fit around work. At least Paige's and Chrissy's unwavering positivity helped ease some of the defeat that had settled so solidly on Alice from the moment Blue had cleared the jump, but her spirits remained low.

She left the Arms with a promise to chat again in the morning, hoping a good night's sleep would bring more ideas.

Alice threw open her bedroom curtains. A southerly change had moved in and Monday morning rose bleak and grey. Flipping it two fingers, she marched to the bathroom where she washed her hair and loofahed all over with her favourite pink grapefruit shower gel. A blow-dry and a slick of deodorant later, she padded back to her room and tugged on a clean Lindner's uniform.

So what if her cause was hopeless? That didn't give her permission to wimp out. If she failed to catch Eddie, at least she'd have given it her all and raised a ton of money for the Show Queen. Stung pride or not, that was what mattered.

She would be queen in action if not title.

'Hey, Dad,' she said, walking into the kitchen and raiding the cupboard for a sachet of quick oats. She tipped them into a bowl, poured over milk and set it in the microwave.

Ross was at the kitchen table, reading glasses perched on his nose as he scrolled through his tablet. Like Alice, he was neatly dressed in his Linder's uniform, the cuffs of his shirt already rolled up in anticipation of a busy day.

'Hello, love.' He set the tablet down and regarded her over the top of his glasses. 'Sleep well?'

'Not too bad. You?'

'Not so great. Bit worried about my princess.'

'I'm fine, Dad. Really.'

He pursed his lips and sipped his coffee. Alice could feel his eyes following her as she set the automatic espresso machine to make a large latte and fetched honey to drizzle over her oats. Her breakfast ready, she carried her mug and bowl over to the table and sat down.

'Any interesting news?' she asked, using her chin to indicate the tablet.

'Nothing out of the ordinary.' He took another sip from his mug. 'Tough day yesterday, Eddie winning.'

'It was.' Alice stirred her spoon through her oats and smiled reassuringly. 'But I'm not done yet.'

Ross stroked her hair, his expression warm with love. 'Ah, princess, you're so like your mum.'

Heat prickled at the back of Alice's eyes as it always did when her dad said things like that.

'Whatever happens,' he said, his voice slightly husky, 'win or lose, your mum will still be proud of you. I know I'm proud.'

Her swollen heart was too big to form speech around. In a few words her dad had countered all her secret fears. Her neediness and ego didn't matter. Queen or not, she was loved.

She glanced at the rows of family photographs lining the dining-room cabinet and caught her mum's smile. Though Alice knew it was her imagination, the air seemed to vibrate with her mum's presence, as if she were reaching across the ether to comfort them.

Alice refocused on her dad and squeezed his hand. 'Thank you.'

They shared a smile, then he indicated her bowl. 'Better eat your breakfast before it gets cold.'

Warmed beyond measure, Alice did as she was told.

He watched her for a moment, then made a show of staring around the open-plan kitchen-living area. 'You know, I reckon it's about time we gave this place a bit of a spruce-up. Hasn't been touched since your mum died and it's looking a bit worn out. A coat of paint, maybe new cupboards.' He jerked his chin at the laminated kitchen benchtop – a stained and rather ugly avocado-green affair. 'That's certainly seen better days.' He regarded the sombre farming-scene print that had hung on the wall near the fridge since they'd inherited it from Alice's great-grand-mother some twenty-plus years ago. 'And that miserable thing can go to the dump. We'll hang something bright and modern. Cheerful. What do you think?'

'I think it's a great idea.' Alice had been wanting to liven the house for a while, but had been too worried about upsetting her dad and losing precious memories of her mum to suggest it. It had been four years, though, and their grief had lost its sharp edges. The time was right.

'That big art auction is on this week. Might be able to pick up something cheap.' Ross lifted the tablet and pushed up his reading glasses. 'I'm sure the *Leader* had a link to the catalogue.' He swiped a couple of times. 'Bingo.'

Alice scoffed the last of her breakfast and leaned closer to look at the paintings on offer, her eyes bulging at some of the estimates.

'Bloody hell,' said her dad. 'We're in the wrong game.'

They laughed at one particularly hideous cubist-style picture of a dislocated Friesian cow that the catalogue described as 'a vivid and expressive allusive abstraction of contemporary rural life from an exciting new talent'.

But when her dad scrolled to the next lot, Alice's laugh died. The painting was one from Scarlett's feminine series – albeit less confronting than those Alice had viewed in her studio – and the estimate for it was gobsmacking.

Ross enlarged the page to read the details. 'Isn't that the woman who did your t-shirt?'

'Mm,' said Alice, her gaze distant as her mind scrambled with a forming idea. An idea that had her skin tingling more and more as she poked and prodded it for flaws and found only benefits. It was a gamble, but with a litre of gin and a bit of sweet-talking, they might be able to pull it off. 'Dad, you're a genius.'

'Why? What did I do?'

'You, my clever daddy,' she said, grinning wildly and kissing his cheek, 'might have found me a way to win the Show Queen!'

TWENTY

MONDAY NIGHT'S final Show Queen meeting was compulsory for all contestants, even those who'd dropped out long ago.

Alice arrived early and took a front-row seat, the closest she could get to Mrs Wallace's usual perch. Smiling hello, Steph quickly filled the chair to her right, the Phillips twins settling soon after into the seats on Alice's left. Alice forced herself to exchange pleasantries, which wasn't easy when her attention was fixated on the door.

Mrs Wallace had gone incommunicado since early morning and Alice was going crazy.

Chrissy strode in, head swivelling as she searched out Alice. Finding her, she lifted her eyebrows. Alice shook her head. Chrissy frowned and checked behind herself, but Mrs Wallace was clearly intent on torturing them all with a last-minute arrival.

'Entries for the auction have closed,' Mrs Wallace had said when Alice had phoned her after breakfast with a proposal that they auction Scarlett's original t-shirt artwork. The hour hadn't been exactly civilised, but this was an emergency. The old lady had been up anyway, enjoying a cigar if the puffs Alice had heard were anything to go by.

'Oh,' said Alice, flattened. She could have smacked herself for not realising. Of course entries had closed. The catalogue had been out for ages and the auction had been advertised for months. It was part of the town's major event calendar.

'However, that is easily remedied. It's convincing Scarlett to donate her work where you are most likely to come unstuck.'

'With proceeds going to charity, she might be amenable. And she did allow us to use the original design for free.'

'Licensing for limited use is one thing, transferring ownership quite another. You do realise that her work commands many thousands of dollars?'

Alice slumped miserably on her bed. 'I saw the estimates in the catalogue.' She cuddled her pillow to her belly as she tried to remember how much was in her bank account. Not a lot, and with her car registration and insurance due soon there wasn't much fat to play with. The rest of her savings were locked away in less liquid investments. 'I could offer her five hundred, maybe.'

Mrs Wallace gave a throaty cough, which told Alice all she needed to know about that proposition.

'It's my last chance,' she said, unable to keep the wobble from her voice. 'Eddie's so far in front it'd take a Lotto win for me to catch him.'

'Has it ever occurred to you that Edmond might deserve to be Show King?'

Alice's chest tightened at her words. Perhaps she was right and Eddie had earned the crown. He'd worked hard, caught up an extraordinary amount of ground despite his late entry, was always on hand to help, joining in and charming everyone with his easy manner and farm-boy can-do practicality. But he didn't truly care about the Show Queen, not like she did, and his current lead was purely thanks to a canine miracle. The injustice of it made Alice want to pummel her fists on the floor.

Mrs Wallace sighed. 'It's a very good thing I like you. All right. Leave it with me. I shall be in touch.'

Except she never called back. Alice phoned multiple times throughout the day without response. By late afternoon she was desperate. Cadging yet more time off work, she drove to Camrick, but no one answered the door at the house or the flat over the old stone stables. She supposed it should come as no surprise. This was one of Levenham's biggest weeks of the year, in which the entire Wallace clan was heavily involved. Alice contemplated scouring the town and dismissed the idea. Mrs Wallace had her expensively ringed fingers in so many pies she could be poking holes anywhere.

Alice waited twenty minutes before growling and marching back to her car. She shot an update to Paige and Chrissy, followed by a last-ditch pleading email to the address Scarlett had used when she sent through the digital files. It was a risk, if Mrs Wallace's opinion of the artist's temperament was anything to go by, but Alice felt they'd developed a small bond at the studio, and a direct appeal to Scarlett's altruism might be the nudge that pushed her the right way. She returned to the nursery, praying that Mrs Wallace was saving her good news for tonight. It'd be just like her to make Alice sweat.

To Alice's dismay, Mrs Wallace – immaculate in cream trousers, matching trenchcoat and a tortoiseshell-patterned silk shirt – strode through the door of the Mechanics' Institute with her arm looped through Eddie's and her expression benign. After a pat of thanks, she shooed him towards the chairs. A few long strides and Eddie plonked in the seat behind Alice.

His big hand gripped the back of her chair as he leaned close, bringing with him the wonderful scent of freshly mown grass. It was too early for hay cutting. Eddie must have mowed the lawns for his mum.

'Hey. You okay?'

Alice suppressed a shiver as his breath tickled the delicate hairs of her ear and neck. 'Of course.'

Eddie's voice lowered. 'I tried to give it back. They wouldn't let me. Kept insisting it was Show Queen money, that I'd let everyone down if I didn't accept it. I couldn't even donate it directly to the hospital.'

'It's fine,' she said, twisting to give him a brief, not-very-well-executed smile.

'It's not.' He swallowed and glanced at the others. Their gazes might be elsewhere, but from Steph's and the twins' concentrated expressions it was obvious their ears were well tuned in. He bent closer, his voice softening even further. 'This was meant to be for your mum.'

'It doesn't matter now. Truly.' Alice smiled properly to show she meant it. 'Besides, I still intend to win.'

'How?'

'You'll see.' At least she hoped he would. Mrs Wallace was still refusing to make eye contact and Alice wanted to throttle her.

'If you don't?'

'Then I'll still have raised a lot of money for charity.'

For a few heartbeats he was quiet. 'And us?'

Good question, and one that would have to wait. Right now, all Alice wanted to do was make it through this final week knowing that she'd given the Show Queen her all.

Besides, their future was too important to rush and Eddie had suffered enough hurt already from Alice's distraction. The Show Queen wasn't on the same scale as her mum dying, but she wasn't about to risk it.

'We'll sort that out after.'

Movement as Sarah, Tiffany and Chrissy broke from their huddle drew Alice's gaze forward and set wings fluttering through her insides. The meeting was about to begin and with it news of her Show Queen chances. She crossed her fingers tightly, then crossed her toes for extra oomph.

Eddie said nothing more, though his hand stayed on the back of her chair for a long while. Then he gently stroked a curled finger down her neck and sat back.

Sarah opened with congratulations to Eddie and Blue, which Eddie acknowledged with a brief lift of his hand and nothing more. Mrs Wallace kept her expression neutral and her gaze everywhere except where Alice needed.

Sarah handed over to Chrissy, who ran through the Saturday agenda, along with a stern reminder to take it easy at the wine-tasting stands. They might be contestants, but they were also ambassadors for the Wine Show. There'd be no drowning of sorrows until after the presentation. Then, with the exception of the winner, who'd have queenly duties, they were free to party themselves silly.

'Don't you mean kingly duties?' piped up Margot. If Alice hadn't been so occupied glaring at Mrs Wallace, she would have speared the girl a filthy look. Not that Margot would have been any more responsive than the model-thin Buddha at the front of the room; she was too busy batting her lashes at Eddie. 'I mean, it's pretty obvious who's won.'

'A lot can happen over the next four days,' Chrissy countered with acid sweetness. Then she sneaked an encouraging wink at Alice, causing the twins to giggle and Steph to elbow Alice and whisper, 'No bias there ... *much*.'

Sarah reclaimed the floor. 'Quite right. There are still events scheduled for this week. Anything can happen. Chelsea and Willow, you have a cake stall on Thursday?'

The twins nodded their confirmation.

'Fairy cakes,' said Willow.

'Chocolate-brownie cheesecake slice,' said Chelsea.

'Really?' asked Eddie, who'd always been a sucker for brownies.

'Uh-huh,' said Chelsea. 'I'll save you a piece. Two pieces, if you like.'

'And a caramel slice,' said Willow.

For God's sake. What was with all the Eddie sucking up? The man wasn't Show King yet.

'Banana bread?' asked Mick. 'It's Missy's favourite.' A claim Missy backed up with a woof.

'Of course,' the twins chorused.

'Sounds wonderful as always, girls.' Sarah regarded her list and frowned. 'Funny, I thought there was more. Eddie, didn't you have something planned? A meat raffle, wasn't it? For darts night at the Arms?'

'Cancelled,' he said, his brownie perkiness lost. 'Unforeseen circumstances.'

Alice leaned around. Eddie shrugged and gave a wry smile, but the weariness of it had her frowning and wanting to reach for his hand.

'Anyone else?'

Tearing her gaze from Eddie's, Alice looked desperately at Mrs Wallace.

'There is one late addition,' she said, finally gracing Alice with eye contact. 'Alice will be auctioning an original artwork by Scarlett Ash on Wednesday evening, with the proceeds going to her fund.'

Alice squealed, then slapped a hand over her mouth while her feet beat a happy tattoo on the floor. She'd done it, the wonderful, exasperating woman had done it!

Chrissy threw Alice a not-very-subtle thumbs-up behind Sarah's back.

'Oh,' said Sarah, flipping up a sheet on her list to check beneath then letting it drop. 'It doesn't seem to be written down anywhere.'

'Well, I did say it was a late addition. Alice telephoned me this morning with the proposal, and I approved it.' Mrs Wallace stared down her nose at the committee women, daring them to challenge her.

No one did.

'Ah ... good, then,' said Sarah. 'Yes. Um, well done, Alice. And good luck.' Her composure recovered, she grinned at Tiffany and Chrissy. 'What a development. Looks like we're in for an entertaining week after all. Tiffany, you'll chase this up?'

'I certainly will,' replied Tiffany, pink-cheeked with excitement. 'Scarlett Ash, what a coup! With no one knowing the latest numbers, this will add real tension to the crown announcement and its lead-up. The *Leader* is going to love it, so will the Vigneron's Association. Eddie, are you sure you can't put on another event, just to spice things up further?'

He shook his head. 'Nope, I'm done.'

'Something little, perhaps?' She smiled winningly and pinched her finger and thumb together, but even her pretty appeal didn't change Eddie's mind.

Sarah pursed her lips at him, then glanced at Alice before moving on. 'Right, then, I think that covers everything. Any questions?' With none raised, she closed the meeting. 'See you all at six o'clock on Saturday. Don't forget to bring your dancing shoes!'

Bursting with excitement, Alice shot for Mrs Wallace, only for Eddie to block her with a sidestep.

'Can we talk?'

'I'm sorry, I really need to catch up with Mrs Wallace.' She needed details, like how much the painting was going to cost and, more importantly, how much Mrs Wallace thought it would fetch.

'She'll keep.'

Alice ducked her head to the side. Mrs Wallace had shrugged on her trenchcoat and was now extracting a cigar from one of its pockets. 'I'm not so sure about that.'

'Alice, please. It's important.'

She stared at him. Eddie had that bruised look only lack of sleep brought. Lines furrowed his brow and his lovely mouth was grim. Alice's heart squeezed with anguish for him. Poor Eddie, he must have been fretting over her loss all night. But there was hope now. Lots of hope.

Though she wanted to do more, Alice took his hand and squeezed it. 'We'll talk when the Show Queen's over, okay?'

'No, it has to be now. It'll be too late then.'

'Are you sure about that, Edmond?' Mrs Wallace tapped Alice with her cigar. 'Do hurry along. One is rather in need of one's restorative. So very irritating these smoking bans.'

'I need to talk to Alice.'

'It's fine,' said Alice. 'Really.'

'So do I,' said Mrs Wallace, as if Alice hadn't spoken. 'And as patron of this event, I take priority. Now, please stop distracting my young friend. She has a very busy week ahead.'

A muscle flexed in Eddie's jaw. 'Tomorrow, then. I'll come around after work.'

'I can't.' Eddie's cancelled raffle had given Alice an idea for tomorrow night. 'We'll catch up after Saturday, okay?' She smiled to soften his disappointment. 'I promise.'

'But—'

'No one likes a groveller, Edmond.'

'I'm not—' He rubbed his hand over his face then flicked it at them. 'Forget it. I'll see you on Saturday.'

Mrs Wallace kept a tight grip on Alice while they headed for the door. As they passed through, Alice looked back. Eddie was slumped in a chair, head down, gaze fixed on his palms.

She faltered. 'I should—'

'No, you should not. You and I have matters to discuss.' Mrs Wallace smiled in way that made Alice's skin prickle. 'I'm sure you're rather anxious to know Scarlett's terms, aren't you?'

'SHE DID IT, PAIGE,' said Alice, flopping backwards onto her bed and cycling her legs like an upended beetle, her phone beside her on speaker. 'We're in the auction.'

'That's brilliant!'

'I know. Guess what else?'

'What?'

'She conned Scarlett into handing over the canvas for nothing!'

'What? Like, for free?'

Performing a sort of splits, Alice levered up and tumbled onto her belly. She dragged the phone closer, curled her legs up behind her and rested her chin on the backs of her folded hands. 'Yep!'

'No catches?'

'Nope, and the devious old duck has even convinced the auction house to waive the seller's premium.'

Paige erupted into laughter. 'Look out, Eddie, we are back in the game! What was his reaction when he heard?'

At the mention of Eddie, Alice's soaring high took a nose-dive. Poor Eddie, he'd looked so forlorn when she left.

Perhaps she should have stood up to Mrs Wallace and stayed with him, but they'd waited this long to piece together their broken relationship, another week wouldn't matter.

'Nothing,' she said, plucking at her doona cover. 'I don't think he cares anymore.'

Paige considered a moment. 'Well, we do. Down to priorities. How much will it make?'

'Mrs Wallace wasn't sure. One of Scarlett's crazy self-portraits sold for several thousand at an auction in Adelaide recently, but this is different. It's a commercial piece, conceived specifically for the Show Queen and done in a hurry, so lacking the meticulousness of her usual stuff. Apparently, it also lacks all those arty-farty themes that get collectors in a lather.'

'In other words, no dirty bits.'

'No, no, they're not dirty bits, they're essences of womanhood. Scarlett's art isn't rude, it's – and I quote – "A rich visual treatise on female sexuality and feminism".'

'Ugh. Spare me.' Alice could hear her friend's eye roll. 'Hang on, that doesn't sound like Mrs Wallace.'

'Because it's not. According to her, that was how the auction-house director described Scarlett's work. Reading between the lines, I think Mrs Wallace thinks he's a complete wanker. Anyway, Scarlett doesn't always include dirty bits. The two she has in the auction are pretty tame ... for her.'

'What does all that add up to in dollar terms? Will it fetch enough?'

'I don't know. Not even the auctioneer was sure, but Mrs Wallace expects it'll clear at least fifteen hundred on name alone.'

'But that's fantastic!'

'It is.' Alice couldn't keep the disheartened sigh from her voice. 'But it'll still leave us short. By a lot.'

'You can quit with your negativity right now, Princess Piker. Anything could happen on the night, and we have other tricks up our sleeves.'

True. And while Mrs Wallace had been careful to hedge her bets, she'd seemed confident Alice was still in the game.

'I wonder how she convinced Scarlett to donate the painting,' mused Paige. 'Scarlett's a bit odd, but she's not exactly a pushover. That girl's got brains. Reads loads of biographies and art-history titles, and last week she came in asking about an intra-library loan for a book on intellectual property law.'

'Mrs Wallace probably just scared the pants off her like she does the rest of us.'

'She is terrifying, isn't she?'

'She is. Except it's more a nice kind of terror. Like, I don't know ... benevolent terror.'

They broke into giggles.

'God,' said Paige, sniffing back the last of her laughter, 'please let me be like her when I get old. I'd be brilliant at it.'

'You would.'

'I would indeed,' said Paige, mimicking Mrs Wallace's regal tones. 'There's just that little problem of lacking a posh husband with a vast fortune to help me on my way.'

'You mean the one who'll not only keep you in fine jewels and clothes, but insist you spread his largesse throughout the land?'

'That's him,' said Paige. 'Although, you forgot to mention his impressive jigglestick. Very important those jigglesticks.'

'So she told me.'

They cracked up again.

Paige let out a long sigh. 'How is it that you scored an upper-class fairy godmother and I didn't?'

'Because I'm friends with Chrissy?' Alice rolled onto her side and raked the edge of the doona close to her chest, cuddling it like a makeshift soft toy. 'I don't really know. My suspicion is that she has a thing for enterprising women. Look at what she did for Chrissy.'

'Hmm, maybe. But she's not afraid to demand her pound of flesh in return. Poor Chrissy's working herself stupid.'

'And having a wonderful time doing it. I can't remember the last time I saw her so happy.'

'That's just a permanent post-orgasmic smile from all that Nick sex.'

'*Jealousy*,' teased Alice.

'You bet I'm jealous. And don't you dare tell me you're not because I won't believe you. Now, the auction. Anything we need to do?'

'Nothing. It's all organised. All we have to do is turn up and smile prettily at the bidders so they'll spend more.'

'I'm sure we can manage that.'

'One other thing. Eddie's cancelled the meat raffle he was supposed to be running at the Arms tomorrow night for the darts competition. Why don't we slide into his spot? I doubt anyone will mind, and every bit counts.'

'Great idea.' A smile entered Paige's voice. 'We are going to nail this thing, Your Highness, you just wait.'

'Don't count your chickens.'

'If I had chickens, dearest Alice-friend, I'd raffle them.'

Tuesday evening's raffle at the Arms raised two hundred and thirty-five dollars after expenses. Not a lot, but better than nothing.

Just before the draw Alice received a message from Eddie chastising her for not letting him know she'd taken it over. He'd already paid for his raffle prizes and would have happily donated them to her cause. Instead, his mum's freezer was now full of chops, sausages and steaks they didn't need, and the pantry loaded with six dozen eggs on top of the farm's Australorp's usual production. His mum was not impressed, threatening Eddie with quiche for a week. *So unmanly*, he'd texted.

Alice grinned and messaged back her thanks for the offer. It hadn't crossed her mind to check. Between work, setting up the raffle and organising locations to sell the last of her merchandise, she'd barely had time to think about anything else.

I'll forgive you if you'll forgive me, he replied.

'Draw time,' said Paige, and in the action following, Alice completely forgot to message back. By the time she staggered home, yawning and spaghetti-limbed from another long day, it was too late to respond. She fell asleep intending to answer in the morning.

Only to forget again on waking.

♔

Art Week was a big deal in Levenham. Unlike the Wine Show, which was Mrs Wallace's baby, Art Week was supported by the entire Wallace family, and as such sparkled with even more glamour as their many posh and artistic friends flew and drove in from all over to support the event and socialise. Word around town was that, urged on by their hosts, many were staying for the weekend, guaranteeing a photogenic crowd for the Wine Show and more press interest.

The auction had been scheduled originally for Ryan's Winery, but after the fire another venue had to be found. With few suitable, the committee was forced to relocate to the council auditorium, which made no one happy. An unattractive early-seventies brutalist concrete cube that some fool had allowed to be attached like an unburst boil to the rear of council's historic and elegantly fronted chambers, it was hardly the ideal place to glorify Levenham's artistic culture. Worse, the venue was dry, a situation that could have been resolved with a temporary licence to serve alcohol had not Mrs Wallace's archenemy Councillor Herriot blocked it.

Three generations of Wallaces graced the front row of the auditorium. Their matriarch was her usual resplendent self in a slim-fitting cobalt Jacquard-weave pantsuit with an eye-popping diamond wreath necklace around her throat. Her daughter, Adrienne Wallace-Jones, sat alongside, dressed in forest-green silk, her plain gold jewellery an understated but stylish match. Next to Adrienne was Emily Wallace-Jones, now Sinclair since her marriage to the Gerrinton Giants' super-hunky captain Josh, who, given his absence, was likely babysitting their daughter tonight. She looked lovely in an off-the-shoulder white blouse and burgundy skirt, and her hair up in a loose bun that showed off the glittery amethysts in her ears. Digby Wallace-Jones occupied the last seat, handsome as ever in a charcoal suit and blue tie.

'I feel like such a dag,' whispered Paige as she and Alice hovered at the edge of the room. 'Look at them. All those perfect genes and jewels.'

'Shush. You look wonderful.' And her friend did. Paige's coral-coloured dress might be simply cut, but on her athletic body it looked stunning.

Aiming for maximum cuteness in case she was singled out as the Show Queen entrant whose lot they would be bidding on, Alice had opted for a sleeveless crimson frock patterned with white love hearts that she'd ordered online ages ago and never had a chance to wear. Paige had laughed uproariously on seeing her, and immediately nicknamed her Show Queen of Hearts.

Paige smoothed a hand over her waist. '*You*, missy, look wonderful. *I* look like a frump.'

'You do not. You're beautiful. Now, whatever you do, don't twitch a muscle when the auction is on or you might end up buying a Picasso look-a-like.'

'Yes, Your Majesty.'

Alice elbowed her. 'Shut up.'

'Yes, Your Majesty.'

They slipped into vacant seats a few rows from the back. Dark-suited men and women lined the walls, phones at the ready and papers and tablets in their hands. Another woman sat behind a desk near the auctioneer's podium with a laptop in front of her, poised to take internet bids.

'I had no idea it was such a big deal,' said Paige.

'Me either.' This time it was Alice's turn to rub her hands down her pretty skirt. 'I mean, Mrs Wallace warned me it was, but this is beyond anything I imagined.'

More people continued to wander in; Levenham's arty crowd, locals curious to see what the fuss was about, landowners descended from the settlers whose holdings had made them ridiculously wealthy, glamorous out-of-towners, and nervous-looking types whom Alice pegged as artists with lots up for sale. She spotted Willow and Chelsea as they made their way to a couple of vacant seats several rows in front. Both gave her silly smiles and thumbs-ups and Alice's heart warmed at their good sportsmanship. Margot and Steph were also present, which made Alice wonder where Eddie was. He'd supported every other event.

Chrissy appeared at the end of their row. Alice beckoned and patted the seat they'd reserved, but Chrissy held up her index finger in a 'one-moment' gesture. She strode to the front row, capturing the admiring attention of several men as she passed, and greeted the Wallace family individually before leaning close to Mrs Wallace and speaking in her ear. Mrs Wallace gave a regal nod, and with her face a mask of poorly hidden glee, Chrissy disappeared through a side door.

'What was that all about?' Alice asked when Chrissy finally arrived at her seat.

'Oh, nothing.' She waved a hand. 'Just some last-minute wine-show business.'

Paige leaned across Alice to give Chrissy one of her severe librarian looks.

Chrissy poked out her tongue, only to be caught by Mayor Barry McClintoff as he arrived, causing her face to turn almost as crimson as Alice's dress. The mayor grinned and winked, demonstrating the likeability and easy nature that had helped keep him in power for over a decade.

A few more minutes passed with Chrissy constantly checking the doors and her phone, and refusing to respond to Alice and Paige's pestering. The mystery was solved when a waitress backed into the room holding a tray of white, red and sparkling wine, and Chrissy let out a sigh of relief.

'Oh goodie,' said Paige. 'I could do with a drink.'

From the furrowed brows of the auction-house staff, this

was not an appreciated development. The scheduled start time was only a minute away, and drinks would delay that further.

Mrs Wallace rose, faced the room and gave a single clap. Immediately, everyone fell silent. She bowed graciously in acknowledgement of their civility and began to speak. 'Thank you, both for your attention and attendance to this special event, which, as I'm sure you have heard, is not the only special event our wonderful town will be hosting this week. This weekend Levenham will hold its inaugural wine festival. As many of you are aware, thanks to our passionate and talented winemakers, and the blessing of a truly unique terroir, our small but growing region is rapidly becoming an industry darling. With good reason. Our wines are exceptional.' She smiled and indicated the waitstaff. 'Please, don't take my word for it, sample for yourself. I defy you not to be impressed.' The auctioneer began to sidle towards her, the tips of his fingers tapping his watch face. Mrs Wallace withered him with a glare. 'Tonight, we will also be auctioning a lot for one of our Show Queen charity fundraiser contestants, Alice Lindner. It is a remarkable work from up-and-coming local artist Scarlett Ash, and the cause is excellent. I'm sure you will not let myself, Alice or Levenham down, and will prove once again how generous the art world can be.' With a regal nod to the now shiny-browed auctioneer, she sat.

As the wine began to circulate, the exasperated auctioneer turned to Barry McClintoff, who shrugged, happily snagged a glass of red from a passing waiter and raised it to a triumphant Mrs Wallace.

Chrissy was vibrating with suppressed laughter.

'Your idea?' asked Paige.

'Granny B's. I just sorted the logistics and Barry resolved the licence. That's why we're late.'

With official welcomes and speeches taking up more time, it was another twenty minutes before the actual auction started, by which time Alice was fidgeting like a two-year-old, flushed and buzzing from the sparkling wine she'd drunk. Chrissy stayed busy checking emails on her phone, while Paige attempted to distract Alice from her nerves by assessing all the suited men for potential jiggle-sticking, none of whom lived up to Eddie, and which made her even more aware that he still hadn't showed.

The first painting, a stunning seascape by a local artist of significant talent, went for five thousand dollars. The next made four figures, too, as did several subsequent lots. Clearly, the room was in a buying mood, no doubt helped by the uninterrupted supply of alcohol.

With so many artworks on offer, it was another hour before Alice's lot was set on its easel and an enlarged image of it projected onto the screen behind. To her delight, the auctioneer invited her to stand.

'Thank you,' said Alice, moving out into the aisle to accept a microphone from one of the auction-house staff and beaming her best smile. 'I think you'll all agree the Show Queen initiative is, as Mrs Wallace said, something very special. It's captured the heart of Levenham, built community spirit, and through its events given many people a lot of pleasure. Yet where it truly shines is in its unique charter. Show Queen money stays in the district. We are locals looking after locals, helping and supporting charities and services that tend the heart of our community. Every dollar raised makes a difference. Maybe not directly to you, but now or in the future, perhaps someone you know, someone you care about, will have their life changed thanks to your generosity tonight. A happy and healthy community is a strong one. Please dig deep and help us thrive. Thank you.'

She sat and hoped like crazy that the murmurs and nods meant something positive.

Paige took her left hand, Chrissy her right, and they shared a smile before focusing on the auctioneer.

The bids started at a thousand and quickly rose to fifteen hundred, then two thousand.

'Omigod,' whispered Alice on a shaky breath.

'Go, baby,' muttered Paige as another hundred was bid then quickly trumped by two more bids.

At two-and-a-half thousand, Alice's heart began to pound. If it made four, there was a good chance she could win the Show Queen this very night.

'Please, please, please,' she mouthed as the price jumped to two thousand, eight hundred, then three thousand, only for momentum to then slow.

'Don't you bloody dare,' growled Paige.

One by one the room bidders dropped out, leaving a single phone bidder against the internet.

At three thousand four hundred, the staff member relaying the phone bids shook his head. The auctioneer gave the sale every chance to keep going, allowing fifty-dollar bids then twenties, but even a stern scan of the room by Mrs Wallace had no effect. The gavel came down. It was over.

For a long moment the girls remained silent, then Paige let out an enormous whoop, and Chrissy was cheering and Alice was on her feet laughing and half crying as she yelled, 'Thank you, thank you, thank you!' and blew kisses across the room.

Applause broke out and the auditorium shone with smiles.

Bouncing crazily, Alice hugged Paige then Chrissy before blowing even more kisses. Tears leaked over cheeks that were beginning to ache from the broadness of her grin. They weren't over the line, but Eddie's lead had been eroded significantly.

And Alice still had two days up her sleeve.

TWENTY-TWO

EDDIE SLID his phone into his pocket and dragged his sleeve over his sweaty brow. He'd been to a few auctions in his time – cattle, property, clearance sales – and none had been like that. Hell was the only way to describe it, and as the bidding rose higher and higher he'd been caught in its hot flames.

He'd exceeded his limit by two hundred dollars before sanity resumed. Even then, it had been hard to pull out. The auction had lost its momentum and the total remained short of where he needed, but Eddie simply didn't have the cash to drive it on and he couldn't risk another bid in case he ended up buying the work.

Eddie ducked from his hiding place to check the auditorium. Alice was bouncing up and down in Paige's arms, crying and laughing at the same time. Indulgent faces were turned to her. Except for one. Granny B's sharp gaze was squarely on Eddie.

Her mouth curved knowingly. Eddie shrugged and with a final glance at a still-bouncing Alice, strode quickly for the exit before anyone else caught him.

Eddie drove home feeling sick and not just about the auction. He'd been feeling crappy since Monday morning and had put it down to worry and lack of sleep, but the sweat that kept sheening his brow and the headache that wouldn't budge suggested more. God, he hoped he wasn't coming down with the flu. The strain the twins had caught in the winter had knocked them flat for a fortnight. Eddie couldn't afford a day out, let alone two weeks.

He tried to focus on the road, wary of kangaroos and wombats. Summer had hit a kangaroo on her way home from work a week ago and damn near had totalled her car. Adding to the carnage would really top off his night, not to mention condemn him to weeks of sledging from Harry.

Even with the danger, Eddie's thoughts kept drifting back to the auction. Had she raised enough? If Alice's and Paige's reactions were anything to go by, they seemed to think so, whereas Eddie wasn't so sure. He was sitting on just over twenty-one thousand. The last time he'd seen her total, Alice had been around sixteen. She'd had events since then, and maybe she'd been lucky and made a grand, perhaps stretched it to fifteen hundred, but with Scarlett's painting only raising three thousand four hundred dollars, that still left a shortfall.

He smacked his palm on the steering wheel. Stuff his bank account, he should have pushed higher. What did a few hundred dollars matter when compared to losing Alice?

Eddie slid his ute into its bay in the shed, turned off the engine and stared at the corrugated-iron wall in front of him, trying to find hope. Despite Alice's protest otherwise at Monday's meeting, he hadn't believed for a second that she was fine. He'd seen the downward curve of her mouth when he'd mentioned her mum. As for when he'd asked about their future, her answer that they'd tackle it after the Show Queen had been hardly encouraging, and he still hadn't had a response from Tuesday night's message. Which was, he was beginning to think, an answer in itself.

Granny B was right. Alice was never going to forgive him for stealing her dream. They had too much baggage, too much hurt and blame still hanging over them.

The girl he loved, and he'd failed her twice.

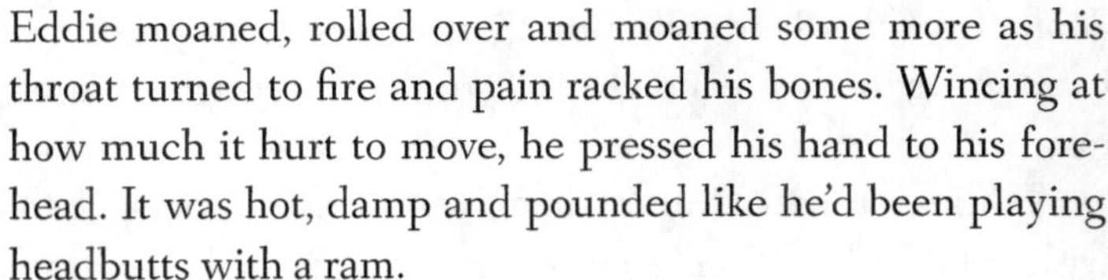

Eddie moaned, rolled over and moaned some more as his throat turned to fire and pain racked his bones. Wincing at how much it hurt to move, he pressed his hand to his fore-head. It was hot, damp and pounded like he'd been playing headbutts with a ram.

He slid his eyes to his bedside clock and grated out a curse. It was after seven. He should have been up ages ago. Eddie was already in the shit with his dad for all the time he'd taken off work with the Show Queen, and today he intended to take more to visit Alice. They had to talk. He'd go crazy otherwise.

The thought of getting up made Eddie quail, but he had to try. Cautiously, he lifted his head only to plonk it straight down as the room pitched. He lay for a moment, painfully panting air through his blazing throat as his heart drummed its fear. He had to get up. He had to. He had no time for this. An experimental slide of one leg towards the bed's edge had him groaning. Frigging hell, it was like he'd been run back and forth through a mangle. Every movement was a protest. Even breathing was a challenge.

A knock sounded at the door. Eddie managed a hoarse, 'Yeah' in answer. Hit by a sudden shiver, he reached for his doona and found only sheet, and a damp sheet at that. Brilliant. Just brilliant.

The door swung open. His mum stood in the frame and assessed him with a glance. 'I see.'

'What?'

'You're sick.'

Another shiver racked Eddie's body, shaking his achy bones with it. 'Not sick,' he juddered out. 'Dying.'

She smiled. His own mum actually smiled at his distress, the heartless woman.

'You're not dying, you big sook.' She scooped up his doona from the floor and fluffed it over him, then pressed a hand to his forehead and cheeks. 'You're suffering a bout of man flu.'

Eddie returned fire with a 'very funny' sneer then wished he hadn't when even that movement made his head throb.

'Need ... up,' said Eddie, not making any move. The pain in his throat was horrible and he wasn't sure his body would obey anyway.

'No upping for you, Edmond Argyle. What you need is rest.'

'But ... Dad.'

She cupped his face. 'Don't you worry about your father, he'll be fine. You, on the other hand, won't be if you don't stay in bed.' She stroked her thumb fondly over his cheek and gently patted it. 'I'll fetch you some cold-and-flu tabs.'

Eddie pointed to his throat.

His mum smiled. 'And some lozenges.'

'Phone?' He'd stuck his on a charger in the kitchen when he came home last night.

'Eddie, you can hardly talk.'

A reedy, childish '*Muuuum*' formed in Eddie's throat before it was killed by the germs raging there. He made do with a sulky look instead. Eddie might not be able to talk, but he could message.

'Don't you give me that look. You need to rest and that means no phone.'

He wanted to protest, except his mum was using *that* voice and any argument would only make her more intractable. It was too early to message Alice anyway, and his head felt full of fog. Better to hold off until the drugs kicked in.

His mum returned with the tablets, a packet of lozenges and a mug of honey, lemon and ginger-steeped hot water. Eddie swallowed the tablets and water, and nestled into his pillow to suck on his lozenge and wait for relief. Within minutes of the lozenge dissolving, he was asleep.

It was almost eleven when he woke up, groggy, still aching and sweaty, and not one hundred percent sure where he was. He'd been dreaming about Alice. They were at Talanga and Eddie was dragging her from one end of the farm to the other, looking for a place to have sex while Alice complained that she didn't want to. It hadn't been good.

He reached for the bedside table and his phone, and knocked over a water bottle his mum must have left. Exhausted from the effort, Eddie closed his eyes and tried to sort out his brain. He needn't have bothered. All he could focus on was how deathly he felt.

'You're awake, then,' said his mum. She came in and placed a hand on his forehead. 'Still a bit hot. Some paracetamol might help.'

'Doctor?' Getting out of bed would be a challenge, but doctors had good drugs.

'No point if you have the flu. It's just rest, and cold-and-flu tablets.'

Eddie closed his eyes and fought an urge to cry. This was a disaster.

'Not much you can do about it, I'm afraid. Good thing you don't have anything important on until Saturday.'

But he did. The most important thing in the world: Alice. He had to talk to her. He couldn't lose her again.

There was only one thing for it. Eddie heaved up his too-heavy body and swung his legs over the side of the bed. He sat for a moment with his head spinning, then, allowing no time to chicken out, forced himself upright. His mum watched him with folded arms and a 'this ought to be interesting' expression.

Eddie glanced at the door. It was so far away, but he had no choice. Lurching like a zombie, he shuffled towards it, teeth chattering. His sheet caught around one foot, causing his boxer shorts to be dragged halfway down his arse. He would have tugged them up if it hadn't taken so much effort. Besides, his mum had seen it all before and Eddie really didn't care. He needed a shower, clean clothes, and then someone to drive him to Lindner's.

'Having fun?' his mum asked, when Eddie reeled into the wall.

Eddie didn't answer. He was too busy trying not to slide to the floor.

'Eddie,' she said on one of her mum sighs, 'you're in no state to go anywhere, and you're more than likely contagious. Passing on the flu won't win you Alice.'

He managed to look at her. 'How?'

'I'm your mother. I know everything.' She jerked her head at the bed. 'Now get your backside into bed where it belongs before I smack it like you deserve.'

Eddie stared out at the hall, his momentary determination lost. His mum was right. He probably was contagious, and from the disgusting taste of his mouth he bet his breath was rotten, too. Given the way Eddie was sweating, he'd be stinking like a summer-bloated carcass by the time he made it to Lindner's. Not a winning state in which to plead his case. Not that he could plead anything with his throat the way it was.

Head down, Eddie let his mum shuffle him back to bed.

'Sleep now. I'll bring you more drugs in a couple of hours. Anything else you want?'

'Phone?'

'Not a chance.'

'Please?'

'Nope.' She tucked his doona around his shoulders.

Eddie's already oversized throat thickened further, and he began to blink. As if things weren't bad enough, now sickness was turning him into a snivelling little kid. 'I'll lose her.'

'No, you won't.'

He turned his face to the wall. Easy for his mum to say.

She stroked his hair, her voice gentle. 'You're just upset because you're sick. Things will look brighter when you're feeling better.' She kissed his cheek. 'Rest now. I'll bring you some soup later.'

But Eddie didn't want soup. The only thing he wanted was Alice.

It was evening before Eddie got his hands on his phone, though even he wasn't sure it was a great idea. Despite the day in bed, cold-and-flu tablets and half a packet of lozenges, he still felt sledgehammered. His fever had eased a fraction, but the fresh sheets his mum had put on the bed when he'd staggered off for a late-afternoon shower already felt scungy, and his skin had the clammy texture of a frog. Worse, he felt newborn weak, his legs so jellied he'd had to drag himself along the length of the hall wall to the bathroom.

That his phone was devoid of messages didn't help Eddie's mood either. His mum had made a post-lunch chemist trip into Levenham, where she would have bumped into at least a dozen people she knew. That Eddie was sick should have flown around town. He was the leading Show Queen contestant. It would send a lot of plans awry if he was too sick to attend the crowning.

He stared at the screen. He'd been hankering for this moment all day and now he had no idea what to say. Maybe his mum was right and his flu was feeding his fear, except Eddie had been panicky before he got sick.

His thumbs hovered over the keypad. What could he type that would make a difference? What would make Alice understand?

Eddie took a deep breath.

I love you. Always have, always will. Please give us a future.

Then with a silent prayer he hit 'send'.

TWENTY-THREE

HANDS SHOVED deep in his pockets and shoulders hunched, Eddie trailed his mum and dad to Civic Park. His plan to make the trip on his own had been vetoed the moment his mum saw him reach for his keys. Despite it leaving him without the means to make a speedy escape, Eddie hadn't put up a fight. He was too sick, weary and heavy with despair. Putting one foot in front of the other was hard enough, without having to coordinate his feet with his hands and eyes to drive.

Though the early evening was fine, Eddie couldn't shift the cold that had settled into his bones. He wished he'd put on heavier clothes than the navy blazer, brushed cotton checked shirt and moleskin jeans he wore. The fever and aches from his bout of flu still lingered, but it was Alice's silence that was killing him inside.

There'd been nothing from her. Not a message, call or email in response to his 'I love you'. Talk about being kicked in the goolies. Except it wasn't his manhood that was crushed, it was his heart.

His mum had seen Alice, even chatted, on Friday when

she had ducked into Levenham for groceries, then ventured down McArthur Street to the newsagency for the latest *Stock and Land*. Alice had set up a stall nearby, where she was selling the last of her merchandise. Eddie's hope had ballooned at the news then collapsed when his mum had nothing for him from Alice other than a 'get well soon'.

'She's tired, Eddie,' his mum admonished, when he grumbled that she might have at least offered to visit. It was a stupid thing to say, but Eddie was too down and sick to think straight. 'And busy. With the auction and all the mad scrambling, it's been a big week. She was out with Paige until eleven last night, collecting donations at every pub in town, then up early again this morning to help Ross in the nursery. She told me she was going to keep that stall open until every item was gone, then dump her takings at the bank and head straight home to bed.' His mum smoothed his damp hair from his forehead. 'She didn't sound like a girl who was worried about losing.'

Not losing him anyway.

People smiled and waved as their little group passed, a few yelling their 'good lucks'. Eddie nodded and made listless 'thanks' gestures in return. When a bloke had a broken heart on top of the flu, friendliness took effort.

If his mum had her way Eddie would be tucked in bed, but he'd made a commitment to the Show Queen when he signed on and didn't want to let anyone down. The situation wasn't the committee's fault and they'd worked hard to bring the show together. And he wanted one last chance with Alice. A face-to-face plea. If she fobbed him off this time, he was done for good.

Eddie rubbed his chest. God, the thought of that hurt.

They passed through the ticket booth. His mum stepped to the side and waited for Eddie to join her. 'We'll see you after the presentation, okay? Now, remember what I said about drinking. It won't go well with those tablets.' She fidgeted with the lapels of his jacket, tugging and smoothing and picking at fluff that wasn't there. 'Try not to breathe on anyone. If you don't feel well, it's okay to leave. Your father and I will handle Audrey.'

'Yes, Mum,' said Eddie, experiencing a warm rush of love for this funny, fiercely protective woman.

His dad shook his hand. 'Good luck.' Then he clapped Eddie on the shoulder and gave it a fatherly joggle. 'With everything.'

Eddie watched them wander off, his mum checking over her shoulder twice before they melted into the crowd. He scanned the park for Alice, his pulse thrumming as nerves set in. He still hadn't figured out what he'd say to her. There didn't seem to be words. He'd opened his soul and she hadn't answered. Twice in the same week, if he counted Tuesday's 'forgive me' message.

It seemed like half of Levenham had turned up for the trade part of the Wine Show. People swarmed the little white winery tents and food stalls like honey bees. Entry included a tasting glass and lanyard to hang it from, as well as tickets to sample wines. When those were used up, more could be purchased, with proceeds going to the same charities as the Show Queen competition. Chrissy said ticketing also helped prevent the guzzlers from treating the show as a cheap way to get hammered.

A few of the tents had hastily drawn signs advertising their success in Friday's professional tasting competition. Others promoted special 'today only' offers, wine clubs and other deals. A cooking demonstration was underway in one of the food tents, while to the rear of the fenced area kids ran amok on a bouncing castle.

Eddie began to wander, his progress slowed by well-wishers and friendly faces. He caught a glimpse of Chrissy hurrying in the distance but couldn't see Alice anywhere, and Paige proved as elusive. Spotting the twins and Cam at a plastic table near Digby Wallace-Jones's Gratia tent, Eddie headed over.

'Eddie,' chorused the twins, 'you're here! We heard you were sick and we were worried you wouldn't make it.'

'I nearly didn't.' He pinched a stray chair and sat opposite them, keeping his distance. 'I'd say hello, but I might be still germy.'

'That's okay,' said Willow. 'How are you feeling?'

He shrugged and inspected the crowd. 'Not great. Don't suppose you've seen Alice?'

They shook their heads.

Cam checked his watch. 'She can't be far away. You guys are due on stage shortly.'

Eddie checked his own watch. It was quarter to six. It wasn't like Alice to be late. Or maybe she was deliberately cutting it fine so they wouldn't have time to talk before the presentation.

'We'll have a look while we fetch another glass,' said Chelsea, jumping up, Willow shooting up with her. Clearly, neither was interested in obeying Chrissy's lay-off-the-booze instruction. 'Back in a tick.'

Before Eddie could protest, they were gone, leaving him alone with Cam.

'Good wine?' asked Eddie for something to say.

Cam inspected the pale-yellow contents of his tasting glass and screwed up his nose. 'No idea. I don't know the first thing about wine.'

Neither did Eddie, but right now he wished he could stick an entire bottle of it down his throat.

A stage had been set up in front of the council chambers upon which a female singer-guitarist crooned easy-listening music, adding to the relaxed, friendly atmosphere. Eddie listened as he continued to scan for Alice. After the Show Queen presentation was complete and the sun had set, Chrissy had promised a proper band and music they could dance to. Eddie could only hope he'd last that long.

'Do you think you'll still win?' asked Cam.

Eddie shrugged. 'Hope not.'

Cam nodded a few times as though confirming something to himself. 'You and Alice are an item, then?'

'Not looking like it. Excuse me.' Eddie plunged back into the fray. He'd been rude but didn't care. He'd had enough inaction, and not a chance was he about to discuss Alice with the bloke who wanted her for his own.

He threaded his way around the tents, peering over heads, searching for blonde hair. He spied the twins in the distance, glasses topped up and chatting to Mick, an ever-obedient Missy at his heels. Harry and Summer, who'd come from the farm in Harry's car, were at the tent behind them, waiting to be served. Harry had his arm slung around Summer's shoulder and was kissing her temple. Eddie quickly looked elsewhere.

'Eddie.'

He turned behind to find Alistair Haynes, the physio he'd gone to for rehab when he'd busted his knee playing football a few years before. Eddie shook Alistair's extended hand. 'Alistair, how's things?'

'Oh, you know. Up and down.' Alistair glanced around him and sidled closer. He was an older man, in his sixties, who'd famously worked for both Adelaide AFL teams before semi-retiring to Levenham, his home town. 'Look, I was hoping to run into you.'

'Really?' Eddie's gaze flitted from the physio to the stage. The singer was packing up. He didn't have time to waste on Alistair.

'Uh-huh.' Alistair lowered his voice, forcing Eddie to bend down to hear him. 'See, I got this message the other day.'

Eddie did his best to sound interested. 'Oh yeah?'

'Uh-huh.'

'Anything important?'

'Well, that's the thing. I don't know.'

Eddie's patience hit zero. 'Probably spam. Good to see you, Alistair.' He pointed at the stage where the twins and Mick were heading. Granny B, Sarah, Tiff and most of the other contestants were already at the meeting point, near the stairs. 'I've got to go.'

'It was from you.'

His body stilled. Slowly, he turned, a chill that had nothing to do with the flu scuttling over his skin. 'From me?'

Alistair nodded. 'Wasn't sure what to do about it. Thought about phoning you, but I was a bit embarrassed to tell you the truth.'

The chill hit his chest and speared inwards, a painful shard of realisation. *Shit, shit, shit.*

'Something about ...' Colour flooded Alistair's cheeks. He looked left then right and softened his voice even further. 'Giving you a future?'

Heys! Carefuls! and other grumbles followed Eddie as he barged his way towards the stage. He'd have some apologising to do later, especially to Alistair, whom he'd abandoned without a word, but he didn't give a rat's arse right now. All that mattered was Alice.

Alice who never received his message.

'Never stopped.'

Her mouth opened.

'For God's sake, go!' Chrissy loud-whispered behind him.

Panic crossed Alice's gorgeous face, then she whirled around and ran up on to the stage.

Something whacked Eddie on the back. Chrissy with her folder.

'Seriously, Eddie, could your timing be any more rotten?'

'I had to tell her.'

She regarded him like he was an idiot. 'It could have waited, you know.'

No, it couldn't have. Eddie glanced upwards. Even with his height he couldn't see the stage, but he could hear the ongoing applause. Everyone wanted Alice to win.

'Has she won?'

'You know I can't tell you that.'

'Please?'

The no-nonsense professional mask Chrissy had been wearing finally dropped. 'I know you're scared she won't forgive you, but have a bit of faith. That tiny body hides a heart the size of Australia, with room enough spare even for you. Now get up there.' She gave him a push. 'And no falling over. Knowing Granny B, she won't be able to resist giving you mouth-to-mouth and that is something none of us need to witness.'

If Eddie had had time and wasn't so germy, he would have kissed Chrissy in thanks. She and Paige were Alice's best friends. If Chrissy believed he had a chance, then maybe he really did.

He took the steps two at a time. The other entrants had their heads turned to the rear of the stage, questioning looks on their faces. Clearly he was late. Again. Eddie hurried to the front as whoops and wolf-whistles erupted from the crowd, and lined up alongside Alice.

Eddie glanced at the front row, where the Argyles had taken position. His mum looked peacock proud in her blue dress, while his dad's shirt strained from the pressure of his puffed-out chest. Harry's and Summer's grins were so huge and silly they looked like they'd been raiding the wine tents harder than Steph.

In front of the entrants, on a velvet cushion atop a stool, sat the crown. It was a plain, almost ugly thing, woven out of grapevine canes and reminding Eddie more of a crown of thorns than a coveted prize. It was hard to believe they'd put in months of work for it, but as Alice had maintained all along, it wasn't the crown that mattered.

'As I mentioned earlier,' continued Granny B in a crisp, resonant voice, 'the Wine Show Crown competition has proved to be an outstanding success. Our contestants not only took on this challenge with enthusiasm and aplomb, but surpassed all expectations in their fundraising efforts. The committee is grateful and proud. Every one of them deserves a crown for their efforts.'

More applause broke out. Eddie glanced at Alice. She was staring at the crown with her lips pressed together and her brow furrowed. If it wouldn't have caused a ruckus and embarrassed his family, Eddie would have snatched up the stupid thing and crowned Alice with it himself. She reflected everything the crown stood for – passion for the community, goodness, enthusiasm. It should be hers.

With a quiet sigh, he went to shove his twitchy fingers into his pockets only to brush against Alice's hand. His heart thumped. Being tiny, her hand should have been well below his. The touch had to be deliberate.

He waited, not breathing, then she carefully curled her little finger around his, hooking them together and shooting electricity through his body, as if a long-broken connection suddenly had been rejoined.

He looked down and found Alice smiling at him. A proper Alice smile, like she used to.

A love smile.

TWENTY-FOUR

IT WAS a good thing Alice's little finger was locked with Eddie's or she might have floated away. Her heart was huge, yet feather light and pulsing with joy.

Eddie loved her. He'd never stopped.

Despite everything, she couldn't help but wonder if she'd ever stopped loving him, too. Her feelings about Eddie since their breakup had always been confused, mixed with her grief at losing her mum and her anger over his behaviour afterwards. Maturity had given her better insight into herself and him, and the mistakes they'd made when they were hurting. Now the soil she'd buried her feelings in was fertile with understanding and forgiveness. It was time for the dormant seeds of their original love to burst through and flourish.

She broke eye contact with Eddie and tried to focus. Mrs Wallace once more was praising the contestants' achievements, jewellery glittering as it reflected the sun's low rays. Alice checked on Paige. Noticing her attention, Paige pointed at Alice and Eddie's joined fingers and inclined her head. Alice returned with a crooked smile and mouthed, 'Couldn't help myself.'

'Now?' mouthed back Paige, spreading her arms to indicate the stage.

Alice gave a half-shrug, although she supposed Paige had a point. The Show Queen presentation wasn't the most appropriate time for a public display of affection, but Eddie had looked so sick with flu and worry she'd been desperate to comfort him.

Plus an 'I love you' deserved it, and more. Much more. Kissing ... cuddling ... jigglesticking.

A giggle bubbled in Alice's chest. She bit her lip to hold it down, only for Paige to press her thumb to the end of her nose and mash her face into a tongue-poking, squinty-eyed contortion of idiocy. Alice made a noise like a stepped-on squeaky toy. Barely breaking stride, Mrs Wallace stabbed her with an ice-pick glare that punctured both squeak and giggle in an instant.

Too chastened to respond to Eddie's inquiring look, Alice squeezed his finger. Eddie squeezed back. Alice repeated her squeeze until their fingers were flexing and unflexing like little pumping hearts. Another dangerous bout of giggles frothed.

Nerves, it had to be. Alice wasn't normally this silly.

On the other hand, it had been a long time since Eddie had told her he loved her. Alice might have melted into a mushy puddle, if she wasn't trying to stop herself from hee-hawing like a donkey.

'In total,' announced Mrs Wallace, 'our group has raised an extraordinary seventy-six thousand, five hundred and eleven dollars.' She began applauding, nodding at the crowd to give them approval to join in, and faced the contestants. Her beady gaze zeroed in on Alice and Eddie's linked fingers. Alice could have sworn she saw a smile flicker at the elderly lady's mouth.

'You should be very proud,' Mrs Wallace said, when the applause had quietened. 'All of you.'

Missy gave a loud bark, causing a cascade of laughter.

'The Wallace Foundation is so delighted with your achievements, that we have decided to donate an extra twenty-three thousand, four hundred and eighty-nine dollars to bring the total funds raised to one hundred thousand dollars.'

Silence followed, then raucous applause exploded, along with several whoops and wolf-whistles. Though reluctant to lose contact with Eddie, Alice joined in and swapped amazed expressions with the other contestants. Sarah and Tiffany had their heads together, laughing and wiping fingers beneath their leaky eyes. Chrissy stood alongside, smiling wryly and shaking her head at Mrs Wallace.

The applause died down. Alice's hand dropped to her side and was quickly folded into Eddie's. She leaned closer until her shoulder touched his arm, wishing they could connect everywhere.

'Thank you,' said Mrs Wallace. 'Now we progress to the most important part of the evening. As I mentioned, it has been an exciting and entertaining competition, complete with last-minute twists that saw some extraordinary resilience and fortitude from our frontrunners. I'm sure, like myself, you'll be amazed to discover that only fifty-five dollars separates our two leaders.'

Alice's eyes widened. Fifty-five dollars? Oh, that was close. Too close. She glanced at Paige. No funny face-making now, only pursed-lipped pensiveness. It was always going to be tight, but after working their backsides off with the raffle, panhandling and tees and totes sales, they thought they'd done enough.

Murmurs broke out among the crowd. Every bubble of Alice's lovesick silliness was gone now. The skin of her scalp had grown tight and sweat greased her palms. She pressed her teeth into the soft inside of her bottom lip and hoped her desperation to win didn't show.

Eddie's grip on her hand firmed.

'But first, to our third placegetter.'

Alice swapped a look with Eddie. Placegetter? Singular? Surely the twins were third, unless it was Mrs Wallace playing games. Alice wouldn't put it past her.

Tiffany passed Mrs Wallace a thick envelope, complete with red wax seal. An unnecessary drama, but Mrs Wallace did like to put on a show, and while the competitors had had the advantage of knowing the tallies, at least for most of the competition, their audience had not. Third place was a big deal.

Mrs Wallace popped the seal, glanced at the card inside and quickly slid it away. 'In third place, having raised the commendable total of sixteen thousand, nine hundred and twenty-six dollars, are ...' She paused to run her gaze down the line of contestants, drawing out the tension. She needn't have bothered. Having recognised the total, the twins were already celebrating. 'Chelsea and Willow Phillips. Congratulations, ladies.'

The girls hugged one another. The Phillips family hooted their joy. Missy woofed as the crowd was momentarily hidden behind a salvo of camera flashes. Even though the result was no surprise, Alice breathed out in relief. The twins had been formidable competitors and might well have won had Eddie not entered the field. They deserved the kudos.

Chelsea and Willow bowed and waved as they made their way to Mrs Wallace and Julian, who was standing by with two white satin sashes over his arm, the ends of which were held together with a large gold wineglass-shaped brooch.

Adorned with their sashes, the girls held hands and bowed again to the audience, before heading to the top of the line and Eddie, who, apparently having forgotten his germy status, hugged them close.

'Thank you,' said Alice, when it was her turn.

'What for?' asked Willow.

'I don't know. Being supportive, being great sports.'

'No need to thank us, we loved it.' Willow winked. 'But next year we're going to win.'

Alice laughed. 'I feel sorry for your competitors already.'

'You won't be trying again?'

'No. Anyway, who says I haven't won this one?'

'Pity you both can't win,' said Chelsea, glancing at Eddie. 'That'd be so romantic.'

'King and queen,' said Willow.

'Ladies,' warned Mrs Wallace, her hand over the microphone.

'Oops,' said the twins, and hurried on.

In seconds, Willow and Chelsea had completed their triumph and were back in position next to Alice, grinning at each other and admiring their sashes. Mrs Wallace turned to the crowd again. Silence fell. The air thickened, and with it Alice's pulse. Blood thudded past her ears. All the work she'd put in, all the longing and emotion and passion, were condensed into these slowly passing seconds. Clasping her hands at her belly, Alice concentrated on taking steady breaths. If she lost, she lost. The real pride came from playing the game well.

Besides, what she'd gained was worth more than a crown of woven sticks. She had Eddie, who'd loved her through all her screw-ups and meanness. The gorgeous, kind and funny man who'd once been her world and would be again.

'Eddie,' she whispered suddenly.

He glanced at Mrs Wallace and bent close, concern etching his handsome face. 'What?'

'I love you, too.'

Eddie blinked, then broke into a huge grin. Alice grinned back. Then they faced the front with their hands as united as their hearts.

'Now for the announcement we've been waiting for,' said Mrs Wallace.

To Alice's frustration, Tiffany's face remained as smooth as carved marble when she crossed to hand Mrs Wallace the winner's envelope. The old lady accepted it with a nod. If the first unsealing was drawn out, this was even worse. Mrs Wallace unpicked the wax seal as though her life depended on keeping it intact.

'For crying out loud,' muttered Eddie.

Finally, Mrs Wallace slipped the card from the envelope. The contestants craned to catch a glance, but the old lady was sly and used her cupped hand to hide the contents. A smug smile flitted across her mouth and was gone.

Alice glanced at Paige. She had her hands steepled in front of her mouth, like a praying angel. Ross was gnawing a thumbnail, while Melanie Argyle watched her son with worry.

The crowd began to shift and murmur. *What was taking so long?*

Mrs Wallace held up her hand for quiet then placed it across her chest. 'You'll have to excuse me. I feel quite overwhelmed.'

'Be a first,' whispered Eddie.

'Shh!' Alice was having trouble enough with her nerves without Eddie's giggle-inducing asides.

'It is my great pleasure,' said Mrs Wallace, sounding more queen-like than ever, 'to announce that the runner-up for the inaugural Wine Show Crown, having raised the impressive total of twenty-one thousand, two hundred and seventy-five dollars, is Edd—'

Alice squealed and bounced up and down with her fists raised over her head in victory, then she was swept up in Eddie's strong arms and twirled around and around, the two of them laughing.

Mrs Wallace was fairly shouting to be heard over the noise of the crowd. 'Which means our winner, on twenty-one thousand, three hundred and thirty dollars, is Alice Lindner!'

'I'm sorry you lost,' said Alice, easing her head back to look Eddie in the eyes. Her arms were wrapped around his neck, and his were hooked under her bum. From the air circulating around her legs, Alice suspected her dress had ridden up and was likely exposing parts she shouldn't, but her care factor was nil. She'd won. On every front.

'Nah, crowns don't suit me.' Then Eddie kissed her, which brought loud whoops from their audience.

'You'll give me your flu.'

'Sorry,' said Eddie, not sounding remotely sorry, but he set her down.

'If you two have quite finished,' said Mrs Wallace, her hand cupped over the microphone.

'Not even close,' said Eddie, winking at her. 'We're just getting started.'

Alice elbowed him.

Eddie *oofed* and grinned, then kissed her temple. 'Love you, Queen.'

The twins and Steph *awwed*. Even Mrs Wallace couldn't stop her smile.

They walked forward as a pair, Alice waving in a most unqueenly manner and Eddie grinning like a lottery winner.

Flushed on good wine and goodwill, it took a while for the crowd to hush. The sun was low now, casting gold over the park like a blessing. Alice's dad had one arm around Paige's shoulders and was wiping his nose with his hanky with the other. Paige, bless her, was openly crying. Alice wished she could call both to the stage. Without her dad's love and generosity, and her friend's faith and help – all her friends' help – she never would have managed this.

She couldn't wait to tell them how much she loved them.

Julian presented Eddie with his sash first – the same as the twins' but in red satin. Slanted across his navy blazer and big chest, it gave him an almost military bearing that Alice found rather sexy. From the sparkle in Mrs Wallace's eye, she felt the same.

'Hands off,' said Alice. 'He's mine.'

'Indeed.' Mrs Wallace laughed and patted her shoulder. 'You're a very fortunate young woman.'

Alice wasn't about to argue with that.

Finally, it was her turn. Alice was so tiny she barely had to crouch for Julian to crown her, but when she rose, surrounded by her beaming, proud friends and loved ones, Alice felt a hundred feet tall.

'Well done,' he said, shaking her hand. 'A great effort.'

'Thank you.' She faced the applauding gathering, bowed and reached out her hand for Eddie.

He hesitated, then took her hand and stepped alongside.

A king beside his queen.

TWENTY-FIVE

IT CAME as no surprise to Eddie when Alice was struck down with his flu. They'd kissed enough after the Show Queen for Eddie to pass it on a hundred times. Thankfully, no one else succumbed. Eddie felt terrible enough as it was without the twins or, God forbid, Granny B suffering it, too.

Fortunately, Alice's was a milder version – woman flu as opposed to the more debilitating man flu, his mum teased – and she soldiered on like the queen she was thanks to cold-and-flu tablets and medicinal kisses from Eddie whenever he could sneak them in.

Getting away from Talanga to visit Alice wasn't easy, though. After all the time Eddie had taken off with show-queening and illness, his dad was demanding payback. Now the soil was warming, they'd begun planting summer grazing crops and hay cutting was close, too. With a hundred other farm activities on his list, there was little time for play.

He fitted it in, however. Eddie would always find time for play with his Alice of the wonderland.

It was near closing time on a Monday afternoon, a full

two weeks after the presentation, when Eddie sauntered across the bridge and pond and into Lindner's. With its spring flush of growth, the bower was lusher and prettier than ever. Like its owner, Eddie mused, then grinned at himself for being a big sap.

Love tended to have that effect, though, and he was overflowing with it.

A glance at the information desk showed no Alice. Nor was she working on any of the nearby displays. Eddie shoved his hands in his pockets and went wandering.

He found her outside, standing at the edge of a small lawn surrounded by plants and a zoo of resin ornamental garden animals, watching what looked to be an oversized electronic cockroach skitter about.

Eddie wrapped his arms around Alice and nuzzled her neck from behind. 'Nice pet.'

'It's a bit like that.' She turned in his arms and kissed him, blue eyes luminous in the sunshine and full of delight. 'Hello, devilish Duke.'

Eddie grinned. They'd begun teasing each other with 'Queenie' and 'Duke' after a late-night messaging session and it'd stuck. 'Hello, comely Queenie. So,' he said, peering over her head at the motorised cockroach, 'what is it?'

'A robotic lawn mower. Cool, isn't it?'

Eddie screwed up his nose. Cool wasn't the term he'd use. It looked pretty rickety to his farmer's eye. Those plastic wheels would bog in a shallow puddle and he bet that whiny engine would conk out from the strain the moment it hit a bit of capeweed.

Alice gave him a friendly thump. 'You're as bad as Dad.'

'It is a bit ...' Eddie tried and failed to think of a less disparaging word than pathetic.

'It's awesome,' said Alice, jiggling out of his arms. 'Look, it even goes back to base when it's done.'

The robo-pet had executed a multi-point turn and was trundling towards a recharging plate with creepy determination. Eddie had a strange urge to stomp on it before it found a mate and bred.

'Good robo-roach,' said Eddie.

'Laugh all you like, but I bet I sell at least two of these this spring, and they're nearly fifteen hundred dollars a pop.'

'No bets from me.' He held up his palms. 'I learned my lesson the last time I took you on.'

Alice seized his hand and led him inside. 'It wasn't that bad.'

'Oh right. You weren't the one who got waxed in front of all his footy mates.'

'Stop being a sook. I get waxed every month and you don't hear me bleating.'

'Can I feel?'

'Maybe later, if you're good.'

Oh, he planned on being good. Very, very good.

She left him on the other side of the counter to work on the tills. Eddie knew from experience she'd be a while yet and settled in to watch her. With the nursery quiet, they could have some fun. A tease here, a touch there ...

'Where's Ross?'

'Fruit trees, I think.'

That was towards the back of the nursery. A reasonable distance. Enough time for a bloke to act innocent if he saw trouble coming. Yeah, Alice and Eddie were adults, but he'd rather not get caught with his hands up Alice's top. They'd been together a fortnight. Eddie wanted a lifetime and wasn't about to screw it up by upsetting her dad. Or her.

Alice waggled a pencil at him. 'You can quit that thought.'

'How did you know what I was thinking?'

'Because I know you, Eddie Argyle.' She finished counting the notes she held and wrote down the number on a cash sheet. 'Your mind is not pure.'

'Neither's yours. I have text messages to prove it.'

'No,' said Alice on a sigh. 'It's getting worse, too.'

'Tell me about it.'

She slid him a look from under lowered lashes. 'That bad, huh?'

Alice had no idea. Eddie's want was driving him crazy, in more ways than one. The physical craving he could handle – he'd managed well enough for a long time already – but sex with Alice came with baggage. As much as Eddie ached for her, he wasn't going to do anything unless it was right. No doubts, no regrets, only love.

He shrugged. 'Nothing I can't handle.'

'You sure?'

'Yep.'

She leaned her elbows on the counter and rested her chin on her hands. There was a wicked glow in her eyes that made Eddie's blood surge. Something was up. Besides what was in his jeans. 'What if I said I might have a fix for that?'

Two could play her coy game. Eddie bent to mirror her, their faces centimetres apart, his tone as teasing as hers. 'What sort of fix?'

'Oh, nothing major. Just an empty house, an empty bed ...'

A naked Alice.

The image went straight to his groin. Eddie swallowed, but his response still came out hoarse. 'When?'

Alice bit her lip, unable to hide her smile. 'Tonight.' She

gave a little shimmy of joy. 'Dad's got a Chamber of Commerce meeting. Those things go on forever.'

Cautious of sounding over-eager, Eddie played it cool. 'Sounds like a good fix.'

Which was rubbish. It sounded like a fantastic fix. His mind shifted to practicalities. Condoms, for starters. Once upon a time, he'd kept a supply in his car, but it'd been a while since he'd bothered. Then there was his mum. She'd made lasagne, and though the meal would keep, his mum's temper wouldn't if he didn't ring to let her know he wouldn't be home for dinner. Manners mattered in the Argyle house, as he and Harry had well learned.

Eddie scratched his jaw and checked the time. Enough, if he left now. 'I'll need to visit the chemist.' The supermarket would be cheaper, but he'd likely bump into someone's mum there.

Alice leaned closer and made a show of inspecting either side of him. 'You're off the hook. I bought a box this morning.'

'Oh.'

That she'd bought condoms surprised him. She'd been shy about it in their previous time together, but she'd been a lot younger, too, less confident in herself and probably guilty about how buying condoms would look when her mum was so sick. Eddie had been so randy and in love he couldn't have given a toss.

'Just "oh"?'

'Yeah. I mean, that's good.'

Alice's smile disappeared. She edged back from him. 'Do I sense a "but" here?'

'What? No!' He shook his head. 'Trust me, there's nothing I want more. It's just that ...' Eddie took a breath. Was it weak to admit he had hang-ups? Such a stupid thing, but it preyed on him. All those times before that he'd thought were special hadn't been that way for her. 'Are you sure about this?'

'God, yes.'

'You sure? Because I don't want—'

'Eddie.' She reached for his hand and squeezed it. 'I want this. I promise.'

He blew out a breath. 'Good.' Eddie nodded, then grinned. 'What time does your dad leave?'

Alice laughed and went back to reconciling the till. Overcome with restless energy, Eddie killed time fiddling with counter displays – little cacti in terracotta pots, small sachets of flower food, a tin bucket of colourful garden whirligigs on metal stakes.

A raffle book with a pen jammed in the fold lay next to the bucket. It was for one of the tennis clubs. The sight made something niggle in his mind only for it to whizz out of reach.

'Yours?' he asked. Maybe she was taking up summer sport, although he doubted it. Winter netball was okay because the nursery was quiet, but Alice was needed in the summer months. He had a brief image of her in a tennis outfit, all slim legs and tight bum and bouncing ponytail. A bloke would skip a cricket match or two to watch that.

'No. That's Noah's.' Noah was one of the nursery's casual workers, a capable, if scrawny, seventeen-year-old schoolkid who was filling his pockets in preparation for university the following year.

Eddie checked out a stub to see what the prize was. Nothing to get excited about; a five-hundred-dollar voucher for Levenham's one-and-only sports store. He'd buy a ticket anyway.

He started filling in his details, still plagued by that

mind niggle, then forgot about it as his brain sauntered off onto thoughts of Alice naked, and the wonderland that awaited.

Eddie stared up at Alice's bedroom ceiling. Sensational didn't begin to describe how he felt. He tipped his head to look down at her, curled up against his chest with her leg hooked over his hips, blonde hair loose and cascading over her shoulders and back.

He skimmed his knuckles down her toned arm. Her skin was blushed with pink, like a ripe peach. She smelled as delicious as one, too.

'Not going to sleep on me there?' he asked.

She made an incoherent '*nnngh*' noise.

'Was that a yes or no?' When she didn't answer he hoisted her up his body until they were chest to chest. Her face was sleepy, satisfied and sexy as hell. He knew the feeling. 'Wake up, Queenie, your subject needs you.'

She dropped her head to kiss the tip of his nose then flopped against him. 'You've already had me.'

He had. Twice. And it was bloody fantastic.

'Don't tell me you're worn out already?'

'Getting there.'

'Only getting there? Clearly, I haven't been doing my duty.'

Alice giggled, the sound vibrating against his neck.

He cuddled her, wishing he could absorb her somehow, his lovely, gorgeous happy Alice. 'We've got a lot to catch up on, you and I.'

'I know.' She pulled back and rested on her folded arms

to regard him. 'And it might be ages before we get another chance.'

'Not keen on the back of my ute?'

She smiled. 'Your ute smells of sheep and dog. Not known aphrodisiacs.'

'Blue will be devastated to hear that. He still thinks he's the duck's guts after winning the high jump. Demanding steak every night. Rolling on his back, expecting belly scratches.' Eddie tsked and shook his head.

'Still getting rid of your raffle meat from the freezer, huh?'

'Yeah.'

They rested a bit, Eddie half mesmerising himself with strokes of Alice's silky skin. He wished he could stay all night. Maybe he could have a man-to-man with Ross to see how he felt about that. Or he could ask Alice if she'd like to move in somewhere with him. It'd be a commute back and forth to the farm, but nothing he couldn't handle and they'd have privacy.

Eddie pondered that for a bit. Too soon, perhaps. Maybe in another week.

He kissed the top of Alice's head and gazed around the room. Except for a double bed replacing her old narrow single – thank God – it hadn't changed much. A couple of fluffy toys on the shelf above her old desk-cum-dresser. A silver laptop. Family photos. Her Lindner's uniform and his clothes in a trail from door to bed, where they'd tossed them in their hurry to get naked.

A large frame leaning against the blanket box she used to store jumpers caught his attention. 'What's that?'

'What's what?'

He pointed at the frame.

'Oh that. That's Scarlett's painting.'

'How did you end up with it?'

'Digby Wallace dropped it around this morning on behalf of his grandmother. He said the guy who bought it wanted to donate it to the Show Queen winner. Some old friend of Mrs Wallace's from Adelaide.'

'Generous of him.'

'Very, given what it's worth. And could be in the future if Scarlett turns out to be the next big thing that everyone's predicting. I suspect it was more that he didn't like it. It's not as good as her other stuff.'

'Not as sexy, you mean.'

'Don't be so sure about that. I swear I found a stylised clitoris when I checked it over this morning. I'm going to give it to Paige as a thankyou present. She deserves it after all her hard work. I couldn't have done half the things I did without her.'

Eddie sneaked a hand down her belly. 'Speaking of clitorises ...'

'You're insatiable.'

'Only when it comes to you, my precious queen. You rule me. Mind ...' He sucked on her earlobe, causing her to squirm. 'Body ...' The squirms became gasps as his lips wormed down her throat and chest to her nipple. 'And soul.'

Eddie was hunting for his trunks when the niggle that had been bothering him since he spotted the raffle book in the nursery finally took form. He smiled and shook his head.

'What's tickled your fancy?' asked Alice, who was perched on the bed, threading a leg into her underpants. 'Besides me.'

'Nothing really. Just irony.'

She scrunched her nose. 'Irony?'

'Yeah. Remember that day I came in with Mum? When I bought your raffle tickets and you dared me to enter the Show Queen?'

'How could I forget?' Alice stood and wriggled the rest of her way into her pants. 'What about it?'

Distracted with her jiggly boobs, Eddie momentarily forgot what he was talking about. Alice had perfect breasts, pert but soft and with pale-pink nipples that puckered cutely when he sucked on them.

'Eddie?'

'What? Oh, right. Sorry.' He grinned, mind still not on the job. 'Can I take your boobs home with me?'

'Not without the rest of me, and I don't think your mum would approve.'

'Yes, she would. She adores you.' His mum was still beaming over the news that Eddie and Alice were back together. Just as well Harry and Summer looked close to getting engaged or he'd be copping all the pressure about wedding planning and grandkids. Not that Eddie would mind either with Alice, but all in good time. Tomorrow would work fine.

'What about that day?' asked Alice, spoiling his view by putting on her bra.

'Yeah, the raffle. Remember what you won the Show Queen by?'

'Of course. Fifty-five—' For a second her brow furrowed, then she slammed her hands over her mouth and did one of her funny, over-excited stompy dances. 'Omigod, so it was!' She stilled and dropped her hands, her eyes huge. 'I won because of you. Because of the tickets you bought.'

'Yep.'

The fifty-five dollars' worth of tickets that Eddie had

purchased that fateful day had been the exact figure that had separated them.

'But ...' Pure amazement lit her face. 'It's like it was meant to be.'

Eddie crossed to gently cup her jaw, his thumbs brushing her cheeks and lips. 'We were always meant to be. We just lost our way a bit and needed to find a road back.'

Her eyes were limpid with unshed tears. 'I'm so glad we did.'

'Me too,' whispered Eddie, leaning in to kiss her. 'Me too.'

Rocking
HORSE HILL
CATHRYN
HEIN
A Levenham Love Story

Who do you trust when a stranger threatens to tear your family apart?

When Emily Wallace-Jones's brother Digby arrives home with a secretive new fiancée, no one knows how to react. The Wallace-Jones are old-money rural aristocracy and Felicity Townsend is from a very different side of the tracks.

But Em is determined not to treat Felicity with the same teenage snobbery that tore apart her relationship with her first love, Josh Sinclair. A man who has now sauntered sexily back into Em's life and given her a chance for redemption.

As Felicity settles in, suspicions are raised about her intentions toward Em's beloved Rocking Horse Hill, the historic family property that Digby owns but has promised will be Em's home for as long as she wishes. Though worried for her future, Em sides with her brother and Felicity, until a near tragedy sets in motion a chain of events that will change the family forever.

An emotional story of family turmoil and second-chance love played out against the dramatic landscape of rural South Australia.

Thank you so much for reading *Eddie and the Show Queen*. I hope you enjoyed Alice and Eddie's journey to love and happiness. If you did, and you have a few moments, I'd be very grateful if you could leave a rating or few words in review to help others discover my books.

If you'd like to know when my next release comes available plus gain access to exclusive content, news and giveaways, please subscribe to my newsletter via my website.

More information about me and my books, including the inspiration behind *Eddie and the Show Queen*, along with plenty of other fun stuff, can be found at cathrynhein.com.

Web: cathrynhein.com
Facebook: facebook.com/cathrynhein
Twitter: @CathrynHein
Instagram: cathrynheinauthor

'What is it?' asked Alice when they were out of sight. 'Are you still worried about winning?'

Eddie nodded, his mouth drying as the words he needed to say shrivelled on his tongue.

'Don't be.' She shrugged. 'If I lose, I lose. I know I did my best.'

'What about us?'

But before she could answer, Chrissy rounded the corner. 'What the hell are you two playing at?' She jerked her folder at the stage. 'Get your backsides to the bottom of those stairs. Your names are going to be called any second.'

'We're coming.' Alice's smile gentled as she turned back to Eddie. 'Now really isn't the time for this.'

'I don't care.'

'Now!'

'Coming, twisty-knickers.' She smiled again. 'We'd better do as we're told before Chrissy pops a vessel.'

And like that, Alice slipped from him.

'You called me twisty-knickers,' Chrissy complained as she pushed Alice forward. Eddie stayed where he was, rubbing his hands up and down his face, his emotions a mess. Seconds later Chrissy was back. 'Don't think I haven't forgotten you.' She jerked her thumb. 'Move.'

Alice was looking up, hand on the rail in readiness, when Eddie reached the steps. Across the grounds, Granny B's voice described her delight in her next introduction. Then came Alice's name, followed by an outbreak of applause and cheers. Alice grinned and bounced up the first three steps with her dress flaring prettily around her slim legs. Three more steps and she'd be gone.

'I love you.'

She jerked to a halt and looked back at him with huge eyes.

bright eyes, appeared to have spent even more time in the wine tents than the twins.

'Don't worry, we'll help you,' said the twins, dissolving into giggles.

Margot snorted. 'Yeah, like that wouldn't be the blind leading the blind.'

'Fortunately,' said Mick, holding up Missy's lead, 'I have a guide dog you can borrow.'

Which had everyone laughing except Eddie. His concentration was on Alice and the nerves that were threatening to swamp him.

Chrissy tapped her watch and addressed Mrs Wallace. 'You're up.'

'Thank you, Christina.' Chin held regally high, Granny B swept towards the stairs in a grape-coloured trenchcoat and matching plaid fedora that made her look like a cold-war spy. She paused near Eddie. 'Do stop looking so fretful, Edmond. You're frightening Tiffany.'

'Break a leg,' he said, then felt shitty for his petty get-you-back joke. 'Sorry.'

But Granny B gave a bark of laughter. 'I rather think you're not at this moment. But not to worry, I still enjoy you.'

With Granny B on stage and Chrissy busy with Tiff and Sarah, it was now or never.

Eddie clasped Alice's hand. 'We should be safe for a couple of minutes.' He nodded past the stairs. 'Let's go.'

He led Alice behind the stage. Alice kept glancing behind as though she too could feel the stares of the others. Above him, Granny B paused for applause, then moved on to the committee introductions. She was powering through. They had moments.

Eddie was almost at the meeting point when he spotted her. She was running on the toes of her high-heeled shoes past the front of the council chambers, a slash of brilliant pink against the white limestone, hair streaming like a golden banner. Paige was alongside, and both were laughing.

Alice looked beautiful, happy, carefree. God, he loved her.

'Edmond,' said Granny B archly, 'nice that you could make it.'

Eddie didn't bother to respond. His focus was on Alice. Alice of the wonderland in a bright-pink dress that matched her flushed cheeks and lipstick. Alice who'd caught his eye and grinned, rocketing his heart into orbit and giving him hope that today might still work out.

The two girls slowed as they moved onto the grass. Alice spoke to the security guard monitoring the staff entrance then hugged Paige tightly. Seconds later, every one of them beaten out by Eddie's pounding heart, she was skipping towards their group.

'Hi, everyone! Sorry I'm late. It was chaos at work and hard to get away, then Paige's car decided to cark it in the driveway and we had to pinch one of the nursery vans, which might not be a bad thing if I buy lots of wine later. Not to worry, I'm here now.' She paused for breath, her breasts rising sexily behind the 'V' of her neckline, and wagged her hand in front of her face. 'Flustered, but here.' Her eyes widened as she finally took in the show. Prompted by an announcement, the crowd was slowly shifting towards the front of the stage, making it look even thicker than it was. 'Omigod, look at all these people!'

'Yes, an excellent turnout,' said Granny B. Eddie noticed that her voice held none of the annoyance he'd been lashed with. Favouritism for the Show Queen? He could only hope.

'Eddie,' said Alice, finally turning and beaming at him. 'You poor thing. Your mum told me how sick you were. She seemed quite worried about you.' The beam dimmed and she reached up on tiptoe to put her hand to his forehead. 'Are you okay? You look awful.'

'I'll survive. Can we talk?'

She glanced at Granny B, who was making zero effort to hide her interest. 'I don't think we have time.'

'It's important.'

Alice nodded, but as he went to steer her away Chrissy descended the stage stairs.

'Where are you two off to? We're on in two minutes.' Chrissy waved her clipboard, which had a watch secured under the clip. She hugged Alice briefly, whispering, 'You look amazing,' before joining Granny B and using the end of her pen to count off entrants.

Eddie pressed a hand to Alice's back. She shook her head. 'You heard Chrissy. We're on in a couple of minutes.'

'Good,' said Chrissy, having finished her count. 'You're all here. Hey, eyes forward please. I know we went through this on Monday, but a refresher never hurts, and we don't want any hitches. First on stage will be Mrs Wallace. She'll do the welcome and acknowledgements, and introduce the committee and Julian Koch, president of the Grapegrower's and Vigneron's Association, who'll be crowning our winner. Each of you will be introduced individually, with a brief rundown of your fundraising efforts. If you could smile and wave that'd be great. Happy people make for good memories and we want this show to be truly memorable. Oh, and please try not to fall as you go up the stairs.'

'Thanks for that,' muttered Steph, who, from her over-